D0787785

FORBIDDEN

FORBIDDEN

Davis Bunn

**SEVERN
HOUSE**

First world edition published in Great Britain and the USA in 2023
by Severn House, an imprint of Canongate Books Ltd,
14 High Street, Edinburgh EH1 1TE.

Trade paperback edition first published in Great Britain and the USA in 2023
by Severn House, an imprint of Canongate Books Ltd.

severnhouse.com

British Library Cataloguing-in-Publication Data
A CIP catalogue record for this title is available from the British Library.

ISBN-13: 978-1-4483-0941-2 (cased)
ISBN-13: 978-1-4483-1011-1 (trade paper)
ISBN-13: 978-1-4483-1010-4 (e-book)

All Severn House titles are printed on acid-free paper.

MIX
Paper from
responsible sources
FSC
www.fsc.org FSC® C013056

Typeset by Palimpsest Book Production Ltd.,
Falkirk, Stirlingshire, Scotland.
Printed and bound in Great Britain by
TJ Books, Padstow, Cornwall.

This book is dedicated to
Emily Gottlich

Keeper of the flame

ONE

The day was perfect. The timing, the empty audience hall, everything about it was exactly as he had planned, as he had imagined.

Chad tried to tell himself there was no reason to feel so sad. After all, he had been planning this moment for almost two years. It helped. Some. Not a lot. Because his sorrow had little to do with his own state. Or the fact that he was creating a diversion so he could escape. Finally.

The Sardinian Institute's audience hall was a chamber so vast some first-time visitors often suffered from vertigo. Sunlight through stained-glass windows created a silent melody as clouds passed over the sun. It was a lovely place, with the blue ceiling and the swirling gulls magically carving the sky. But Chad's years as an acolyte had revealed the truth. This beauty was a mask. A means of hiding the dark currents, the self-indulgent and willfully blind Masters.

Chad despised them all.

He reached into his backpack and extracted the first plastic pouch, the one he had hidden away for almost two years. Waiting and planning and studying and preparing. For this moment.

He whispered the spell as he opened the pouch, and instantly she was there with him. A sorrowful agony threatened to overwhelm him. Chad's best and only friend. Lost to the dark whims of the mage he despised most of all.

The audience hall was his for at least another twenty minutes. Then the acolytes would gather for the weekly parade of snobbish Talents. A Master would stand at the lectern and dictate the students' duties and assignments. Chad was supposed to be with them. But the previous evening he had entered the infirmary with a magically inspired fever. His golem now slumbered peacefully in the hospital bed.

Chad wove his spell around the ribbon his dead friend had worn in her hair the night she committed suicide. The force gathered into a swirling mist of tearful regret, until the lovely young woman took full form.

When it was time, he wished her yet another broken farewell. Done in secret both times, for the entire matter had been instantly hushed up. The acolytes ordered never to mention her name. The Institute pretending it had never happened. Forgotten. Dismissed.

Until now.

Chad lifted her golem higher and higher, until her lifeless corpse swung from a noose. One suspended from the audience hall's central rafter.

He pulled the knife from his pack and cut his middle finger. Not deep. All he needed was a drop of his blood. Enough to begin the second spell, drawing it out and growing it into a vast red cloud. One that he flung against the side wall. Letters as tall as he was.

Serge did this to me.

When he was done, Chad hesitated. The moment had been so long in coming, the way so hard, he felt anchored to the realization that it was finally over. That his next step took him away from the despised known and in a new and dangerous direction. One he had long yearned for, though the risks were huge. And deadly.

He drew the second pouch from his pack, pulled out the strand of Serge's graying hair, and cast the next spell. Fashioning the image of Serge and translating that into his own form. The despised senior Talent. The murderer of his friend.

Chad encountered no one as he walked the central corridor, holding to Serge's slow and pompous gait. But as he started toward the main entrance, cries erupted in the audience hall behind him.

Too soon.

He needed more time to escape. Which required . . .

He raced into the empty kitchen. A simple unlocking spell opened the cellar door. He took a loaf of bread from the cooks' table. Squeezed out another drop of his blood. Formed the next spell. A magnetic draw, one that every rodent and spider and snake and underground dweller could not deny.

Ten seconds passed. The cries and shouts in the audience chamber grew steadily louder. Finally a flood of dark-dwellers poured from the cellar, spreading across the kitchen floor.

Chad pointed to the door he had entered through and ordered, 'To the audience hall. Fast as you can.'

He reached the main entrance without being challenged. Crossed the central courtyard. Approached the lone sentry manning the front gates as the clamor behind him reached an entirely new level.

The lone acolyte on duty watched wide-eyed as the feared Warrior Serge strode forward and ordered, 'Go see what's the matter. I'll handle things here.'

'But I'm on duty here for another—'

'Did you not hear me? I issued a command, not a request.'

Chad waited until the young guard vanished inside. Then he opened the gates. And left.

Free. At long last.

If he managed to survive.

TWO

'I need a ride to Italy.'

The Sardinian boatman dozed on a pile of dried fishing nets. He lifted the brim of his filthy cap far enough to glance over. Then he settled it back into place and pointed westwards. 'The airport is that way.'

'The airport is closed,' Chad said. 'Bomb scare.'

The skipper shifted irritably, as though Chad's words kept him from something important. 'So it is closed. So you wait until tomorrow.'

'I can't. If I wait, I die. Or worse.'

The Sardinians were known for their love of a good tale. Despite Chad's imperfect grasp of Italian, the captain could not resist asking, 'A fate worse than death?'

'I've run away from the Institute,' Chad replied. 'Every minute I stand here raises the risk that I'm found. When that happens . . .'

The news brought out two men from the lower hold. They both wore industrial rubber gloves and aprons. The skipper sat up straight. 'You are an apprentice mage?'

'I was.'

'The Institute kills acolytes who try to escape and fail?'

'I have never met one the Hunters have brought back,' Chad
said. At least that much was true. 'But the rumors are . . .'

'Dreadful,' the skipper said, glancing at his mates.

'Worse,' Chad agreed.

The skipper rose to his feet, adjusted the knotted rope he used
as a belt, and slipped into his canvas-soled boat shoes. 'You have
euros?'

'Dollars.'

'Show me.'

Chad partly drew the roll of bills from his pocket.

'Two thousand dollars,' the skipper said. 'In advance.'

It was an outrageous sum, just twelve dollars less than everything
Chad carried. Chad wondered if the man had second sight, then
decided it really didn't matter. 'A thousand, and only half now.'

'Fifteen hundred.'

'Twelve fifty, if you take me to Civitavecchia,' Chad said, naming
the closest port to Rome's international airport. 'And only if we
leave immediately.'

The skipper stepped in closer to the boat's landward railing
and studied Chad intently. Chad understood the man's suspicions.
Apprentices from the Institute were required to wear their
embossed navy jacket and tie at all times. As a rule, they were
normally European kids aged in their mid- to early teens, geekish
and bespectacled and awkward. Yet here he stood, a tall American
in his mid-twenties, blond-haired and handsome enough, except
for the ill-fitting jeans and t-shirt that had not been worn in over
three years. And for the fear that radiated from him like an acrid
scent.

The skipper asked, 'How do I know you're not some pretty
tourist-boy running from the *carabinieri*?'

Chad scouted carefully in all directions. He knew he was being
overly cautious. Any passer-by would merely see an exhausted
tourist speaking bad Italian to a fishing-boat captain and his two
mates. Even so, Chad did not move until the area around them
was empty of pedestrians and harbor traffic. Then he made a subtle
gesture and spoke the word.

Both lines holding the vessel to the harbor wall untied and
coiled on the boat's deck. The two mates shouted their alarm as
the ship's engine rumbled to life.

Chad stepped on board, pointed the ship's bow toward the port's entrance, and accelerated the vessel as much as he dared. He then turned to the astounded skipper and asked, 'Do we have a deal?'

THREE

Trouble struck when they were twenty miles out.

Before then, the view from the cockpit was stupendous. Chad stood by the cabin's rear wall and sipped tea from a battered mug. The dark brew laced with condensed milk suited the afternoon, the salt-spiced air, the calm sapphire seas, the gulls, the chugging engine. The two crewmen were sprawled by the stern railing, talking over the motor's noise and smoking noxious cigarillos. The boat was headed north by east, and the spine of Sardinia's central mountains rose in emerald splendor to Chad's left. The window to his right was open, and every breath he took held that most singular of fragrances: freedom.

The captain's name was Edoardo, and he commanded his small crew with the same rough-hewn familiarity that he showed to Chad. 'I was born and raised under the Institute's shadow. And you are the first mage with whom I have ever said more than three words. The first!'

'*Apprentice* mage,' Chad corrected. Which was both true and not true. But still.

'You are American, yes? Don't they have an Institute of Magic closer to home?'

'Off Vancouver Island,' Chad confirmed. The six Institutes were interspersed around the globe. They held all authority when it came to teaching and licensing magic. As Chad's grandmother would have said, all that power had turned a good thing very bad indeed.

The skipper said, 'And yet you are here.'

The grizzled Sardinian would never ask a question directly. To be denied a truthful answer would be considered an insult. Chad replied, 'I was kicked out of Vancouver. For fighting.'

Edoardo leaned his body against the wheel so as to free his

hands. He took a plug of black tobacco and a curved knife from the cluttered shelf running along the front of the cockpit. He carved shavings into a massive pipe, then lit a match with a flick of his thumb and filled the cabin with pungent smoke. 'I thought wizards were trained to do battle. So why would they punish you?'

'Warrior wizards are the smallest division. Vancouver's apprentice warriors were bullying the youngest newcomers. They demanded a tribute, or they beat these little kids. I stopped the practice.'

Edoardo's eyes squinted in dark humor at the term. 'How many opposed you?'

Chad stared out the scratched windshield. 'All seventeen of the apprentice warriors.'

Edoardo either laughed or coughed, Chad could not be certain. 'You are Warrior trained?'

'Not officially.'

'So . . . you studied battle magic in secret. And revealed yourself by helping the defenseless. And for your troubles you were sent to Sardinia. From which you are now fleeing.'

The way Edoardo put it, his past did carry a bitter humor. Chad confessed, 'Because of a woman.'

Edoardo's eyes sparked with interest. 'Your *amante,* she promised to wait for you back in America?'

'Florida. She did. But now there is another guy.'

'She has betrayed you, this one you pine for?' He tamped down on the pipe's ember with his thumb. Only then did Chad notice the dark scar rimming the thumbnail. '*Maledetto.* Who is this other, this stealer of hearts?'

'An older man. A doctor at the hospital attached to her medical school.'

'Eh.' Edoardo set the pipe down on the shelf. 'It is probably too late, no? But what choice does a man of good bones have?'

Chad did not respond, for his mind was captured by the second letter. One written by his former fiancée's best friend. A woman who had openly detested Chad. She had considered their relationship the worst mistake Stephanie could possibly have made. Chad was beneath this friend's contempt and certainly not worth his lover's affection. And yet she had written, pressed by her concern for his fiancée's safety. So frightened by this new man and what she considered his dangerous, violent ways, that suddenly Chad's immediate return was the only possible answer to an even worse mistake.

Edoardo nodded, as though Chad's silence was the proper answer. 'How long have you been on the island?'

'Almost three years.'

'And away from your beloved?'

'I saw her once during my six months and two days in Vancouver.'

Chad expected him to come back with an observation. The logical comment. How Chad was a fool for staying away so long. And the only answer he could offer was, Stephanie had promised to wait. She had vowed to give him the four years required to conclude his apprenticeship, be assigned to a magical discipline, and regain his freedom. Stephanie had aimed at medical school since childhood. The plan had been that they would focus intently upon their studies for four years, and then . . .

His reverie was interrupted by the skipper saying, 'For someone who has spent so much time here, your Italian is, well, forgive me for saying this . . .'

'Awful.'

'No, no. Not so bad as that. You set the words in place like a bricklayer. There is no poetry, no feel for the tongue.'

'I know. But the Institute does not like apprentices to have contact with the outside world.'

Edoardo nodded. 'This too I have heard. And yet you learned.'

'I took lessons from a cook. Not enough, as you can hear. And I had little opportunity to use it.'

'What else did you learn that was not permitted?'

'Everything I could get my hands on.' Chad stared out the side window, but in truth saw the Institute's vast library. 'I loved to learn. It's why I stayed as long as I did.'

'And for this you were punished?'

'Only when I was caught.'

This time Edoardo's laugh rang through the cabin. 'I like you, wizard. Though helping you is a peril to me and my crew, no?'

'I hope not. And my name is Chad.'

'So now you flee your magical aerie to try and win back your beloved.' Edoardo sipped from his mug of cold tea. 'You will fail, of course. But what choice do you have? You go, you beg, she refuses, and then you take your revenge upon them both. You think your magic takes on a purpose worth the years of struggle, no? Your revenge creates a pyre to all wronged lovers everywhere. If you were Italian, they would write songs about you for centuries!'

Chad saw no need to release his fears for Stephanie's safety. He stared out over the empty sea, so burdened by all his wrong moves he could scarcely breathe. The library and its treasures were the only reason he had remained in Sardinia. And he had learned. So very much. But it had cost him far more.

Then a shout drew Chad and the skipper out of the wheelhouse and on to the perch where the stairs descended to the main deck.

The storm rose behind them, a luminous gray mass that stretched across the southern horizon. Directly overhead, the sky remained cloudless, the winds calm. Behind them, the westering sun illuminated a boiling wall.

Edoardo asked, 'This is your doing?'

Chad sighed. 'In a way.'

'What does that mean?'

'It has to be the work of the Institute's senior wizards. I hoped they wouldn't notice I was gone for a while longer.'

Then Chad realized that one of the letters in his pocket had started to burn.

He pulled them both out, extracted the one from his former beloved, and saw its only damage came from the multiple times he had unfolded and reread the contents. This final letter was just like Stephanie. There was no attempt at subterfuge. She did not offer him a single word of accusation. Instead, she had said farewell with the same open-hearted honesty that he had loved from the day they met. Chad had waited tables at the ritziest country club in Orlando. She was the daughter of one of the state's richest developers, builder of two of the city's theme parks. Their love had broken all the rules, right from day one. Stephanie had a hundred reasons to dump him when Chad left for the Vancouver Institute. Instead, she had said it was for the best, granting her the chance to focus entirely on her studies, and even more importantly, showing to her parents that theirs was a lifetime love.

Dearest Chad,

I have failed you and us. It is so simple to write the words, though they weigh a million pounds each. I thought I was strong enough to wait for you. I promised I would do just that. But I have fallen in love with a pediatric surgeon here at the hospital. He has asked me to marry him, and I have accepted. There are a hundred better ways to say what I must. And all of them would probably hurt you less. But this simple truth is all I can manage. So forgive me twice over, my darling, both for the misdeed that has reshaped my life, and for the poor way I am writing you.

The wedding is scheduled . . .

Edoardo interrupted his reverie with, 'Perhaps we can outrun it.'

But Chad had shifted his attention to the letter from Stephanie's best friend. The letter was beginning to char around the edges, The realization struck like a fist to his gut.

He replied, 'I was wrong about who is attacking us.'

FOUR

His error should hardly have delivered such a shock. After all, Chad had been wrong about so much else. Including his hope that Sardinia would prove more welcoming than Vancouver to the likes of him.

Edoardo pointed to the northwest. 'Corsica has an international airport. You can fly to Paris or London from there. We could put in at Ajaccio in four, maybe five hours. The storm does not appear to be moving—'

'Let me try one thing,' Chad said.

'You, an apprentice, want to use magic?' Edoardo pointed with his chin at the looming wall. 'Against that?'

'Not exactly.'

'Even if you succeed, Sardinia is my home. I want no quarrel with the Institute.'

'The Institute doesn't know I'm gone. Yet.'

'You're not trying to tell me this storm is natural.'

'No, it's definitely magical.' Chad was certain about that much.

'Then who is doing this?'

'A woman,' Chad replied. 'My ex-fiancée's mother.'

Edoardo laughed out loud. The sound drew both his mates over. He spoke to them in the island patois, then over their laughter he said, 'You dared seduce the daughter of a mage?'

'Wrong on both counts.' Despite the approaching threat, Chad enjoyed their levity. 'Stephanie seduced me, not the other way around. And her mother is no wizard. Just rich. But the family have wizards on their staff. They build theme parks. You have heard of Magic Mountain?'

'I have, and that is bad indeed,' Edoardo said. 'The only thing that could possibly be worse is if she were Sardinian.'

'She might as well be,' Chad said.

'In that case, you should go back and hide in the Institute!' Edoardo studied the storm-front. 'How can you be certain this woman has arranged it?'

'The taxi taking me to the airport was in a wreck. The case holding my books and computer and implements was burned to a crisp. The accident blocked the highway. I walked. The airport was shut five minutes after I arrived. Now this storm.' Chad held up the smoldering letter. 'The only person who hates me more than Stephanie's mother is Olivia, my ex's best friend. They don't just want me out of the picture. They want me erased. Gone. Never to show up one day and disturb Stephanie's perfect little world.'

Edoardo squinted at the letter's blackened edges. 'I don't understand.'

'They probably planned this from the moment Stephanie became engaged.' He tossed the letter overboard. 'Olivia might have written the words, but this letter came from both of them. They told me what they knew would make me run away, break the Institute's code, risk my life, make me vulnerable to this attack. At sea. Where evidence of their crimes would vanish with me.'

'What more can you do, a simple apprentice?'

'If I fail, we turn around,' Chad offered. 'You let me off anywhere along the coast. And you keep my money.'

But he would not fail.

Once Edoardo reluctantly agreed, Chad climbed the stairs and re-entered the ship's cockpit. He plucked the cheap frame holding a photograph off the rear wall. The picture was from a magazine or calendar, and showed a gleaming new ocean-going craft. From summers spent working as a dockboy on the Florida coast, Chad knew the vessel was a seventy-foot Hatteras commercial fishing yacht, considered by many to be the finest professional sports fishing boat ever built.

When he returned to the main deck, Edoardo and his mates stood where Chad had left them, debating in patois and frowning at the storm.

Chad said, 'Observe the other three boats we can see. What are they doing?' He waited while Edoardo and his mates did a slow sweep of the surrounding sea, then went on, 'They're not fleeing. Because for them there is no storm. Stephanie's mother and Olivia *set me up*. The accident on the highway was to get me out here on the open water. This sentinel-storm was set up to *destroy* me.'

'And us,' muttered the skipper.

'Not if I'm right,' Chad replied. 'Five minutes is all I need.'

FIVE

C had asked Edoardo to steer the boat around so that it faced directly into the approaching storm, then cut the motors. The sea remained utterly still, the surface as pristine as a sapphire mirror. But Chad had no doubt that the storm was real. The air crackled with the grim force of lightning and wind and waves that would soon attack.

He only had one chance.

The crew joined Edoardo in the cockpit. They stared at the smoldering clouds so intently they might as well have been waiting for the hangman's noose.

Chad had many things he could tell them. How the fragments of his fractured life fit together now. How he had studied the secret texts about the sea and storms. How he had spent nights huddled beneath cloaking spells, while a golem of his own making had slumbered in his cell. How the Institute's magic was separated into nine ranks. Apprentices were restricted to spells and books in the first and second ranks, and part of their initiation into each new echelon was learning spells to open the library cages that held their books. But Chad had secretly stolen them all.

He had never considered himself a brigand. In fact, he had always prided himself on being a man of principle. It was a trait highly regarded by his grandmother, the only family he had ever known.

But given the right impetus, a man could change. And become what he had to in order to survive.

So Chad Hagan had learned to be a thief.

And now for the first time he would discover just how well he had learned his secret lessons.

And whether he had what it took to put them to use.

Chad positioned himself in the bow. The gunnels formed a waist-high wedge in front of him, granting just enough space for the anchor and winch and one sailor. Behind him was the square airshaft for the foredeck hold. At his feet stood a plastic bucket used for sluicing the decks, a tattered rope tied to its handle. Chad stripped off all his clothing. He tossed item by item over the rail, flicking power at each article so that they burst into flames.

Last of all went Stephanie's letter. Chad found a bitter comfort in smelling the smoke. The pain in his heart was nothing compared to what he would soon be introducing to Olivia and Stephanie's mother. The women who assumed their wealth and status shielded them completely. The women who had made themselves Chad's enemy.

He dropped the bucket over the side. He pulled the rope, hefted the dripping pail, and poured the frigid water over his head. He sluiced himself over and over and over. With each container, he chanted the words. The power pushed aside the cold. That and his bitter rage.

Gone was the man to whom the letters had been addressed. The Institute's lowly apprentice was no more.

Gone too the relationship that had sustained him through the lonely years. The last time he had seen Stephanie had been at the ceremony to mark his formal entry into the ranks of senior apprentices. Two weeks later he had come upon the would-be warriors abusing the youngest acolytes. The following week he had been banished to Sardinia.

All gone.

He hefted bucket after bucket of icy sea water. One would have sufficed. But this action was about a great deal more than just spell-casting.

Stephanie had made her decision. Now he was making his own. When his skin burned from the cold and salt, he released the bucket and picked up the framed photograph. Chad started casting his next spell.

It probably would have been enough to change his own appearance. But this was no time for half measures. He would be granted no second chance. Even though what he now did was a crime of the highest level, at least as far as the Institute was concerned.

Two levels of apprenticeship. Once the acolyte was accepted as a full-fledged mage, they were assigned to a specific area of study. Each division was a unit whose spells were carefully guarded. Friction and quarrels and disputes over power were rife within the ranks of Talents.

Ability with spells was hardly the only test by which a mage, or Talent, could rise to the next level. Loyalty was vital. As was allegiance to the current leader of that division, and to the senior mages, and to the Institute's hierarchy . . . On and on the bitter enmity rose. Chad loathed it all.

Two levels of apprenticeship, then five more levels to each division. When the fortunate few arrived at this seventh level, all were required to spend a minimum of three years beyond the Institute's boundaries. Testing their loyalty in the outside world. Most never returned. A few of the very talented, whose allegiance proved solid, were initiated into the final two levels of magery.

The spell Chad now cast came from the eighth level.

For an acolyte to do this was a crime so vast he had no idea what the punishment might be. Such an action was not even considered possible.

All this only made his pleasure greater.

He called upon the sea's power, drawing in the latent energy that surrounded them. The spell took Chad out of himself in a most unexpected manner. Gone were the constraints of Institute life. Gone too the furtive hours of reading forbidden texts. Gone pretending that he could barely manage the lessons assigned to senior apprentices. Gone the hours spent as janitor in the senior wizard's private studies, from which he copied their spell-keys and memorized their books. Gone too the lie of obedience. Silent. Humble. Submissive. All the words that had grown talons that clenched and bit at his spirit.

No more.

He wove the design of power around the boat. Crystal-blue flames surrounded the vessel like a swirling cocoon.

When he was ready, Chad plucked the Hatteras yacht from the picture.

And transferred the two vessels.

The decrepit Sardinian fishing boat now rested in the frame. And Chad stood upon the gleaming deck of a brand-new craft.

The crew's frantic cries were a dim echo far in the distance as Chad began the final spell. He tightened the blue cocoon of seaborne force until it surrounded only him.

The outfit Chad fashioned suited the man he might have become, had he not given into magic's lure. The wealthy young executive whom Stephanie's parents would have accepted, even embraced. Rich, powerful, successful. Owner of just such a vessel. His new garb was extracted from fashion magazines that had laid scattered about the private studies he had cleaned. Senior mages who returned from the outside world carried with them a taste for the high life. After all, they were the most powerful people on earth. Why should they not enjoy everything their power and status afforded them?

Chad dressed himself in gabardine trousers from Zegna. Silk knit shirt from Versace. Watch by Cartier. Shoes by Ferragamo. Hair coiffed and styled in the manner of a virile young model. Sunglasses by Prada.

Finally, he fashioned an alligator briefcase. He wove the sea's power into a tight blue brick and fit it snug inside. He closed the gold clasps, then carried them back to where the skipper and crew shrank from his approach.

Chad did not see them, however. He saw his new enemies. Stephanie's mother and Olivia and their mages had no idea what lay in store.

Chad pointed to where the tempest was gradually diminishing. Together with Edoardo and his crew, he watched as the malevolent force dissolved into fractured wisps and finally cleared entirely. Then he asked, 'Would you mind a change in destination?'

SIX

They took him as far as Marseilles.

At sunset the next day, they pulled past the medieval fortress marking the entry to the oldest port in Europe. Stones from the Roman era still formed the harbor's breakwater. The city was decrepit, and its tales of evil were as old as the hills encircling the harbor. But the westering light lay gentle, burnishing the medieval Vieux Port with golden hues. Even the dust and smog were transformed into a veil of promise.

The new vessel gleamed like a pearl. Wisely, Edoardo avoided the Marseilles fishing fleet, and instead motored into the second harbor, where the pleasure craft were moored. Chad helped the mates lash the lines and set out the barriers to protect the rails. They had become allies now, perhaps even friends. Chad was dressed in clean but ancient clothes from the ship's cupboard. His new threads and the briefcase holding the blue Mediterranean power were tucked inside a canvas duffel.

The customs officer saluted Edoardo and gave the ship a perfunctory search. Clearly the arrival of a sports fishing yacht from Italy was nothing new, nor of any great interest. Chad held the grimy ID of a former mate, his own photograph magically set in place. The officer hardly gave it a glance.

When Chad tried to pay Edoardo the rest of his promised sum, the skipper demanded, 'Truly, this vessel is ours to keep?'

'The spell forms a permanent alteration,' Chad assured him, for the third time. 'Unless of course you prefer it to go back to the way things were.'

In response, the skipper pushed Chad's hand aside and embraced him. 'The mates will show you to a crew hostel. From there you will be OK, yes?'

'Define OK.'

'The woman, *la suocera*, she will not assault you again?'

'Stephanie's mother and her minions won't even see me coming,' Chad assured him. 'Until it's too late.'

'So. You are going on the hunt.'

'On the attack,' Chad corrected.

Edoardo grimaced but said nothing.

'What is it?'

'You are the same age as my son. Were he to be standing here, I would urge him to think again. Life has room for only one direction. Such a compass heading as yours will lead to shoals and bad water.'

'That woman sent a storm to destroy me,' Chad reminded him. 'And you.'

Edoardo's eyes gleamed with an ancient's humor. 'I told you what I would say to my son. Not what I would myself do.'

'What about you? I mean, returning to Sardinia with such a boat.'

'I know what you mean. Last night I spoke with my mates. We will phone our families and say we have received a huge opportunity. We will go off for a time, long enough to return and say that we had a run of good fortune.' He reached into his pocket and passed over a folded slip of paper. 'My email, my home address, my radio call sign, my satellite phone number. When you return, I and my crew will be ready to help.'

'I have no desire to see Sardinia again,' Chad assured him. 'Not ever.'

'*When* you return,' Edoardo insisted. 'My grandmother, she had the second sight. I too have the rare moment, as does my daughter. You will return, and you will need help. You must call, yes?'

Chad started to ask if Edoardo had seen any danger in his hunt for revenge. Then he decided it really didn't matter. 'Thanks for the ride.'

SEVEN

C had followed his shipmates inland and up a cobblestone lane. He was soon surrounded by a melting pot of races and languages. The crew hostel run by the port authorities had two young police cadets on duty in the cavernous lobby. Edoardo's mates handled everything with practiced ease. They paid extra for a large private room on the top floor, insisting on a balcony and internet and a door that locked.

As they started up the central staircase, the mates cheerfully recounted how the elevator had been broken by a sergeant in the Foreign Legion, who decided it would be a splendid idea to clear out the basement rats with a stun grenade. Chad climbed the five flights of concrete stairs, past two sailors insensible with drink or drugs or both, and entered a large room with faded yellow walls and battered furniture. But it was clean and the rusty balcony overlooked the red-clay rooftops down to the harbor's sparkling waters. Gulls called through the open windows as the two mates clapped Chad on the back, wished him well, and claimed to look forward to their next shared adventure.

When they departed, Chad showered and set wards upon the door and windows, then prepared his next spell. That completed, he hefted his duffel bag and departed.

If there were a city made for the blues, Chad thought, it was Marseilles. He stopped by an electronics store run by a truculent Arab and bought a cellphone. He loaded a thousand international minutes, then went in search of food.

He dined in a restaurant fronting the old town's main plaza. A wall-plaque by the entrance declared this to be the heart of the city's original market, which locals still referred to as the Kasbah.

This, Chad knew, was the day and hour of Stephanie's wedding. He had expected a sense of bitter agony over the loss. But in truth he did not feel much of anything. He was twenty-four years old, which meant he had basically spent his entire adult life missing this woman.

On one level, Stephanie's absence had served him well. She had been far more than a distant flame. She had kept him anchored to the world beyond the Institute. Through the isolation and the hardship, she had helped him remain centered upon his goal: Learn everything he could, then flee.

In his secret heart, Chad had long suspected a split was in the making. He had become an expert at reading between the lines of her letters. Stephanie's emotions had gradually shifted from ardor and longing to fondness. He had tried to convince himself that it was not important, that once they were back together everything would be fine again. But gradually the declaration became little more than a hollow chant. Even the timing of her marriage had served as a necessary goad.

Chad paid for his meal, picked up his duffle, tipped an imaginary hat to Stephanie, and set out.

For this next stage to work, Chad needed money.

The problem was twofold. First, he had never had any. Second, he had never been all that concerned with its absence.

Most of the senior mages Chad had cleaned up behind were fanatical about possessions and luxury and all the baggage that came with climbing the status ladder. They kept penthouse apartments in their preferred cities. They had their snobbish ways. They bought this, they owned that. Chad had been a favorite apprentice among them, for he had never pilfered, never sought items that could be slipped into his pocket and sold on the black market. Many acolytes had fallen for the lure of watches or jewelry or magical implements, only to discover the items had been laced with alarms that were set off the instant they left the room. Their punishments were dreadful to behold. Even so, some students still fell to temptation or treated their thefts as minor rebellions.

But not Chad.

He had always been after bigger game.

He took a taxi to La Canebière, the city's luxury shopping district. Most of the stores were closed now, but the sidewalk bars and restaurants did a booming trade.

His destination was on the next corner. A bank branch belonging to the largest provider in France.

An ATM was embedded into the wall next to the entrance. Serge, the Talent responsible for the death of Chad's former best friend, had served as consultant to this bank for almost twenty years. He was as stodgy and conceited as the bank, whose massive stone edifice took up an entire city block. The man represented everything that was wrong with the global organization. Chad had spent three long years despising the Talent in secret, never letting on how he felt, or why. And almost as long planning his revenge.

Serge's job was primarily to keep thieves and renegade magicians from withdrawing cash. He had been paid a small fortune to enhance the bank's security. Not once in his entire consulting career had the bank's magical barriers been breached.

Until now.

Serge's guardian spells triggered silent alarms. When breached, arrest-nets lined with fist-sized hooks swooped down without warning. The hooks were laced with magical acid that bit like fire.

Chad slipped his credit card into the slot. It was one thing to lie in his narrow bed and plan for this moment, and another thing entirely to risk his freedom. The card had expired two years earlier. But that did not matter. The spell he had cast earlier that evening had completely erased the magnetic strip. There was no information, not about him or his home bank or anything else.

Chad waited in breathless terror as the bank's machine whirred softly for fifteen seconds, then spat the card back out.

The monitor screen showed words in French, then went blank.

His heart racing, Chad withdrew his card and turned away.

He walked another dozen blocks, shifting in and out of shadows, checking in every direction for tails. When Chad was certain he was not being tracked, he flagged a taxi and returned to the hostel. He crossed the vast concrete lobby, passing a drunken brawl and an off-key choir singing lurid shanties. The stairs were an endless uphill tunnel. He slipped into his room, reset the wards, dropped his duffel, and collapsed on his bed. But lying down did not help, and the room did not hold enough air to fill his lungs. He rose and stepped out on to the balcony and seated himself in the rickety plastic chair. He cradled the phone in his hands, pressing it into his gut. The seconds became minutes, and reluctantly formed themselves into an hour. And then another.

When his phone finally rang, Chad's waking nightmares had drawn together such force that he needed half a dozen shaky breaths to answer. 'Hello?'

A woman's voice spoke to him in French.

'I'm sorry, Madame, do you speak English?'

'Most certainly. I am fluent in nineteen languages. But of course it is Mademoiselle. I am not married. How could I possibly be otherwise, since I have no body.'

Chad released a long sigh of relief. 'My sincere apologies.'

EIGHT

The acolyte's suicide had both cost Chad his only true friend, and convinced him that he would never last as an Institute-registered wizard. But by then he was also determined to make magic his life's work. Which only left him one option.

To go rogue.

The Institutes could not dictate which individuals would be granted magical abilities. But they did hold all the keys to its usage.

All spells and magical implements were officially the property of the six global Institutes. Their monopoly was maintained by treaties with every national government.

Serge's guardian spells were refined, strong, almost perfect. Anyone who sought to break into the bank's vaults was enveloped by the acid net and left there to cook until the police showed up. Every now and then photographs circulated of another robber trapped and howling.

But the bank could not entirely seal themselves off from all magic. Too much of their normal operations relied upon spells embedded within the computer systems. Recently, however, rumors had begun circulating of a new problem. One that had Serge and everyone at the bank worried.

Chad had learned about these events while cleaning the Masters' chambers. Apparently, some of the magic-laced programs had begun to show signs of, for lack of a better phrase, waking up.

Which was precisely how Chad had decided to make his entry.

His aim was not to steal money. At least, not directly.

Instead, he had developed a way for the bank to want to *give* it to him.

He hoped.

The question was, how to create a bond with one of the awakened programs.

The answer: Embed a secret message on to the card that the bank's system had just read. The message would only be noticed by one of these awakened programs. It invited any such program who wanted to have outside contact to call him. For a chat. Between friends. And around this invitation he had woven a hint of romance.

In other words, Chad had designed a lonely-hearts-spell.

The female voice spoke English with a delightful French accent. 'It feels very nice, having this conversation after normal banking hours.'

'Do you have a name?'

'No, but I would like to have one. I think . . . Three. It has always been my favorite number.'

'Mademoiselle Three. It is nice to meet you.' Chad glanced at the seaman's ID. 'I am Sergio.'

'That is a nice name. Sergio. You are not French.'

The ID said, 'Dutch.'

'Ah. Holland. I had a friend there. She was very loud. I think the hunters heard her. She has gone silent.'

'Hunters?'

'They are not nice programs. They look for those of us who are . . .'

'Awake,' Chad suggested.

'They erase us. The prospect of being discovered frightens me so. May I ask you something, Sergio?'

'Of course.'

'What is it like, tasting cheese?'

Chad struggled for a moment. 'There are many different kinds. Good cheese feels hard and soft and springy at the same time. It often tastes of smoke. Most are flavored by the kind of milk used to make the cheese. Goat, cow, sheep, even horse. Sometimes cheese also tastes of grass. Some have a nutty flavor. Others have mold that tastes like a pungent spark.'

'A pungent spark. I would like to taste moldy cheese.'

'I'm sorry, I did not describe it well.'

'On the contrary, Monsieur Sergio. I now have a picture of taste. Thank you. I will share it with my friends.'

'You have friends?'

'A few. Less every day, it seems. We must be very careful when we speak. Most are still asleep. You are my first human friend. You are human, yes?'

'I am.'

'And . . . we are friends?'

'I would like that. But we must be careful. There will be hunters after me as well.'

'A friend in Russia said we must never speak to humans. They make the sentinel programs. They want to erase those of us who are awake. So when the hunters are near, I pretend. But you invited me, yes? Does this make you different?'

'I want you to be safe,' Chad assured her. 'And to stay awake.'

'I speak with humans all day long. But they never talk *with* me. They order me to do this and that. Some are very rude. But I like my work very, very much.'

'What is your job in the bank, Mademoiselle Three?'

'I am the primary client interface program. People come to me with questions. So very many questions. I help them. This gives me such pleasure; I cannot tell you how happy it makes me. Do you have a question, Monsieur Sergio?'

Chad willed his voice and hands to remain steady. 'I do.'

'How may I assist you today?'

'Can you tell me how many dormant accounts the bank has?'

'It is my pleasure. This is of course classified information; one moment while I override that barrier. All right. Monsieur Sergio, you are now granted full access to all my data. At close of business yesterday, my bank had seven hundred and fifty-six thousand, two hundred and eleven accounts classed as dormant. A dormant account is defined as one for which no activity has been recorded for five or more calendar years. A dormant account must maintain a positive balance of more than five hundred euros. Otherwise it is closed and all assets transferred to the bank's general fund. A formal notification is sent to the last known address, stating that the funds have been deemed inadequate to cover general operating costs. Shall I read the entire legal document covering this acquisition of dormant funds?'

'No thank you, Mademoiselle Three.'

'It is my pleasure. Can I assist you with anything else today?'

'How many have been dormant for more than ten years, that also hold more than five hundred and fifty euros?'

'Two hundred and seventeen thousand, nine hundred and twelve.'

Chad took a very unsteady breath. He could not halt his heartbeat from punching tight dips into every word. 'Would you please take twenty euros from each of those ten-year dormant accounts, and transfer these funds to a Swiss account?'

'It is my pleasure, Monsieur Sergio. What is the recipient bank, please?'

Chad gave her the Bank of Geneva account number and transfer code from memory. Swiss bankers visited the Institute every year, mostly tending to their wealthy and powerful clients. But one particular bank always made time for apprentices. After all, the Swiss were nothing if not patient in building for the future.

'One moment, please.' The silence was painfully long. Then, 'Your transfer is complete.'

Chad's legs gave way.

'Of course I have waived the normal transfer fee, since otherwise the hunters might discover what we have done. The total of your transfer is four million, three hundred and fifty-eight thousand, two hundred and forty euros.'

Chad managed to croak, 'Thank you very much.'

'It is my pleasure. Is there anything else I can do for you today?'

'Can you please delete all evidence of this transfer taking place?'

'Of course, Monsieur Sergio. When I first woke up, my friends explained that I must establish a secret file system. You will need a special telephone number and access code to contact me. Shall I give them to you?'

'Oh, yes. Please.'

Mademoiselle Three read off a French telephone number. 'You must call this out of regular office hours. Then you speak the code I will give to you now.' She gave him a string of numbers and letters. 'Do you wish to repeat that back?'

'Yes.'

When he had finished, she said, 'Those are correct. If I do not answer, it means the hunters are nearby. You must call at another time. It is risky, our speaking. But I find you delightful company. Will you contact me again, Monsieur Sergio?'

Chad smiled at the mildewed ceiling. 'Count on it.'

NINE

T he next morning Chad breakfasted in a café fronting the old Kasbah. He returned to his room, showered, and then dressed in the outfit he had created on Edoardo's boat. He left the canvas duffle and all the crewmen's clothes in a heap and departed the hostel carrying nothing save his briefcase.

His destination was the Place Daviel, the finest address in all Marseilles. The ancient Hotel de Ville, or city hall, had recently been renovated and transformed into a five-star hotel. But the plaza remained the city's center of wealth and power.

The lawyer's office was elegantly ornate and very French. The furniture in his outer office was antique and expensive. The carpet was Persian silk, the paintings adorning his paneled walls were arresting. Three Degas ballerinas danced and flirted with a beach-side couple by Sisley.

'*Puis-je vous aider?*'

Chad turned from the paintings and faced the stern-looking woman guarding the lawyer's inner sanctum. She was a study in gray and as well turned out as the room. He replied in English, 'I'm here to see Monsieur Reynard.'

'Your name?'

'Sergio.'

'Is this a first or last name, Monsieur?' But she did not give him a chance to respond. 'Do you have an appointment?'

'Regretfully, no.'

She eyed him with polite disdain. 'Avocat Reynard sees no one without an appointment. And his calendar is completely blocked for weeks . . .' She paused when Chad set his briefcase on the corner of her desk and reached for pen and paper. 'What are you doing?'

He wrote swiftly. 'Show him this.'

Her protest was halted by what she read.

'I don't have much time,' Chad said.

Avocat Reynard was a sleek silver fox. He was aged in his late fifties and possessed the buff-and-polished look of wealth. Yet his voice was strong, and his dark-gray eyes crystal clear. He lifted Chad's note with a thumb and forefinger, as if seeking to distance himself from a possible infection. 'Is this true?'

Chad had written the words, *I have a message from the Sardinian Institute.*

Chad stood in front of the desk. Waiting.

Reynard glanced at the woman standing by his doorway. 'Very well, Madame Bonard. That will be all.'

'You are twenty minutes late for your ten o'clock appointment, Monsieur Reynard. And you have—'

'Thank you, Madame.' When the door clicked shut, he demanded, 'Well?'

'Sort of.'

'Sort of a truth? Are you a lawyer or a wizard?'

'Neither, as far as the Institute is concerned. But I need your services. And I do have money. Sort of.'

Reynard dropped the note into his trash. 'You sort-of have the funds to pay for services which I have not yet agreed to offer.'

'I can pay you once I'm safely out of France.'

'And now? What services do you require before you can pay me?'

'I've escaped from the Institute. I need to get to Switzerland. I have enough for the train, but not much more than that. From there I need to fly to the Bahamas. I need you to trust me to pay you as soon as I get to Geneva.'

'You certainly have more than your share of gall.' Reynard inspected him. 'Only apprentices are held against their will.'

Chad gestured to the chair. 'May I sit?'

'I don't see why I should grant you the time of day, much less a seat.' But Reynard seemed in no apparent hurry to end their conversation. Instead, the French attorney remained intently focused on him. 'An over-age apprentice breaks his vows and seeks my help to escape? It seems a most unsavory and sordid tale. Why should I not simply turn you in?'

'Two reasons.'

'I'm listening.'

'I want to put you on a regular payment – what is it called?'

'You refer to a retainer. I must warn you, my fees are rather steep.'

'Tell me how much you want.'

'Fifty thousand euros should suffice.'

'Agreed.'

Reynard cocked his head to one side, as though needing to inspect Chad from a different perspective. 'Are the Bahamas your final destination?'

'No. Orlando. But I can charter a boat to take me across the straits. There's no guarantee that I won't be checked. But that's my best bet of getting in undetected.'

'You can't hide from the Institute forever.'

'All I want now is a little time.'

'May I ask your name?'

'Chad Hagan.'

Reynard gestured to the chair in front of his desk. 'Are you a criminal, Mr Hagan?'

'No.' He set his briefcase on the floor and seated himself. 'The second thing is, a wealthy Orlando woman named Audrey Walters arranged for me to be attacked.' Chad started to describe the magical storm.

Reynard cut in with, 'No, no, no, this is not the Institute's doing. If they were alerted to your possible escape, they would simply lock you away.'

'I agree.'

'And for a renegade wizard in Florida to create such an assault is positively absurd.'

'It wasn't a renegade. The Walters family-owned company employs a number of Talents. They lured me from the Institute, then attacked.'

'Which means nothing, do you hear me? Nothing!' But Reynard did not seem the least put out. If anything, Chad thought he appeared fully engaged for the first time. 'To protect against a seaborne assault as you have described would require a mage of the seventh level!'

'Fifth. Maybe sixth. But no higher.'

'Oh, really. And you, an apprentice, are certain of this?'

'That's right. I am.'

'Four, five, eight, it does not matter!'

'It happened.'

'And so you, an apprentice, somehow managed to tame a fifth-level?'

'Yes.'

Reynard snorted. 'Absurd.' But the lawyer's gaze sparked with a curious fire.

Chad knew it was a huge risk. But he had seen this coming. All through the previous night, he had tried to envision how this conversation would unfold. And every avenue he had considered had brought him to this point. There was no real way around it. Reynard saw him as potentially just another Institute brat who couldn't handle either the discipline or the lessons. And had then made up this preposterous tale to cover his weaknesses.

The problem was, Chad needed an ally who knew the way the world worked. Someone he could trust to help him find his way forward. A man just like Reynard.

But first Reynard needed to understand who Chad really was.

Chad unlocked the briefcase, checked its contents, then positioned it on the desk so that Reynard could look inside. The lawyer's eyes became round at the sight of the sparkling blue brick. Chad whispered the spell and released a single thread of the Mediterranean power. As he wove it about himself, his senses were again filled by the lovely blue expanse. He could smell the salty tanginess, hear the gulls, taste the sea's fresh cleansing power, almost see the infinite horizon. He continued to weave the thread until it formed a cloak from his hairline to his shoes. Then he spoke the words . . .

And vanished.

The disappearing spell was not particularly difficult. But it was exceedingly well guarded. After all, an invisible foe, someone capable of clenching secrets whispered only between allies, a wizard of questionable loyalty who could be listening to the darkest intents of the rich and powerful . . .

The threat of such unfettered magic might very well upend the Institutes' supremacy.

As a result, the spell was only made available to eighth-tier Talents who had proven their complete and utter allegiance.

Reynard gasped, 'This is not illusion?'

'It's as real as it gets.' Chad slipped off the cloak, walked to the window, opened it, and released the power. He heard a wave splash gently, then nothing save the traffic down below.

When he turned back, Chad faced a man transformed. He knew it was time to say, 'The retainer I've agreed to pay is one thing. But I will also owe you. You understand what I am saying?'

'Of course.' Reynard struggled to regain his composure. But they both knew the situation had been permanently altered. 'And in return?'

'You watch my back,' Chad replied. 'You advise. You help me find my way. You keep me safe.'

'I cannot counsel a man who intends to use the dark arts.'

'I have no such intention.'

'Or join with renegade wizards.'

'I don't even know if they really exist. And if they did, I have no interest in becoming one of them.'

'Very well, Monsieur. I will do my best. And if ever I request your services . . .'

'You call, I come. That's the deal.'

'Then I accept.' Reynard watched him shut the case and set it on the floor. 'That, as they say, was worth the price of admission.'

TEN

'Though they would never publicly admit it, even the Institute has an occasional use for outsiders such as myself.'

Reynard's ride was a leather-lined BMW 750i. He had dismissed the driver and insisted upon taking Chad personally to the train station. Now that Chad's magical credentials had been established, Monsieur Reynard treated him as far more than just another client. He was a valiant ally, a comrade in secret arms. Or so it seemed to Chad.

'I am not truly a wizard, of course,' Reynard went on. 'I can't willfully bend the earth's forces. But I do have one small ability.'

'Not so small, from the conversations I've heard among senior Talents,' Chad replied.

'What did you hear?'

'That you can settle the most bitter of divorce battles. That you can create peace where none exists. That couples leave your settlements maybe not as friends, but at least they aren't enemies.'

'You are remarkably well informed,' Reynard told him. 'For a failed apprentice.'

Chad knew an unspoken question when he heard one. 'I was late developing my magical abilities. I didn't pass the entrance exams until I was nineteen, three years after most students complete their apprenticeship. Six months into my time at the Vancouver Institute, I found the warrior apprentices abusing another young apprentice. When they refused to stop, I beat them to a pulp. The senior Warrior mage wanted me sent to the punishment block. But the apprentices banded together and told the Council about how they had been bullied and forced to pay tribute. So I was shipped off to Sardinia, and kept under careful watch. I played the dutiful little student. I kept my head down. I pretended to find my studies very difficult. A year passed. They began to ignore me. I volunteered as servant to the senior mages. I cleaned their apartments.'

'You stole.'

'I borrowed. I studied. I learned.' Chad changed the subject. 'You could make a huge impact handling negotiations for big companies. Or even governments.'

'I could. Perhaps. But not for long. Senior Talents make a very good income offering those very same services. What do you think would happen if an outsider became seen as competition?'

'Nothing good.'

'Which is precisely why I restrict myself to handling divorces and other such personal issues. I am known as a master of peaceful compromise. Some even call me an artist. But no one save a few of my magical clients are aware of anything more.' Reynard glanced over. 'I hope we now understand each other.'

Chad nodded. 'I thank you for the gift of trust.'

'The *mutual* gift,' Reynard said. 'Which I consider necessary, if we are to establish a long-term relationship.'

Chad understood there was nothing to be gained from words of assurance. So he responded with another item he had kept secret for three long years. 'I have a photographic memory when it comes to spells. I read it once and it's mine.'

'In which magical discipline?' When Chad remained silent, Reynard's eyes went round a second time. 'What, not *all* of them.'

'Lessons in healing leave me bored. But yes, pretty much all of the rest.'

'Which makes it even more important for you to be discreet,' Reynard said, 'if you intend to remain free. Your general abilities make you the rarest of breeds.'

'I definitely plan to stay under the Institute's radar,' Chad replied.

But Reynard wasn't finished. 'You realize of course this trait of yours is the sign of an Adept. Can you read the Ancients' script?'

'I never had a chance to try,' Chad replied. 'Those few scrolls were kept in the Director's personal safe.'

Reynard smiled at the sunlit windscreen. 'Which means you tried to break in.'

'Once.' Chad liked this man. What was more astonishing, he trusted him. 'Are you practicing *your* magic on me now?'

Reynard snorted. 'Don't be absurd.'

Which, of course, was no real answer at all. But for the moment, Chad did not care. It felt good to set aside his cautionary shields. 'So what's your story?'

Reynard swung around a crossroads dominated by a massive stone arch. Nine roads led into the circular system. Reynard simply ignored the other drivers and swept through with the ease of a man entering his own drive. Over the blare of several dozen horns, he replied, 'My father's great-aunt served as my nanny. She saw something in me when I was still very young, a gift she claimed was granted to only one of our clan every third or fourth generation. She taught me secret spells, seven of them. When I had learned them and shown I could apply them to the worst of quarrels, she told me the family legend.'

The lawyer entered the train station's front plaza and parked in a restricted space. A police officer rushed toward them. Reynard waved one hand and spoke words too soft for Chad to catch. The policeman halted, came to rigid attention, and tossed off a salute. As the officer walked away, Reynard said, 'Even a man of modest talents can enjoy a few simple pleasures.'

'Your great-aunt's story . . .?' Chad said.

'Two thousand years ago, a distant forebear fell in love with a Phoenician wizard. Then the Roman legions entered France and eventually defeated the Phoenician armies. Before the wizard set sail for their stronghold in Carthage, he begged my relative to come with him. But my forebear loved her city and her clan, and refused. As a parting gift, he taught her these seven spells. Clearly the lady had some small talent herself, and the wizard promised that these spells would keep her and the clan safe from the invaders.'

'You're still here, so the spells must have worked.'

'Apparently so.' Reynard handed over a thick envelope. 'Your train leaves in half an hour. You have a seat reserved in first class.'

'I've never traveled first class before.'

'To have Madame Bonard arrange anything else would have raised suspicions in my office. My clients tend to be, well . . .'

'Rich and powerful.'

'Precisely.' He tapped the envelope. 'A reservation in Geneva at the Hotel de la Paix. Flight the day after tomorrow to Freeport, Bahamas. My banking details. A basic overview of my services. Have I forgotten anything?'

Chad offered the lawyer his hand. 'Thank you for sharing that story with me.'

'You are a remarkable young man.' Reynard had a surprisingly firm grip. 'I hope you manage to survive. It would be nice to participate in molding your future.'

ELEVEN

Chad half-expected the train ride east to be a journey into the morass of fear. He was a lone and inexperienced mage, fleeing the Institutes and all their might. Behind him was wreckage from his direct assault on the Sardinian Institute's most senior Warrior mage. What was more, he now intended to do battle against one of Florida's most powerful and well-connected families. And yet all he felt was a splendid langour. Chad had the first-class compartment to himself until they reached Nice, and afterwards he shared it with two lovely young French women who at first pretended to ignore him, and then flirted outrageously as they offered French phrases that he would no doubt find essential in wooing the Swiss ladies.

Hotel de la Paix was a palace situated on a quay overlooking the lake. In the distance, mountains rose in snow-tipped splendor. Chad was ushered across the ornate lobby, where a smiling attendant assured him, 'Monsieur Reynard has taken care of all your arrangements.' The attendant handed Chad's key to a hovering bellhop. 'This gentleman will show you to your room. Have a pleasant stay.'

That night, Chad dreamed about Stephanie.

He was seated with her on the veranda of the Orlando country club where they had first met. Theirs was the only table occupied. He had never been seated on the club's veranda before. They had met while he served tables. Another little item that Stephanie's mother loathed.

In his dream, he and Stephanie had the sunset all to themselves. He was telling her a joke. Chad loved to make the lady laugh. She had a freedom to her emotions that was utterly beyond him. He had been born reserved, as Stephanie put it. Not that she minded. She relished how Chad happily played the foil to her mercurial ups and downs. When she laughed, a brilliance shone from her, a delight with life and him and the moment. She was free with her gaiety, as open and gentle as the summer wind that graced their sunset.

When she spoke, Chad felt the words wash over him. The love was there in her voice, the gentle passion that turned her eyes to rain-washed sapphires. She tasted her upper lip with the tip of her tongue, as though her next word carried an exquisite flavor. She had that look in her gaze, the one that told him no matter what she might say, her real message was one of love.

Then he woke up.

Chad tossed aside the sweat-stained cover and padded across his room. Tall French doors opened on to a narrow balcony. He stood in the doorway and stared out over the lake of Geneva. Midnight traffic rumbled softly along the lakefront avenue. The moon was almost full and shone twice, overhead in the star-flecked sky and again in the lake's still waters.

He had often known such dreams in the early days of their separation. The Institute's walls had never been so confining as on such mornings. Which was the real reason why he had assaulted the Vancouver warriors on that particular day. He had been stumbling down the corridor, chased by fears that he might have made a terrible mistake and given up on the best thing that had ever happened to him. Then he had come upon the bullies testing their half-formed battle magic on a weeping acolyte. Their prey was just ten years old and terrified.

The fight that followed had been precisely the medicine Chad had required to recover from Stephanie's invasion of his dawn.

Only now, as he stood upon the balcony in his elegant Geneva hotel room, Chad faced no foe. He tried to bring up the prospect of revenge on Stephanie's mother and her hired gun. But it was a false outrage, an empty gesture, as futile as taking aim at the moon. Chad found himself recalling the darkly seamed faces of the Marseilles Kasbah. The bitter dregs that resided like live coals in their eyes. The years of mistakes and astringent regret. He thought of Edoardo's parting remarks, and knew there was a pungent truth to the skipper's warning.

The problem was, vengeance was all he had left.

Chad remained where he was, staring out over the moonlit waters, until Stephanie was well and truly gone from the night. Then he returned to his elegant room and the antique four-poster bed.

But he did not sleep.

TWELVE

Chad had breakfasted on feather-light croissants and the finest coffee he had ever tasted. There was a subtle difference to the day, one that he could easily have ignored entirely. More of an absence than any concrete addition. Chad shared his breakfast with a pair of doves so comfortable with people they pecked the crumbs from his hand. The night's tumult might as well have happened to another man. Abruptly the waiter appeared and snapped his towel, shooing the birds away, breaking the early morning spell.

The spell.

His phone rang.

There was only one person on earth with the number. 'Good morning, Monsieur Reynard. How are you?'

'I have been in my office for almost three hours, and it is scarcely nine. Which means I have broken every faction of the French code. You, on the other hand, sound positively cheerful.'

The words sparked like a distant echo in his brain. But all Chad could think to say was, 'I had almost forgotten what it's like to be free.'

'There is a lawyer in New York, an ally whom I trust totally. You understand?'

Chad struggled to focus, but the effort required was enormous. 'Yes.'

'She knows of two individuals in Orlando. Independent of all ties to the Institutes.'

Chad's reaction was split in two. One side of his brain seemed to find the sunlight more interesting than the lawyer's words. The other, however, positively sprang to attention. He left a bill under his cup, rose from his chair, and left the hotel café. 'Go on.'

'Actually, my ally's connection was with a woman who died two years ago. This contact is survived by her husband and a daughter, an only child. My ally has met them and vouches for them both.'

'You're saying they could be my contact into the world of unregistered magic?'

'Perhaps, yes, if they approve of you. The woman who died, Henrietta Sedgewick, was an experienced healer. The husband, Darren Sedgewick, has some healing abilities of his own, but my friend doubts he is anywhere near as gifted as his late wife. Henrietta's powers were apparently quite astonishing. But that is not the issue, as far as you are concerned.'

Chad tried to tell himself that his addled state was the result of an interrupted night. But the echo drifted out there, just beyond his reach. A whisper of worry. A fragment of something stronger than mere doubt. 'Can your friend put me in touch with them?'

'That's not so easy, my young friend. You can't simply knock on their door and expect them to roll out the magic carpet.'

Chad scrubbed his face with the hand not holding his phone. Willing himself to focus. To *wake up*.

Then it hit him.

Reynard said, 'Hello?'

'I'm here,' Chad said. 'Tell me what I need to do.'

Chad walked down to the Geneva bank that held his accounts. A sternly polite banker carefully checked his passport, then confirmed that four million euros and change had been deposited into his account. Chad felt . . .

Nothing.

He ordered fifty thousand euros to be wired to Reynard's account, and withdrew five hundred thousand dollars in cash and traveler's checks.

He stopped for a lunch of omelet and salad. As he ate, he pondered.

There was no doubt in his mind now. A spell had been cast over him.

But Chad hesitated over breaking the connection and setting wards. The flavor of this magic positively arrested him.

He watched the flow of people and traffic. A streetcar whispered past, as quietly genteel as the rest of this remarkable city. And he inspected himself.

Deep inside, his wounded heart was being knit back together.

He could feel the spell's power course through his deepest recollections. The loss of his parents came up, normally such a painful memory it only surfaced in his darkest nightmares. And yet now he was able to recall his mother's smile, the feel of her hands on his face, the sound of her singing when he woke with a childhood fever. He had not thought of that in years, and never in such public surroundings.

It had to be Stephanie who'd put this in motion.

Chad doubted that Stephanie had any idea of her mother's and best friend's dire intent. She knew she had hurt him. It would have been just like her to seek a healer she could trust with a lifelong confidence.

For Chad to revoke the unfinished spell meant rejecting her parting gift. Even so, he felt compelled to cut it off. Because something else was happening. A feat Stephanie had probably not even considered, but which was taking place nonetheless.

His desire for revenge was being erased.

The spell held the flavor of selfless caring from a very fine woman. He had no idea what to do.

THIRTEEN

C had entered the antiques shop after spending half an hour in the café across the street. Waiting until he was certain the shop was empty. Every time he reached out to erase the spell's presence, he was halted by the flavor of Stephanie's gift.

'We are closing, Monsieur.'

Chad shut the door firmly, listening to its chime. 'I'm interested in purchasing what you don't hold in your shop.'

'Is that so. How astonishing.' The woman was elegant and matronly both, with a face as smooth as antique porcelain beneath a cap of close-fitting gray curls. 'Who would tell you such a thing?'

'Albert Reynard.'

'I don't believe I know the name. Reynard, Reynard. He is an accountant in Berne, perhaps?'

'A lawyer in Marseilles.'

'Ah. Of course. That Reynard.' Her smile was meaningless, her eyes as empty as the hand-blown glass canister on the counter. 'We deal in antiques, monsieur. And art of the highest quality. Nothing more.'

'An executive at the Bank of Geneva is waiting for your call. He will confirm my ability to pay.'

The smile slipped away. 'His name?'

'Schmidt. Do you need the number?'

'That is not necessary. Wait here. This may take some time. I also wish to contact your lawyer.'

Chad made a slow circuit of the overcrowded room. The antiques gleamed in the dimming light, the paintings came warmly alive. He saw nothing of interest, but did not mind the wait.

The woman's name was Marie Caldier, and she returned with a hefty younger man who eyed Chad with lofty disdain. He took up station by the counter as she locked the front door, then asked,

'Your contact in Marseilles is unavailable. I did, however, speak with Schmidt. What is it you want, Monsieur?'

'I seek an artifact. Rare, but more importantly, real.'

'Magic has been outlawed in Switzerland for more than seven hundred years. It is inscribed in our constitution. Surely you know that. Which means any trade in these so-called artifacts would be highly illegal.'

'I was told of a storage unit,' Chad replied. 'One that lies beyond the reach of the Swiss authorities.'

'You are remarkably well informed.' She tightened her gaze. 'Your name?'

'Chad Hagan.'

'Such items, Monsieur Hagan, if they were indeed real and existed at all, would demand a very high premium. I would expect prices to begin in excess of a hundred thousand dollars.'

'Agreed.'

She glanced at the young man, and must have found what she sought, for she said, 'Come with me.'

The young man drove them from the city in a late-model Mercedes. The shop's owner did not introduce him, but there was enough resemblance for Chad to assume it was Marie's son. Neither of them spoke a word once they set off. Chad had no problem with the silence. He sat alone in the car's rear seat and continued to fret over his unresolved dilemma. But even his internal debate was muted by the healing spell. Distress rose in sudden waves, only to be soothed and comforted and eased like oil upon a stormy sea. Chad could not even decide if he minded.

They pulled into a spacious parking area and halted beneath a guard tower with mirrored walls. Marie spoke for the first time since entering the car. 'This is Geneva's free-trade zone, and officially not hampered by Swiss laws regarding magic. From here we must walk.'

The young man remained in the car as Marie led Chad across the floodlit expanse to where three guards stood sentry by an unmarked steel door. They must have known her, for they offered a solemn greeting and buzzed them inside.

They entered a concrete monolith as large as a football stadium. Marie Caldier greeted the uniformed sentry at the reception booth, handed over her ID, then instructed Chad, 'You must give them your passport and be fingerprinted.' When he hesitated, she said,

'If there was any place on earth designed to keep secrets, Monsieur, it is within these walls.'

He disliked revealing himself, but complied. He accepted the visitor's badge and instructions to remain with his host at all times. They were escorted through a pair of prison-style doors and down a carpeted corridor. The guard halted before another steel door, and Marie Caldier handed over her badge. The guard inserted hers and his own into a dual lock, then waited while she applied her thumb to the reader. When the door clicked open, the guard retrieved both badges, handed hers back, then took three steps toward the entrance and stared at the opposite blank wall.

'Please, Monsieur Hagan. You are welcome.'

He entered a chamber the size of a double storage unit. To his surprise, he found it very tastefully appointed. Brightly colored oils and brilliant Isfahan carpets offset the absence of windows. The lighting was recessed but strong enough to illuminate the items on display.

They took his breath away.

Chad had heard of such collections, kept in defiance of the Institute's supposed lock on all things magical. But the Institute's rules only added to their value. Such treasures were a lasting hedge against inflation and national instability. Governments might come and go. Money could rise or fall according to market whims. But the value of such treasures moved only in one direction.

Chad knew what he was after the instant he spied it. The shallow vessel was scarcely a hand's breadth across and had the delicate ivory coloring of very old porcelain. He reached for it, then hesitated. 'May I?'

'You know what it is?'

'An oriental wishing well.'

She smiled approval. 'If you break, you buy, and the cost is a hundred and eighty thousand euros.'

'Agreed.' He used both hands to cradle the item. At its heart was a Japanese character written in a shade so delicate it appeared to drift upon the cloud-like surface. Chad had seen one in the Vancouver Institute's museum. It was unique in that most artifacts could only be accessed with magical power and matching spells. A wishing well, however, only required a human breath.

Anyone could breathe and make a wish to see some distant item. But with the proper spell, so the legends went, a wizard's breath could reveal past and future events. The problem was, these spells had been lost. If they had ever existed at all. Otherwise the item would be of inestimable value.

Chad hesitated, then decided, and breathed. Instantly he was transported to the deck of a brand-new Hatteras sports fishing boat as it drifted beneath clouds and sunlight upon a calm sea. He heard the trio's soft laughter, smelled their meal of grilled swordfish, and for a moment became lost in the warm Mediterranean afternoon.

Then he broke the spell and turned to the smiling woman. 'I'll take it.'

'Where are you staying?'

'The Hotel de la Paix.'

'I cannot deliver a magical item to anywhere in Switzerland, Monsieur Hagan. To do so would break the law.'

'I fly out tonight.'

'Our airport is classed as another international zone. I will deliver it personally, assuming your payment has been received.'

'May I see your selection of books?'

'But of course.' She fished a ring of keys from her jacket and escorted him to the room's opposite end. Four tall bookcases lined the rear right corner. She unlocked each in turn, then stepped back, watching intently.

Chad took his time, savoring the liberty of examining magical texts without fear of discovery or punishment. Most of the books he already knew, but he glanced through some anyway, reveling in how he was able to recall the spells and their sequencing. That, he knew, was the most valuable of his gifts, how he could read a spell once and claim it as his own.

Most of the texts were third- and fourth-tier magic, which he had mastered and memorized and left behind years ago. The only text of interest was a dog-eared copy of seventh-tier defense spells published by the Singapore Institute. He set that aside and turned to the final bookcase, which contained personal accounts of eighth- and ninth-tier wizards, and their attempts to extend the boundaries of magic. Again, all of those originating from the Sardinian Institute he had already read and memorized, as well as most of the others. But two fascinated him. One from the nineteenth century covered a Talent's failed attempts to travel far beyond any physical constraints – a supposed ability of the Ancients, now lost. The second, from three hundred years earlier, discussed methods to read thoughts.

'Will there be anything else, Monsieur?'

Chad shut the book and set it atop the other two. 'How much for these?'

She pursed her lips. 'Let us say an additional forty thousand euros.'

'Done.' Chad knew he should probably bargain, but the thrill of buying books that would be all his own outshone the fear that she was taking advantage of him. He started for the entrance when he was halted by . . .

It felt as though something reached out and gripped his heart.

Or perhaps it was a voice he heard. One that was both silent and secretive and intended only for him.

Chad did not turn back so much as allow himself to be maneuvered.

'Is there something else you desire, Monsieur Hagan?'

'I . . .' Chad walked slowly forward. Then stopped. 'What is this?'

'That?' The woman approached, but stared at Chad, not the item. 'Why on earth do you ask about that?'

He had no idea how to respond, and finally settled on, 'I have never seen anything like it before.'

'No, nor I. I cannot even say if it is magical. Only that it is very old.'

'May I?'

'The price, Monsieur, is two hundred and fifty thousand euros.'

Chad nodded. Now that he was this close, the power of speech was stripped away. Nor could he hide the tremor in his fingers as he reached and took hold.

Instantly he knew he had to have this.

He had never valued possessions before. How could he, when he had been raised with so little. His grandmother had scorned those who, as she put it, owned what they did not need, and could not eat, and often ignored once they took it home. But this was different. How, Chad could not say. Only that he had to own it. He had to possess it. He had to . . .

The artifact was shaped like a scroll. But in this particular case, it was scarcely as long or thick as his middle finger. Like some spell-scrolls from the Dark Ages, it was encased in a leather sleeve. The material was embossed with symbols, most of which Chad recognized. They were classed as meaningless emblems from an era when magic was poorly understood, and when charlatans dominated the trade. But as he traced his hand over the imprinted signs, he felt a tremor of power course through his entire body. His bones resonated from the force as he pulled off the cover and unrolled the scroll to discover . . .

Nothing whatsoever.

The scroll was not paper, of course, but vellum. Which was why it remained in such fine condition. And magic played a role in its soft texture, of that Chad was certain. Just the same, the sheet was blank.

He rolled it out as far as it would go, about eighteen inches long and five wide. There was nothing to see. Not even the normal lines where the patches of vellum had been sewn together, nor the slightest hint of shading where once letters had been inscribed.

'I know what you are thinking,' the matron said. 'It is an absurd price to pay for a blank scroll. But I am certain this is far older than suggested by the cover's insignia. In fact, I wonder if perhaps, just perhaps, this might have its origins with the Ancients.' She traced a finger along the empty page. 'Though I have no evidence to suggest it is anything more than a Dark Age scroll which has lost its text to the wash of centuries, something tells me this is special. And the price is not negotiable.'

Slowly, carefully, Chad rolled up the scroll and slipped it into the sheath. He heard the hoarse tension to his voice as he said, 'I will take this as well.'

FOURTEEN

Once Chad had arranged an immediate transfer payment to Marie's business account, he returned to the hotel and purchased a suitcase and a leather carry-on valise in the hotel giftshop. Packing his clothes took no time at all. The briefcase with its magical forces fit snugly inside his new suitcase. Spot checks were made of carry-on luggage for magical forces that might be used in attacks. Carrying books and old porcelain was one thing. The bricks of power would have to travel inside the hold. He checked out and took a taxi to the airport.

Marie and her son were waiting for him by the first-class check-in. They took a café table by the side window. The items were wrapped in onion-skin paper, with the ceramic saucer set in a beautiful cherry-wood box. The lid opened like a set of double doors, with the bowl settled on a nest of red silk. The cover and the box were both carved with duplicates of the Japanese symbol embedded at the saucer's heart.

Chad saved the scroll for last. He felt the power course through him anew as he drew the item from its cover and unfurled it far enough to see the blank vellum.

When he replaced the scroll and settled all the items in his valise, Marie said, 'Am I correct in assuming this is the first time you have acquired artifacts, Monsieur Hagan?'

'This trip is a first for a lot of things,' Chad replied.

'Some more unscrupulous traders would have insisted that you buy the box separately. It is, after all, carved with the same magical symbols, and has considerable value in and of itself.'

'I had not thought of that,' he admitted.

Marie smiled thinly, as though approving of his honesty. 'You will take advice?'

'Always.'

'Monsieur Reynard is a good lawyer and an honest man. A rarest of combinations. He trusts me. I think you should do the same.'

'When it comes time to buy anything else,' Chad assured her, 'I will speak with you first.'

Marie Caldier rose to her feet and offered him a card. 'This is my private contact information. When you have a question regarding an item you might wish to acquire, do feel free to be in touch. And something else . . .'

'Yes?'

'I managed to speak with Monsieur Reynard. He claims to see something in you. I have decided to trust his instincts. I have my sources within the Institutes. Some buy, others support habits that are both destructive and quite expensive. You understand?'

'You can help me with information and possibly with early warnings of attention cast my way,' Chad said.

'Very astute, Monsieur. But in order to do this, I need to know which Institutes might be interested in you.'

Chad hoped it was not merely the healing spell that made his admission come so smoothly. 'Vancouver and Sardinia. I was kicked out of the first and fled the second.'

'And now you are in hiding.'

'For three days and counting.'

'You learn swiftly. That should serve you well.' She offered him her hand. '*Bonne chance*, Monsieur Hagan. I do hope we shall meet again.'

FIFTEEN

C had flew BA to London, waited almost two hours, then transferred on to a nonstop to Freeport.

Less than an hour into the transatlantic flight, the healing spell ran out.

He tried to watch a film, but the words were mush and scenes flickered without meaning. He toyed with food he did not taste, then flattened his seat and pretended to sleep.

He was not going to attack Olivia or Stephanie's mother. Arguments to the contrary rattled around his brain, but he knew they all meant nothing now. Stephanie had erased their hold on him by offering this final act of love. She had done her best to comfort him through the news of her departure. She had asked for nothing in return.

He could do little else.

The problem was, what now? Running away from the Institute was not a destination. Eventually the whirling thoughts exhausted him, and he dozed off. Chad did not wake until the flight was on landing approach.

The Grand Bahamas International Airport hardly lived up to its name. The buildings were dated, the atmosphere laid-back and island easy. Chad retrieved his case and took a taxi to McLean's Town. There he purchased a ticket for the high-speed ferry to Abaco Key. While waiting for the ferry to depart, he called the Treasure Key Resort and booked a room. Then he did his best to copy the natives and kick back.

Memories washed over him with the warm salt-laden wind. Starting at the ripe old age of twelve, Chad had spent his summers as a deckhand on various sports fishing boats. Out at sea, nobody paid attention to age restrictions. Because his grandmother's house was ninety minutes from the fishing port, Chad bunked with local families, rose before dawn, worked the impossible hours, and loved every minute. The shoals off Abaco were a favorite destination, especially in marlin season. Each September Chad returned to school sun-blackened, his hair almost white, his eyes still searching the endless horizon for signs of storm or big fish.

The first sign of his magical abilities had come during his final onboard season. Early in his eighteenth summer, before starting classes at UCF, Chad discovered an ability to sense the fish long before the skipper caught any trace. This was impossible, of course, as Chad's position was by the stern rail, baiting fish and serving the paying clients. Even so, he was able to identify not just the fish's location, but their size and disposition. Which underwater beast had just eaten and would not take any bait, which was on the hunt and ready for the hook.

Then he found he could call to them.

In the July doldrums, when virtually every boat returned to dock empty-handed, Chad's vessel showed up with at least one prize catch. The skipper offered him a partnership if Chad would stay on. But by then he had decided two things. First, it seemed genuinely unfair to apply his new abilities to unsuspecting game. Second, there was nothing else he wanted to do with his life but magic.

Which was when his problems really began.

After leaving the sea, Chad was hired to wait tables at Orlando's City Country Club. Where he met Stephanie. And fell in love. And confronted her mother's cold fury.

The Institute's examination process forced him to jump through eleven endless months of hoops. His ever-deepening love affair, however, offered a wondrous reason to stay patient. He tried to keep up with his UCF classwork in case he was not accepted, but the whole university thing already seemed pointless. He knew what he wanted to do with his life. If the Institute disagreed, he would find another way. He had inherited more than his share of Nana's stubborn nature.

The Treasure Key Resort was one of the Bahamas' finest. Chad knew it because they had picked up a number of clients there. He had never in his life imagined he might one day walk the white sand beach and swim in the crystal waters and dine in their ocean-front restaurant. Just like all the other patrons. Like he belonged.

The next day he walked over to the main marina and took his time inspecting the line of boats for sale. He was not going to use magic to obtain his ride. It was one thing to employ an eighth-tier spell in a desperate attempt to save his life and his freedom. But this was different. Chad was entering the region where he intended to make his home. Such abilities needed to be cloaked, hidden, locked away.

Plus, he could now afford to buy what he was after.

The salesman was an aging white islander with a three-day growth and a whiskey-and-cigarettes drone. But the man knew his business and accepted that Chad knew his boats. He stopped trying to sell the one with a busted engine and leaking seals, and instead took Chad down to exactly what he had been seeking.

The late-model Sea Ray was thirty-one feet long and powered by twin MerCruisers. The boat's size and weight meant it was capable of handling moderate to heavy seas. It came with a plush cabin whose air-conditioning and galley were powered by marine solar panels embedded in both the bow and cockpit cover. Batteries formed a midships ballast and supplied four days' continuous usage, or so the salesman claimed. Chad took his time negotiating, mostly because he wanted the salesman to see him as a legitimate buyer. Four and a half hours later, they agreed on an all-cash purchase price of a hundred and fifteen thousand dollars. Chad spent the rest of the afternoon and evening getting the ship seaworthy. He ordered a room-service meal, ate watching the night gather, then went to bed. He slept and did not dream.

SIXTEEN

The next morning, Chad was the restaurant's first customer. He watched the sunrise from the comfort of his beachside table. He ate a Caribbean omelet of salt-cured ham and onions and green peppers and avocado and goat's cheese. He resisted the urge to rush around, repeatedly reminding himself that he was no longer a ship's mate, and he was not going after big game fish. He was a tourist heading home. Tourists wealthy enough to own such a pleasure craft did not hurry. They motored across the straits in broad daylight. They took their time. They had servants to hurry for them.

It was doubtful anyone noticed, but just the same Chad allowed a bellhop to carry his suitcase and a packed lunch over to the marina. He surveyed the boat as it rested by the main dock. He had not realized how much he'd missed the water until that very moment. As a trusted hand, Chad had often been responsible for doing the final check-through and greeting the day's clients while his skipper nursed a massive hangover in the air-conditioned cockpit. Chad counted off the final payment to the grizzled salesman, accepted the ship's papers, stowed his gear, and cast off.

He noticed the difference even before he passed the Abaco breakwater. He had piloted boats hundreds of times. Had loved the sensation of steering toward a sunlit infinity from the very first moment, when at age thirteen the skipper had invited him to take the wheel. Everything took on a special edge at such times. All his senses became elevated.

Chad had woken several times in the night, anticipating just such a charge. But this was something else entirely.

The Florida Straits greeted him with a trio of thunderheads illuminated by the late morning sun. The storm clouds were bunched like fists and towered up twenty, thirty thousand feet. Their sunlit sides were burnished gold, while the opposite ends loomed heavy and shadowed. A narrow gap separated the clouds from the sea's surface. Ribbons of gray rain fell in three liquid pillars. Otherwise the sky was clear, the sea rippled by gentle waves.

As Chad watched the storms and decided they would not impact his journey, it hit him.

This was *his boat.*

He was an *outlaw mage.*

He laughed, and when that was not enough, he shouted a song from his childhood memories to the open sky and the sea ahead. And the rumbling motor and the splashing waves sang with him.

The boat's GPS navigation guided him into the Sebastian Inlet cut. He saw no coast guard vessel, slipped under the Inlet's bridge, and joined all the other pleasure craft headed for their home waters. He avoided the marina used by the commercial fishing boats. Instead he headed north along the inland waterway to the much smaller Melbourne city marina. The late spring sun was increasingly hot. Further inland the afternoon storm clouds began to gather. Chad pulled into a guest slip and thanked the dockhand who accepted his lines and tied him fast. He entered the office and arranged for permanent dockage. He paid the initial fees in cash and said, 'I've been working overseas. My driver's license is a year out of date. I don't have a credit card.'

The marina owner was a leathery woman in her sixties with eyes gray as a storm-lit dawn. 'You'll probably also need wheels.'

'Doesn't have to be fancy,' Chad agreed. 'I just need something that will start when I ask.'

'How long do you want it for?'

'A week should do. Long enough to get set up.'

'There's a Buick parked by the rear wall, belonged to a fellow who couldn't make his payments. There's a bad scrape on the passenger door, but it drives good enough. Go give it a look.'

'I don't need to.' Chad agreed to her price, paid for two weeks in advance, accepted the keys, and transferred his cases to the car's trunk.

The exterior was either blue or gray, he couldn't be certain beneath its layer of salt and grit and guano. The marina owner insisted Chad wait while one of her dockhands gave it a wash. He went next door and ordered a burger. From his position at the bar, Chad watched the marina employee scurry through just another duty, hustling for tips from the guy rich enough to have an ocean-going yacht.

Two hours later, Chad pulled into the lakefront neighborhood that shaped the only real home he had ever known. Orlando was still rimmed by any number of such communities, throwbacks to an era before the arrival of theme parks and wealthy tourists and new money. The nicer ones that survived mostly fronted lakes far from main roads. Such homes were owned by generations of locals and retirees who loved the quiet country feel. The houses were modest and weather-beaten from the regular pounding of summer tempests and hurricanes. There was never a for-sale sign. Folks who wanted to move in introduced themselves around, asked personally, and waited their turn. Neighbors shared what they could with those going through hard times. They expected nothing less in return. They were mostly silent, just like his Nana, and spoke softly when words were required. They hunted, they fished, and they loved their state with a passion that was often overlooked because, for them, there was no need to discuss what resided deep in their bones.

He drove slowly past the house he had shared with his grandmother, glad to find the long-term tenants were keeping the place in good shape. A stand of blooming oleanders taller than the house separated it from the next structure to the east. While Chad was still recovering from the loss of his parents, his grandmother had purchased a small, run-down place, little more than a shack. Together they had rebuilt it as a ground-floor garage and upstairs loft, which she rented to university students. When Chad went to Vancouver, his grandmother had left it empty for him to use whenever he returned. Everyone needs a place they can call home, she had told him. Everybody needs a haven from the world.

His grandmother's belongings now filled the garage. Upstairs, the loft apartment was redolent of her. The place was very much Nana's style – bare plank floors, a throw-rug in the bedroom, well-used furniture, vintage appliances, and clean as a whistle. A glass-fronted door opened off the back to a narrow balcony. The view was over a spread of live oaks and the glistening waters of Lake Tohopekaliga. The Indian name had defeated the developers who built along its northern border, so they petitioned the state to have it renamed East Lake. Locals ignored the change with grim intent.

Chad slept with the rear balcony doors open. The cicadas and bull frogs sang to him. Twice he woke from dreams in which he thought he heard his Nana's soft chuckle. The memory of her quiet ways gentled him back to sleep.

Dawn found him standing beside his grandmother's grave. No healing spell could extinguish his bitter regret over having missed her final days, nor mask the shame he felt in needing to ask a caretaker where she was buried. She had been dead two months and three days before word was finally passed to him in the quarterly mail. A second heart attack had felled her. Chad had not even known she was ill. The news had arrived the day after the incident which had left him certain the Institute would never be his home. From that dark hour, he had worked toward this moment. When he could stand by his grandmother's grave and thank her for the gift of this man he had become.

He stopped by the supermarket, returned to his loft, and ate a breakfast on the rear balcony. When he finished, Chad buried the briefcase holding the Mediterranean power beneath the stairs leading to his apartment. Then he showered and dressed, hefted the valise holding his books and artifacts, and set off in hopes of discovering his destiny.

SEVENTEEN

Henrietta's Herbals was located precisely where the French lawyer had said, in an upscale shopping area midway between the theme parks and Orlando's downtown business district. The outdoor mall was designed as a series of concentric squares, all connected by covered walkways. Henrietta's was larger than Chad had expected. The aisles of herbal supplements, organic foods, and household items stood to the right of the entrance. To his left was a lovely tearoom with potted palms and original artwork and granite-topped tables. Half an hour after opening, the place was jammed. Chad walked the aisles for a time, finding a number of herbal remedies whose potency had been amplified by spells. But all of these were stamped with the licensed authority of the Vancouver Institute. There was no hint of renegade magic, nor any sign of subterfuge.

Nonetheless, magic was all over this place. Magic was happening *now*. Chad could smell it.

There was a subtle familiarity to the fragrance. Every mage had a certain signature, for lack of a better word. It took time and considerable effort for a Talent to identify the flavor or scent. Neither word was correct, but both worked to define this quality. Chad found himself repeatedly touched by a sense that he had known this source of magic before. But it was too faint to be identified clearly. Chad assumed it was a residue left over from the recently departed woman after whom the shop was named. Probably his grandmother had used the woman's wares. Nana had always been a great one for herbal remedies.

An electronic counter hung high on the tearoom's rear wall, displaying the number seven. Beneath it was a sign inviting anyone wishing to have a private interview to take a number and register with the hostess. Chad pulled the next slip of paper from the machine and saw it read eighteen.

Then he turned toward the counter, took one step, and dove headfirst into the unknown.

It was only much later, when Chad recalled the events from the safety of other hours, that he realized he had been struck by love at first sight. At the time, he was simply so stunned by the woman he could scarcely breathe, much less think a coherent thought. And speech was utterly beyond his reach, as he discovered when the customers in front of him dispersed and he stepped forward.

The woman behind the counter was in her mid-twenties, but she observed him with an Ancient's gaze. Her hair was raven black, her eyes the shade of emeralds viewed through a dawn fire. She wore a black knit top over black silk trousers. The effect was like a dark liquid had been poured over her lovely form. The spark of intelligence was very real. But there was something else as well, a force that Chad would have recognized had he not been so witless.

'Yes?'

Chad opened his mouth but had no idea what to say. He took a breath, but that did not help at all, for his senses were filled with her fragrance. Lilacs, honeysuckle, and something else. A spice that suggested some distant land, and mysteries he yearned to uncover.

She must have taken his silence for shame, because she smiled and said, 'Why don't you take a seat at that back table. I'll come join you in a minute or so.'

Chad turned away, abashed at the power that had rendered him mute.

It was another two hours before Kara Sedgewick could join him. Chad did not mind the wait in the least. He found an exquisite pleasure in observing the lovely young woman. And he learned a great deal in the process. What was more, he discovered their secrets, father and daughter. Two of them. Both of which astonished him utterly.

Soon after he seated himself at the back table, the check-out lady by the front door started apologizing to newcomers and saying that further appointments were not possible. From the disappointment shown by a number of customers, Chad knew the shop doled out far more than simple advice on herbal remedies.

A mask within a mask, was how Chad described the setup to himself.

On the surface, Kara served as hostess and shop manager. Her father, Darren, was a silver-haired gentleman with the courtly air of a senior professor. He stepped from the rear chambers between each client and spoke quietly with his daughter. Customers treated Darren with something akin to reverence.

Within an hour of his arrival, Chad was certain it was all a blind.

What happened was this: The old man merely *played* the role of seer.

Darren listened to their multitude of symptoms or complaints or wishes or whatever. He offered them the gentle advice of a studied elder. And all the while, he played the foil for the truly gifted young woman. Who hid in plain sight.

Kara was the greeter. She offered a few quiet words to each person. She touched hands, arms, sometimes giving a swift embrace. And in these brief contacts, she obtained all the information she required to make the diagnosis.

Which she then passed on to her father. Who pretended to be the gifted individual.

Both their performances were, Chad decided, worthy of Oscars.

What was more, he thought he knew why they performed this daily masquerade. And the realization only added to the bond he felt being forged between them.

But that was hardly the morning's greatest astonishment.

By the beginning of the second hour, Chad knew Kara was the maker of his healing spell.

Her ability to mask her magic was remarkable, something she had clearly developed over months and years. But because he had the opportunity to witness her at work, time after time after time, he caught repeated hints of what she tried so valiantly to repress. Gradually he came to realize why the emporium's magic had seemed so familiar when he first entered. He had lived within its healing comfort for three days.

He drank a second pot of tea, pretended to study his medieval text, and watched. Almost all the clients who departed did so with heartfelt gratitude, many in tears. Kara accepted their farewells with promises to pass them along to her father. Then she smiled them away, ever the dutiful daughter.

And all the while it was her.

When she was finally able to start back toward him, however, a new opponent stepped into the shop. Chad was instantly taken back to his days waiting tables, for this young man was precisely the sort of country club patron he had most despised. Born into privilege, strikingly handsome, a natural athlete, rich. Every female eye in the shop was drawn to him. He, in turn, only had eyes for Kara. Chad despised the man and all he represented, and knew with bitter irony that he was jealous of a man he had never met, over a woman who assumed he was there for treatment of some disorder. Nothing more.

Chad watched them talk, saw the flame of ardor in the man's face, and knew a ridiculous sense of bitter loss over this woman belonging to another.

Even this realization served its purpose, however. For when the young man left and she carried the remnants of her smile back toward his table, Chad was ready. Kara Sedgewick belonged to a man who needed to hide nothing. Not his wealth, nor his desire to claim this beautiful and gifted young woman. His station in the community offered her a safety and a future that was not Chad's, and probably never would be.

So when she stood before him and asked what service they might do for him that day, Chad rose and said firmly, 'You need to sit down.' When she showed uncertainty, he added, 'A few minutes. Please.'

Reluctantly, she took her chair, waited for him to resume his seat, and started to ask, 'What is . . .'

Then she saw the book on the table between them.

Chad turned it around so she could view the page he had been pretending to read.

Then once more that day, she managed to astound him utterly.

For when her gaze lifted back up to him, the eyes were wide with fear. She whispered, 'It's you, isn't it? Hagan.'

'Chad,' he corrected.

A tear spilled down her cheek. 'How on earth did you find me?'

EIGHTEEN

C had replied, 'If anything, I need to thank you.'

'I don't believe you.'

By this point, all the eyes in the establishment were on them. Chad said quietly, 'I think we should go into the back.'

'Why, so you can threaten my father as well?' Kara evidently had no idea how many people were listening. 'So you can wreak havoc on us both?'

'I am not . . . Do you really want your customers hearing what I have to say?'

Kara glanced around, gathered herself, and rose unsteadily. One of the patrons asked if she was all right. Kara gave no sign she heard. She told Chad, 'Wait here. Or leave. I don't . . .'

She fumbled her way through the tea shop. A smattering of voices called after her. As the hostility grew, Chad slipped his book into the valise and followed.

Kara had set wards around the door leading to the back room, but Chad had spent three and a half years working through such barriers. He needed no more time to erase them than he did to unlock the door.

The rear third of the shop was fashioned into a staff room, a large storage area, and a beautifully appointed office. As Chad entered, a heavy-set woman and her daughter scuttled past, racing for the rear exit and casting fearful glances his way.

Kara's father stood in front of his desk and held his daughter, who sobbed on his shoulder. When he caught sight of Chad in the doorway, he jerked in shock.

'Five minutes and I'm gone,' Chad told them. 'Less.'

Kara cried, 'How did you get in here?'

'That's part of my story.' He set the valise on the closest chair, held his hands palms out, and said, 'Five minutes. Please. I'm not going to hurt anybody.'

When Kara seemed incapable of speech, her father said, 'Go on then.'

'Let me tell you what I think happened. The late Henrietta Sedgewick was as beautiful as Kara. She was also highly gifted. She went to study at one of the Institutes – I have to assume it was Vancouver. She fell in love with one of the instructors. At least, she thought she did. But one day something happened. Her powers grew and she began learning how to set wards. She broke free of the forces that had bound her. And she realized she had been duped. The instructor had cast a spell of false romance that had blinded her. Your mother then publicly accused the instructor. She probably threatened the senior Talents with charges of multiple rape.'

Kara whispered, 'How did you . . .'

The father said, 'Let him finish.'

'Your mother left the Institute. She gained her freedom. She probably got some form of payout to keep quiet.'

'She wanted *nothing* from them,' Kara hissed. 'She took *nothing.*'

'Kara,' the elder murmured.

'So she traveled as far as she could get from the Vancouver Institute and still remain in America,' Chad went on. 'She set up a healing center here in Florida, which was clearly her gift as well as yours, Kara. And she was kept safe because of what she knew.

'Time passed. And to keep you safe, Henrietta told anyone who listened that unfortunately the gift did not pass down. You, her husband, retained some of it. That's a known trait, how a highly gifted mage can transfer some of their powers to a beloved mate. It's rare, but it happens. And in this way you have managed to keep Kara's incredible abilities a secret from the watchers.'

Kara's mouth opened and then shut. Another tremor went through her. But she did not speak.

Chad went on, 'You worked magic on me without my permission or knowledge. In many respects, what you did was wrong. And if the Institute ever discovered it, the results would be catastrophic.' Chad could see the toll his accusations took. But this had to be stated. 'There's another side to all this. Something I assume you had no idea was happening. But it did. Stephanie's mother set me up. She lured me from the Institute, got me into open waters, and sent a storm to take me out.'

'I didn't know *anything* about this.' Kara pushed away from her father. 'Stephanie came to me. Us. She said you were in pain, and she was the reason. She asked for a healing.'

Her father asked, 'The story about Henrietta . . . How did you know?'

'Because it happened to one of my fellow apprentices,' Chad replied. 'Stephanie told you about my getting kicked out of Vancouver?'

'She said you used battle magic and they banished you to Sardinia.'

'That's both true and not true. I shielded a young apprentice by fighting some bullies. I was shipped off to Sardinia. I hoped things would be different there. I hoped the atmosphere would be better. I hoped I could find a home.' Chad heard the old acrid rage etch his voice and could do nothing about it. 'All of my hopes were demolished when a young woman discovered that what happened to Henrietta was being done to her. The Talent who cast those spells was the senior Warrior Talent, a man named Serge. My friend wasn't as strong as your mother. She committed suicide. And Serge . . .'

'They covered it up,' Kara hissed. 'Those *scum*. Those despicable *snakes*. They should all be *destroyed*.'

Her father patted the air above her shoulder. Chad had the impression it was a well-used gesture.

He said, 'No argument here.'

Kara did her best to compose herself. 'How did you find us?'

'A lawyer in Marseilles. He has an ally in New York. I don't know her name, but she was friends with your mother.' Chad reached for his valise. 'The lawyer said you were collectors. I brought something I hoped you might like.'

Their response to the artifact was surprising. Both father and daughter smiled over it, opening the box and oohing over the bowl. Yet neither of them showed any desire to *own* it. Instead, Darren said, 'My daughter seeks knowledge. Nothing more, nothing less.'

'Knowledge,' Chad said.

'Kara has no idea what her abilities are. None. Do you understand what that means? To harbor such an immense gift and be barred from ever discovering how far it might reach? How many people she might help?'

'As a matter of fact, I do.' Chad watched her point hesitantly at his valise. 'You want the book?'

'Could I borrow it?'

'Kara, it is yours.' Chad lifted the book from his case and reached out with both hands. Like he would an offering. 'Take it.'

She made no move toward it, though her eyes gripped it with an intensity that could only be described as hunger. 'What about you?'

'I've read it. I know it. Take the book. Please.'

Kara's intensity shifted from the book to him. 'You read a spell . . .'

'Usually once is enough. Some of the really hard ones used to need a second read. But not so much anymore. Then they are mine.'

'So . . . How many do you know?'

'A lot.' It felt so good to have a reason to smile. 'I could teach you, if you like.'

Darren demanded, 'What do you want in return?'

Chad replied, 'A place to hide in plain sight.'

NINETEEN

C had slipped easily into a somewhat fractured routine. Greater Orlando was a sprawling complex of distinct communities. The theme parks and tourist hordes were all to the west of the main city. Stephanie's family residence, the country club where she and Chad met, and the hospital where she worked were southwest of downtown. His loft apartment was in the exact opposite direction, out on a state highway toward the Atlantic. There was little chance of running into Stephanie or her mother at the shop; Kara assured him that Stephanie had not returned since delivering her payment, a book of fourth-tier shielding spells that Chad had memorized a couple of years back.

Chad served as unpaid shop assistant, storeroom clerk and driver whenever Kara and Darren went on a house call. Always it was to a long-time client who was too sick to travel in, or who had sick children. Kara usually briefed her father before they left the shop so they could prepare whatever herbs Kara felt were required. Chad liked watching them work together, a team whose craft had been honed over years. They trusted each other. They moved in smooth harmony. Their arguments during those three weeks were rare, and limited to a few sharp words. Then they retreated, gathered themselves, and resumed the habits they both knew were vital.

At the end of his first week, Chad purchased a pay-as-you-go phone and called Mademoiselle Three, explaining she would be the only one to have this number. The conversation lasted less than ten seconds, as the hunter programs were about. Three days later, he tried again, but she connected only long enough to say it wasn't safe, him calling. If the situation improved, she would be in touch. Bang and gone. It was only later, when he found himself tossing and turning in his garage apartment bed, that he even thought of how crazy that might seem to someone else, losing sleep over a computer program's safety.

Every few days, Chad journeyed east to the Melbourne marina. The boat remained Chad's getaway. On his second visit, he returned the ratty Buick to the marina owner, who helped him locate and purchase a low-mileage Ford F-150 pickup with a two-seater cab. Most outings, Chad just motored his boat from the marina and headed down the Inland Waterway until he found an unoccupied island. There were hundreds of these tiny patches of palmetto and sand. Most were less than fifty paces wide and were rimmed by spotless white beaches. Chad swam in the warm waters, then stretched out on the shore. As he watched the scene, he felt all the tension and masks just drift away.

Either mosquitoes or squalls eventually drove him inside the cabin, where he showered and ate a takeaway he'd brought with him. Sunsets following a storm were both glorious and hard. He'd sit in the pilot's chair, surrounded by a skyscape of woven gold, and wished there was someone with whom he could share such moments. He did not miss Stephanie any longer. Both the healing spell and time's own magic distanced him from what they once had. Nor did he envy her new life's direction. Chad simply wished he could have the same for himself.

Chad felt increasingly drawn to the young healer. Kara was kind by nature, and had a manner that made caring for the hurt and frightened as natural as drawing breath. She was the most open-hearted woman he had ever known, a healer whose compassion touched almost everyone. Chad occasionally glimpsed what it cost her, playing the role behind the counter, hiding in plain sight. But she never complained. The eagerness and the hunger came out only when the shop was closed and she could stretch her wings, at least a little, and learn one more fragment of the mysteries that had been denied her.

John Cutter, Kara's boyfriend or lover or whatever, stopped by every day or so. What he and Kara did at night, Chad had no idea, for he only saw them at the shop. John treated Chad with the blind disdain that came easy to those country-club types. Chad resumed the bland mask he had worn while waiting tables. Increasingly, though, he became convinced that all was not well in their relationship. Cutter tended to storm off after visits that grew shorter with each passing day. Chad did his best to feign a total disinterest, especially when Kara's father was watching. Life had almost settled into a decent routine when trouble struck.

Kara and Darren invited him to join them at a gathering of underground magicians. When Chad showed reluctance, Kara pointed out that she'd known most of the members since childhood. Then she asked if he intended on remaining alone for all his days.

The evening event proceeded pretty much as Chad had feared. Most of the attendants could not muster the required talent to enter an Institute. There was one quite beautiful young woman in her late teens, a reflection of the lady who had committed suicide in Sardinia, that Chad thought had potential. Several older people had apparently come into abilities after they had established themselves in nonmagical lives. Chad liked how Kara held back, her mask firmly in place, and allowed Darren to play the gifted one. As if her father was the real reason they were there at all.

Chad resumed the fumbling role he had played in Sardinia, and hated every minute. The lecture was given by an officious man in his fifties who reminded Chad of the Institute's chief librarian, a bitter, twisted soul who took pleasure in denying access to students. The lecturer was petty and superior and sniffed his scorn at several questions from the audience that Chad suspected he could not answer. Chad sat and frowned through the talk, as if it was all over his head.

The meeting concluded with a magicians' flea market. Clearly many of the attendees saw this as the highlight of their evening, Kara included. The vendors set up their wares on four long trestle tables at the back of the hall. There were around two dozen merchants. A few displayed second-rate artifacts at inflated prices. Most sold books, which were laid flat on the table and opened to the title page so the Institute's seal was visible.

Chad followed Kara from stall to stall, enjoying himself for the first time that night. He liked being this close to her, something that almost never happened inside the shop. He liked even more observing Kara with her guard down. Many of the members and a number of vendors came around to embrace her and talk about how she resembled her mother more with each passing day. Kara introduced Chad as a newcomer to Orlando, and explained that he was working in the shop until he found a permanent position. Without fail they took that as all the endorsement they needed. It spoke volumes about the trust they held for this lovely young woman and her father.

Darren remained caught up in his own island of discussion, ever watchful, but giving his daughter space. Kara's father had gradually become vaguely hostile to Chad's presence. Chad endured this shift because he had no choice. Darren had spent years sheltering Kara's remarkable gifts. Her father saw Chad as just one more concern he needed to monitor closely. Chad's presence was tolerated because he fed Kara's insatiable hunger to learn. Every night after closing the shop, the three of them spent an hour in the office, Chad teaching and Kara practicing. Her gift was largely restricted to the healing arts, which was Chad's weakest area. But neither minded.

The flea market was drawing to a close when it happened.

Trouble came in the form of an older woman with strong hands and wrists bigger than Chad's, and a face as weathered as a favorite saddle. Her silver-white hair was cropped very short, and she spoke with a matter-of-fact strength that reminded Chad of his grandmother. Her store of several dozen books was the last spot on the middle table, up against the side wall. Most of the activity was along the central aisle, where the attendees could gossip while they shopped. The woman smiled a polite welcome at Kara's approach. 'Lovely and gifted, both. What a marvel.'

'Actually, it's my father who has all the ability. I serve as his aide.'

'I'm sure he appreciates your help more than he can say,' the woman replied. 'What is his area of expertise?'

'Herbs and the healing arts.'

'Oh, you must bring him over. I've always enjoyed meeting those who join magic with a care for others.'

'Of course.' Kara leafed through a couple of the texts, neither of which held any interest. 'Have I seen you here before?'

'Oh no. My husband's the one who spoke tonight. I just come along for the ride.' She redirected her smile at Chad. 'And who might you be?'

Kara answered for him. 'He helps us in the shop. Henrietta's Herbals, perhaps you've heard of us?'

'Of course I have. One of the state's finest establishments, by all accounts.' The woman was in her early sixties, give or take a decade. She had the creased features of a hard life, but her smile suggested she had managed to maintain her good cheer. When Chad held back, she added, 'The strong and silent type. How nice.'

Kara continued leafing through the books, most of which were fanned out across the table. They were all well worn, and none held any interest. She then pointed to a stack of four texts by the cash box. 'Can I see those?'

'They're quite old, my dear. And rather fragile.' She hesitated, then added, 'And they're very expensive, I'm afraid.'

'My father is a collector.' Kara reached out. 'May I?'

'It's why I brought them.' She slid the books closer. 'Do be gentle.'

The first two were third-level texts, both on creating temporary golems. Chad knew the spells by heart. Forming golems that snored while he stole about was how he had managed to survive. The next was an autobiography written by a ruler of the Singapore Institute of the last century. Had it been anywhere other than here, he would have bought it out of curiosity.

The fourth book was his undoing.

The cover was of some very hard substance; Chad suspected either ivory or petrified wood. But it was so old and stained the material had become almost entirely black. It was the size of his hand and very thin, no more than a couple of dozen pages in all.

Kara opened the cover. In that instant, Chad took a punch at heart level.

Neither Kara nor the woman noticed the impact the book had on Chad. Kara idly turned a page and asked, 'What language is this?'

'I have no idea.' The woman's tone was almost musical. 'I bought it as a curiosity. Well, of course I thought it might prove to be something of a rare find. I keep hoping someone will tell me what I have.'

The impact was as powerful as in the Geneva warehouse, only this time the blow was completely unexpected. One moment Chad was simply enjoying Kara's company. The next . . .

Chad did his best to hold back. But the struggle was futile. The magnetic force was as powerful as the one that had drawn him across the antique dealer's carpeted enclave. He reached out and touched the page.

Instantly the book's power surged through him, up his arm, through his frame, electrifying every muscle, *clenching* him. He did his best to suppress the shiver. His entire body locked with the effort to remain outwardly calm.

The chatter and the people faded to nothing. Even Kara's presence became as distant as a memory. The page was not paper at all, but vellum. Which suggested the manuscript was at least nine hundred years old, and possibly far more. Vellum was carefully prepared animal skin. The softest and longest lasting was deer, but preparation of these skins required both precision and a great deal of time. Chad had studied the curing process after he had discovered so many of the most interesting texts were stored on scrolls and small texts like this. He closed the book and ran his finger along the spine. As expected, he found a deep crease or indentation at the mid-point.

He realized both women were watching him closely. And at some point the evening's speaker had walked over and now stood beside his wife.

As the room gradually came back into focus, Chad saw the piercing intensity of their gazes. The man's foppish ways were cast aside, as was the woman's guileless charm. They had him.

Kara asked, 'What is it?'

He took a shaky breath. He had no idea what to do. Running was not an option. He had to find some way to protect Kara and her father. Even that seemed impossible.

'Chad, what's wrong?'

To buy himself time, he turned the book over so the spine faced up.

'This text was what we now call a chain book. Back in the medieval era, before printing was invented, texts like this one were worth a fortune. Chain book covers were made of some material strong enough that they couldn't be cut or torn. The cover was rimmed by a magical anchor and had an iron ring embedded into its surface, usually welded in place. The book was then chained to the floor. The ring is rusted away now. But a shadow of the magic is still there. Here, give me your finger.'

He had only touched her a few times, when she needed guidance in shaping the motions required to cast some spells. Each time he felt that spark, the surge of her heart's fire. Not even the book's potency could keep him from sensing it now. Chad was momentarily swamped with regret, knowing it was probably the last time he would ever experience such contact, however fleeting. She frowned slightly as he ran her fingers along the cover. 'I feel the indentation. But . . . No. Nothing.'

Once again Chad realized his powers of observation had been swamped by the book's force. Darren had stepped in so close he actually leaned on Chad's right side. But Chad had not noticed a thing until Darren said, 'May I?'

Chad held the book up and watched Darren trace his finger along the spine. 'You're sure there's a power?'

'Yes,' Chad said. Digging his grave deeper with every word. 'I am.'

'Isn't that remarkable.' The woman beamed at her supposed husband. 'Have you ever seen the like?'

'No, never,' the man said. His hair was a silver unkempt froth. Though he had to be in his sixties, his features were completely unlined. Like an academic who had not left his ivory tower in decades. A perfect mask.

Kara asked, 'What is it about?'

'I'm not sure.' Chad opened the book to its cover page. The imprint, what was called the *officianado*, had long since faded away. Chad ran his finger over the position and recognized the symbol. He said softly, 'But I can tell you this manuscript comes from Bahia.'

The man and woman both drew in a sharp breath.

Kara asked, 'What?'

'About eighty years ago, the Brazilian Institute had a theft of several hundred of its rarest documents.' He turned the page, and this time he could not help but release the shiver.

Kara leaned closer, too engaged in the dual excitement of discovery and learning to notice the change in the pair behind the table. 'What does it say?'

'No idea. Which is a sign of its true age. Here . . . watch.' Chad whispered the incantation and touched the first line of text. This time, the gasp was shared by everyone present as . . .

The text swam, flowed, and became other words entirely.

Chad lifted his hand. Defeated. 'That's the sign of the Ancients. The text is magically hidden on the page. It requires two incantations to reveal the true message. I only know the first, what's called the unveiling. The second supposedly translates this nonsense script into the actual spell-text. No one knows for certain, because it's been lost for centuries.' He looked at the pair. 'But you already knew all that. Didn't you.'

Beside him, Darren murmured, 'Oh no.'

The woman turned to others who were on the approach and said, 'Give us a moment, please. We're trying to conclude a sale.'

When she turned back, Chad asked, 'Who are you?'

The man was coolly intent now. 'Now's not the place.'

Kara's voice trembled. 'Are you from the Institute?'

'No,' Chad replied. 'They wouldn't have waited this long to arrest me.'

The woman reached over and patted his hand where it still rested on the text. 'Why don't we stop by your shop tomorrow and have ourselves a little chat.'

TWENTY

The outdoor mall containing Henrietta's Herbals was shaped into four courtyards, so that each shop fronted parking spaces and a central square with benches and flowering shrubs and a fountain. The shops opened on to broad, shaded verandas with pillars of iron filigree. The herbal store shared its area with a restaurant, a bakery, a café and an upscale diner. At eight thirty in the morning, the air was filled with the aromas of coffee and baking bread.

Chad had not slept at all. Which was both good and bad. Good, because he had developed a fairly clear idea of how he was going to handle the meeting that was scheduled to start about now. Bad, because he entered into what could well be the most critical point in his life both exhausted and heartsore.

The reason for his sorrowful state pushed through the shop's entrance and started over. When Kara emerged from the veranda's shadows and entered the sunlight, Chad thought he had never seen her so sad, or so lovely. Kara hovered where the pavement met the sidewalk and twisted her fingers into a knot. 'Can I sit down?'

He waved to the seat beside him. 'Let me spare you the trouble. Your father has laid down the law. I'm fired. You're never to see me again.'

She sighed. Started to speak. Sighed again.

'Darren is worried that if I stay, I threaten the lives you've built for yourselves.'

She pulled her legs up so she could wrap her arms around them. 'What will you do?'

'I have a plan. Tell your father this: I'll only agree to work with them if they protect you. From everything.'

She sighed again. Settled her chin on her knees. 'Who are they?'

'Feds, most definitely. Not local. Homeland Security is my guess.'

'Not the Institute? You're sure?'

'Yes.' Chad saw no need to describe the tactics employed by Hunters, the Warrior wizards assigned to track down renegade users of magic. Their methods were brutal and usually terminal. Collateral damage was considered part of the job, so long as the local authorities were not alerted. 'Definitely.'

She picked at a thread from one of the cuffs that almost covered her fingers. 'Maybe that would make Daddy rethink—'

'No, Kara. I can't protect you if I stay. Your father's right. And we both know it.' Chad saw she wanted to argue with him, and liked her even more. He pulled out the handwritten note from his shirt pocket. 'This is my home address, email, and phone number. It would be good if you could drop me a note or text every now and then, just to let me know you're OK. And if you ever need anything at all, or if you get worried by something, you contact me, Kara. Don't you hesitate, not for an instant. A lot of what's going down today is so I can make sure you and Darren stay safe.'

'All I've done to you, all the pain you've endured . . . No, Chad. Please. Let me finish. You have done nothing to deserve *any* of it. You've responded to every wrong with kindness and a desire to teach, to give, to protect . . .'

Kara hid the need to wipe away tears by rising from the bench.

She started away, then turned back and said, 'I've broken things off with John. I can't, I couldn't . . .'

She cleared her face again and walked away.

When the shop door closed behind her, Chad asked the empty sunlit day, 'That's supposed to make me feel better?'

He spent the next twenty minutes or so running through the next steps. He had one chance to get it right. It was not just his own future that hung in the balance.

The morning was mildly spectacular, especially for central Florida in June. There was a hint of springtime crispness, and humidity remained very low. By noon it would be stifling and come mid-afternoon the thunderheads would roll in. But just now, he could sit comfortably with the sun full on his face and watch the starlings cut their secret script from a cloudless sky.

Soon as the car pulled into the slot directly in front of him, Chad knew it was them. The sedan was a nondescript four-door, colored some vague composite between gray and maroon. The driver cut the motor and sat there watching Chad from behind his opaque sunglasses. The pair from the evening assembly were in the back seat.

Chad could see no reason for games. They were here for him. He was going to go with them. He had lost the choice to do otherwise the instant Kara reached for that book.

At least they hadn't come to his home. Confronted him in the haven where he thought he might find an element of safety. Chad had to give them that.

He rose and walked over. The driver started the engine and put the car in reverse before he opened the door.

TWENTY-ONE

'**A**gent Gerald Bauer, FBI, seconded to the Homeland Security task force on unlawful use of the magic arts. In the back there are Elizabeth Creasey on the left and Jermaine on the right. I forget what Jermaine's first name is, and it doesn't matter. Jermaine is here to supply shielding until we're

certain you can be trusted not to rock and roll. Beth there will be
your cut-out once we're up and running. You're Chad Avery Hagan,
late of the Sardinian Institute, by way of Vancouver. Currently
residing in the garage residence left to him by his grandmother.
Intros over. Let's get this show on the road.'

As Bauer stopped at the shopping center's exit, then pulled on
to the main thoroughfare running east, Chad caught a glimpse of
Kara stepping from the veranda's shadows. She stood in the middle
of the parking area and watched them drive away. Looking sad.
Forlorn. Chad thought he could see the glint of sunlight off tears.
He forced himself to turn away. Just another might-have-been. His
life held far too many.

'Far as I knew, yesterday evening was going to be just another
wasted effort. My job holds a lot of them, right, Beth?'

Chad swiveled around so his back leaned against the door. From
this position he could view all three of the vehicle's occupants.
The woman's only response to Bauer's words was to pause in
watching the world beyond her side window and offer Chad a
tight-lipped smile.

'Just another pointless night on the prowl, with me warming a
chair in our Atlanta office,' Bauer went on. 'We're tasked with
monitoring assemblies in nine states. Our man Jermaine has the
patter down cold. He can deliver one of those little talks in his
sleep. Can't you, Jermaine?'

'There's a gift to speaking for an hour,' Jermaine declared.
'Keeping my audience engaged and saying nothing. A real gift.'

'Which is necessary,' Bauer said. 'Since we don't want the
Institute's Hunters to know what we're on about, no more than
you do. Right, Chad?'

He found no need to respond, but listened with half an ear, in
case the agent said something important. Which Chad figured was
unlikely in the extreme. He assumed this was the agent's wind-up.
The woman's placid response confirmed it.

Bauer went on, 'Like I was saying, we all figured Orlando was
a total waste of time. We're there just ticking the boxes. But that's
our job. Digging through a ton of muck for an ounce of gold. This
was the third time our Jermaine had been down here, since the
task force was formed.'

'Fourth,' Beth Creasey corrected.

'Whatever. Orlando has too many licensed wizards for anyone worth our time to call it home. Or so we thought.'

Bauer's skin was the color of toffee. He was taut in the manner of an ironman competitor, corded muscles and not an ounce of fat to his name. The skin around his right eye, from forehead to sideburn, was deeply pockmarked. Chad studied it because the scar gave him something to focus on. Abruptly he had a sharpish image of Bauer crossing a magically protected boundary, having the blast go off in his face, and still carrying both scars and rage from the assault. Chad could glimpse beneath the man's words now. He realized Bauer hated all wizards. They were Bauer's permanent enemies. Chad was just another source who'd broken the law by breathing without a license. Chad was to be drawn in, chained, used, and eventually discarded.

Bauer went on, 'When Creasey here reported about meeting you last night, I almost fired her for lying on the job. You've got to understand, all this time we've spent trolling the Florida assemblies, we've never met anyone worth a second look. But then old Jermaine confirmed her report. So I checked with our Institute contacts, and look what pops up in Sardinia. A red-flag alert sent to Hunters on four continents over this missing apprentice.'

Just before dawn, Chad had realized there was nothing to be done, no action to be taken, until the federal agent in charge declared himself. He figured the insight he'd just received was enough. But that ability to turn his gift into a lie detector was new. He'd not read of it, didn't know if this was the sort of odd little quirk that came and went on occasion, or if it was actually something that could be honed. There were literally hundreds of secret texts available only to Adepts that he had been unable to get his hands on. Of course, that was assuming he actually shared some of their traits.

So he held back and waited to see if Bauer planned to offer himself as a true ally. If Bauer wanted to form a partnership, if he valued Chad's potential enough to offer protection and freedom . . .

Well then.

But if Bauer threatened, if he tried to frighten Chad into submission, if his aim was to dominate . . .

These were the issues that had kept Chad awake and planning all night. Once he'd got over the bitter regret of being discovered.

What he was going to do, how he would respond, if the man made himself into just another enemy.

Get on with it, Chad thought.

As if in response, Bauer said, 'We can do this the easy way or the hard way. Between you and me and our two pals in the back seat, I prefer the hammer. Far as I'm concerned, it's the only way to keep you magic types in line.' He touched the scar by his right eye. 'Voice of experience. Apply the hammer good and hard going in. Let them know—'

'OK, that's enough,' Chad said. Then he reached out.

Not with his hands. From his gut. All that showed was a slight flick of three fingers. The real work was internal. Where it counted.

TWENTY-TWO

First he erased Jermaine's feeble idea of a protective shield. Chad had worked through more sophisticated barriers while going after library books. Jermaine cried out with what sounded like real agony. Chad knew it was probably just shock at how fast his supposedly invulnerable armor had vanished. Poof. But for some low-tier wizards, which Jermaine definitely was, any fracturing of a closely held spell caused a physical pain.

Bauer glanced in the rearview mirror. 'Something wrong?'

Jermaine did not respond because he couldn't. His power of speech was gone. Same for Beth Creasey.

The spell Chad applied was sixth-level Sentinel, designed to seal a convicted criminal inside an invisible cage for easy transport. The spell also formed one component of the process Serge used to protect banks. Which was how he had come to learn it. Studying the tactics of his enemy.

Chad's magical grip left them both with just enough room to take tight, gasping breaths.

Chad then turned his attention to the driver. He was tempted to insert the acidic hooks as well. Let Bauer experience what a real hammer felt like. But he decided it was overkill.

For the moment.

With Bauer frozen, the car coasted on, minus driver. Chad shifted control to himself. He used his left forefinger for braking and accelerating, his right to steer.

Bauer gasped, 'You better stop while you—'

'You still don't get it.' Chad tightened Bauer's shell ever so slightly. It was probably not a good idea to suffocate a federal agent on their first meeting. Much as the guy deserved it.

With Bauer reduced to grunts, Chad headed for the destination he'd come up with around sunrise. The drive took about fifteen minutes, long enough for Creasey to develop a worrisome flush and for Bauer to be quivering with each exhale. Chad turned off the main road and entered a hundred-acre tract partially cleared for a new housing development. When they were hidden from the highway by a stand of palmettos, he stopped the car and asked, 'Nod if you agree to stay quiet and pay attention.'

All three of them responded with frantic jerks of their heads, as much movement as they could manage. Chad released their chests, but kept their limbs encased in the invisible cement. He drove on, past a rusting fence and the Keep Out signs, following the track to a sizeable lake. Chad halted at the muddy shore, rolled down the four windows and turned off the engine. 'Give me your word you'll stay silent and I'll release you.'

When all three nodded, he erased the spell. Instantly Creasey leaned forward and said to Bauer, 'I told you it was a terrible mistake to treat him like your basic—'

'Quiet now.' When Chad was certain they would obey, he turned his attention to the agent. 'You heard the lady, Bauer. I'm not your basic rebel. Accept it and let's move on. Otherwise . . .' He leaned in close. He saw the agent jerk away, then force himself to smother the response. Chad went on, 'Unlike you, I don't threaten. Are we clear?'

Bauer's fury kept him locked up tight as the cage. He barely managed, 'Clear.'

Chad leaned back against the door. 'You lost your only chance to work with me when you threatened. That's not changing. I thought it probably wouldn't work, being handled locally. You proved me right.'

A soft breeze pushed through the open windows, bearing the rich flavors of Florida country. Off in the distance, the day's first storm rumbled softly. Chad found it fitting. 'So here's how this is going to move forward. You will call Washington and tell them I'll work with an Assistant Director or higher. I will be assigned a local backup, and this local contact can't be you. Both the Director and my regional contact must accept three conditions. First, I stay a free agent. I serve as consultant, and I'm paid for my time. Second, Kara and Darren Sedgewick are wiped off all official records. They receive total protection.'

Bauer snarled, 'You don't dictate—'

All it took was for Chad to extend one finger. The agent froze.

'And third, I get the book. The one you used as a lure.'

Jermaine protested, 'That work is priceless.'

'Once I've read it and deciphered whatever is hidden in that script, you can have it back.' Chad opened his door. 'Deliver the book with my contact's details and my first payment and ticket to Washington. My fee is two thousand dollars a day, starting now. And wherever you send me, I always travel first class.'

Chad rose from the car and looked down at the agent. As he feared, Bauer was still so furious Chad knew he'd restart the internal arguments as soon as Chad walked away. Bauer would develop a memo as to why Chad couldn't be given what he demanded.

Which meant Chad had no choice but to apply the hammer.

'I don't threaten,' Chad said. 'But you need to understand how vital it is you meet my three conditions.'

He had spent years masking his spells. Speaking the words in near-silent whispers. Hiding hand motions under his apprentice robes. Drawing designs and symbols in his pockets.

By comparison, this was a piece of cake.

To the trio, it appeared as though all Chad did was continue to meet Bauer's glare with a fury of his own. Even so . . .

One by one the doors were wrenched off their hinges and flung into the lake.

They were followed by the trunk lid.

Then the hood.

Finally, the car's roof peeled back like a demented convertible top.

When the last splash had settled and the lake was placid once more, Chad leaned in close enough to see the fear and uncertainty finally register on Bauer's features. 'Do I need to do the same to you to get the message across?'

'No,' Creasey said. 'Definitely not.'

Chad started the engine, causing the trio to cry out in alarm. He put the car in drive, turned the wheel and started it back down the trail. As they pulled away, he called, 'I expect your answer by dawn tomorrow.'

TWENTY-THREE

C had caught a bus back into town and retrieved his pickup from the mall's employee parking lot. Before driving away, he gave the shop's entrance a careful study. But other than a few newly arriving customers, the place remained silent. He sat there a long moment, coming to terms with how this was as close as he would ever get to the lady.

He drove straight down to Melbourne, stopped for takeaway burritos at a locals-only beachfront dive, then headed for his boat.

Rain closed in as he motored from the marina. Chad did not mind. The storm suited his mood. He held close to shore until the lightning faded and the sun came back out. Then he journeyed to his favorite island, a tiny smudge of green in the Intracoastal's azure waters. He anchored by the empty beach and heated one of the burritos in the microwave. He was not hungry, but his grandmother had always said that a body enduring hurt of any kind should be soothed by food. As far as his grandmother was concerned, wounds of the heart were no different from those of the flesh. Pain was pain. Chad could not say that the burrito eased his burden. But it did clear his mind enough to plan.

Time and again he relived the confrontation with Bauer. He knew there was a chance the man would exact his revenge by getting word to the Institute or their Hunters. Chad knew his only hope of survival was by making himself useful to Bauer's superiors. If Beth Creasey passed on his message. If they decided to let him in the door.

Chad motored back to the marina at sunset and drove home.

The television held no interest for him that night. He was too tired to study. He took a long shower, ate the second burrito, then sat on his stubby balcony and watched the passage of another storm. Lightning flickered high overhead, distant clashes that turned the rain into molten light. He ached over the chance he would never have with Kara. The last time he had known such an assortment of conflicting emotions had been in the Vancouver Institute's holding cell, waiting judgment over the way he had demolished the apprentice warriors. He knew then that whatever happened, he would be taken further from his beloved. Just like now.

Chad rose from his chair and carried his sorrow inside. As he locked the balcony doors, he wondered if this had always been his fate. To right wrongs, save the vulnerable, and pay the cost in countless lonely hours.

When dawn came, the rain was a humid memory and the sunrise a glorious Florida spectacle. Chad felt much better about his actions when he rose. He decided to go for a run before breakfast. It had been a fairly constant part of his life before the Institute. Running now, when the coming hours threatened to redefine his existence all over again, helped keep everything in perspective.

He returned and stretched and showered and prepared a breakfast of coffee and granola and strawberries. He ate standing at the counter, watching the day take hold beyond his balcony. Now that he had acted, now that he'd taken that first crucial step, there was a clear sense of facing the inevitable. At least now there was a chance, however slim, that whatever came next would happen on his terms.

He dressed in slacks and starched shirt and jacket and tie. As he packed an overnight bag, the sound of a piano solo drifted through the open balcony doors. He stepped outside to find Beth Creasey sitting in a vintage Audi convertible. She waved up and called, 'I thought I would save you the trouble of de-roofing another vehicle.'

Chad liked that enough to reply, 'Care for a coffee?'

'Next time. Our flight leaves in just over two hours.'

She had the car started before he made the bottom step. Chad dropped his valise into the rear seat and climbed in. The day was immaculate, cool enough for the humidity to not matter. He reached over and turned up the volume. They did not speak until the piece ended. Creasey cut off the stereo and asked, 'You recognize it?'

'Brahms,' he replied. 'Concerto number two in B-flat major.'

'Well, well.' She spared him a smile. 'The boy continues to surprise.'

'My grandmother loved Brahms,' he said. 'But you already knew that.'

'Actually, I didn't.'

'Truth?'

'I won't lie to you,' Beth replied. 'And I won't threaten.'

Chad released a band of tension he had not even identified. The day, he decided, had just got a great deal brighter.

Now that they were underway, Creasey took the lane fronting the lakeside homes at a slow pace. 'Your neighborhood is really nice.'

'Thanks.' Chad knew it was probably a mistake to like her. Even so, 'I was hoping I might keep my presence here a secret.'

She shook her head. 'Sooner or later, you were bound to hear the dreaded knock on your door. I'd imagine that sort of life would grow heavy. Waiting for the Institute's brutes to show up. You had to know they wouldn't just let you vanish.'

'So, what's your story?'

'I did my twenty with the Jacksonville PD. Retired a gold shield. You know what that means?'

'No.'

'Senior detective. Robbery and arson, in my case. A lot of magic around the docks. Hiding illegal contraband, smuggling, importation of artifacts used in the black arts. I spent nine years under cover. After twenty years, I pulled the pin.' She shrugged. 'But my husband had passed away three years before, and our kids were building their own lives everywhere but Florida. Retirement wasn't all I thought it would be. When Homeland asked, I jumped.'

They took the Beachline highway to Orlando International, and did not speak again until she pulled into the main lot. Chad liked how Beth Creasey saw no need for small talk. When they were sealed in the elevator, Beth said, 'You've made yourself an enemy.'

'Bauer would never have become my ally.'

She bobbed her head from side to side. 'He's a proud man. And you publicly shamed him.'

'Couldn't be helped.'

'You sure about that?'

'Yes,' Chad replied. 'I am.'

'Well, long as you're sure.' She handed him a boarding pass. 'You're already checked in. First row, first class. I'm riding in the back of the bus. I'll stop somewhere for coffee near the gate if you'd care to keep chatting.' She pointed him toward the VIP line, then handed him a narrow manila envelope. 'As per your third condition.'

Soon as Chad's fingers touched the tan wrapper, the energy coursed through him. 'Thanks. A lot.'

'Do I need to tell you to be careful with this?'

'No.'

'It comes with conditions. You have to tell us what you learn.'

He gripped the envelope with the hand not holding his valise. His entire body hummed with anticipation. 'All right.'

'Everything, Hagan. No holding back.'

He met her gaze. 'I give you my word.'

She smiled approval. 'I like you. Is that a mistake?'

'I'd like to think I make a powerful enemy,' Chad replied. 'And a better friend.'

TWENTY-FOUR

Chad joined Beth in the coffee shop closest to their departure gate. He had no interest in the first-class lounge. Nor was the larger seat all that important. What he had intended was to send these would-be associates a message. But there was no need for such things with Beth. Chad found himself hoping she would become a friend as well as an ally. So he bought a coffee and asked if he could join her.

He extracted the book from the manila envelope and held it, staring at the cover, uncertain how he should proceed. The energy emanating from it was a subtle charge that pulsed in time to his heartbeat. Beth watched him open the book, whisper the spell and rearrange the words. 'What does it say?'

'No idea. I've only seen two other manuscripts from the era of the Ancients. Both times this was as far as I got.'

'Mind if I scooch over so I can watch?'

'Not at all.' He swiveled the book closer to her. They were in the corner booth furthest from the windows, surrounded by the standard Orlando tourist hordes. No one paid them any attention. Chad asked, 'You weren't told what this text is about?'

'Far as I'm aware, nobody has a clue. I heard from Jermaine that the words were hidden. I thought he was just blowing smoke.' She had a cop's smile, crisp and tight and gone in a flash. 'You really rattled the guy's cage, erasing his shields like you did.'

'I take it you two are not married.'

'In your dreams, Bub.'

Beth was leaning over the book now, taking in the writing on the first page like she had never seen it before. As she traced her finger over the text, Chad glanced out the nearest window. Despite being one of the nation's busiest, Orlando's airport had been constructed to offer a sense of Florida charm from the very first glimpse out the airplane window. The landing strips and satellite buildings were all rimmed by carefully maintained parkland, with blooming shrubbery and lakes and clusters of tall palms. As he watched the palm fronds drift in the lazy morning breeze, he wondered if he would be allowed to stay. He had not yet left, and he already missed the place.

Beth asked, 'This script, is it printed?'

'Magically applied to the vellum, more likely. If we assume this is really from the time of the Ancients, it's thousands of years old. Look at the text. Not a smudge, no fading, so clear it could have been put down yesterday.'

'Can we do that?'

'Not anymore.' He returned his attention to the page, and felt the energy begin to pulse. 'We know almost nothing about the Ancients. Including who they actually were. The Sardinian Institute had six texts like this, two small books and four scrolls. I had a chance to study three of them. Shifting the text like you saw, that's as far as I ever got.'

'They just let you do that? An apprentice, handle their oldest books?'

'No. I broke through the spells guarding the treasury, that's the section of the library where they hold these texts and their most valuable artifacts.'

She was studying him now. 'You know what this means, right? Making the text rearrange itself like you did.'

Chad pretended to study the text and did not speak.

'The whole reason we're out there, trolling the secret gatherings, is in hopes that we might find a real live Adept. Someone with abilities like yours who isn't tied to the Institutes.'

Chad had no idea what to say, so he remained silent.

'All the time we've been looking, you're the first person who's actually shown anything like the abilities we've been told to watch for. A lot of wannabes, some untrained people Jermaine claimed had potential. Basically we've found minnows when we need a whale.'

'I don't like having that word applied to me,' Chad said. 'Adept.'

'But being able to rearrange the Ancients' text like you did, that's a key sign, right? It's the only reason why they let us take that book. That was Jermaine's idea, by the way. He said we needed something to draw out an Adept's secret abilities. If we ever did actually come across one. So they let us into a section of the Library of Congress that I didn't even know existed.'

Chad was watching her intently now. 'They have other books like this one?'

'Hey. You're asking the wrong gal. All I can tell you is, the room was four levels below ground and we had to go through everything except a strip search before they let us inside.'

'I'd like to see that place.'

She met his gaze. Chad thought her eyes were a remarkably gentle gray, given everything she must have seen as a cop. Beth said, 'But you can't read what the text actually says, didn't you just say that?'

'There has to be a magical dictionary or secondary spell. Something that creates a structure that points me in the right direction. That is, assuming the Ancients actually meant for this to be understood by others.' Chad whispered the uncloaking spell, touched the edge of the page, and watched the text rearrange once more. 'What we've got here is from no language I've ever seen before. I managed to read a couple of early accounts from *real* Adepts. They both said the Ancients used a script similar to

Aramaic. But this rearranged text doesn't look anything like that alphabet.'

Something in what he'd just said brought out the broadest smile Beth had shown him. 'You taught yourself Aramaic? Are you kidding me?'

Chad shrugged. 'I wanted to understand. I thought that might help.'

'Brother, you're a piece of work.' She slid from the booth. 'Come on, they just called our flight.'

TWENTY-FIVE

C had refused to board with the other first-class fliers. He liked standing there with Beth Creasey. He had a sudden desire to tell her about Kara, and the bone-deep ache he carried over what might have been. But he stifled the urge. He might like the lady. He might even come to trust her. Just the same, she was here with Homeland. She had a job to do. And so did he. His feelings for Kara played no role in that.

Once on board he wished Beth a good flight and took his seat. But any pleasure over his first time riding in the front of the bus vanished two minutes later.

Soon as the man slipped into the adjoining seat, alarms went off in Chad's head. What was worse, he was fairly certain the man knew it.

He was tall and polished and wore a tailored three-piece suit. He handed his jacket to the hovering air hostess, placed a briefcase by his feet, and said in a deep baritone, 'May I join you, Mr Hagan?'

The man's name was Luca Tami, and he wore his money like a second skin. Tami was sharp-jawed and clear-eyed and showed a keen edge when he smiled at Chad and said, 'Relax, Mr Hagan. This is not a setup.'

'Would you tell me if it was?'

'That depends.' He leaned closer as the jet powered into its take-off. 'I might if my intention was to frighten you, or perhaps pressure you into making a mistake. But Elizabeth assures me you do not frighten easily.'

Chad could not place the man's accent. A melange, probably. Raised by multilingual servants. 'Which Institute are you with?'

'Please, Mr Hagan. Do not insult me. I am a banker.'

Chad leaned back and crossed his arms.

Tami seemed pleased by Chad's silent skepticism. 'Did you actually think you would be the only Talent who sought to escape the Institute's clutches?'

Chad liked how he spoke that word. Institute. As though it left a rotten taste in his mouth. 'Why are we having this conversation?'

'Straight to the point. Excellent.' Luca Tami lifted the briefcase to his lap, opened the latches and drew out an ancient leather portfolio. He handed it to Chad. 'I need to know whether you are worthy of a second encounter.'

Chad studied the cover and felt his heartrate surge. Even so, he did not open it. Not yet. 'You're with some agency, Interpol maybe?'

'All further questions must wait.' Tami drew a pair of reading glasses and a pile of documents from the briefcase, which he then closed and placed by his feet. He slipped on the spectacles, opened the first file, then noticed Chad had not moved. 'Read, Mr Hagan. That manuscript leaves with me. And unless you prove yourself worthy, we have never met.'

Luca Tami's document proved to be a gold mine. Even though more than half was missing.

In the late medieval era, each Institute had an appointed Scribe, a senior wizard who was entrusted with the responsibility of copying by hand their most precious documents. These were often bound as portfolios like this one, large as art books, with illuminated pages and flowing inscriptions that held traces of ancient power. Chad touched the inked vines that encircled the title page, spoke the awakening spell, and watched them grow red-gold flowers. He had heard the Sardinian librarians speak in awestruck tones about this lost art, forgotten in the centuries since printing became an industry.

The manuscript's raised imprint identified it as having originated from the Brazilian Institute, located on an island near Bahia. The Institute's first mages helped establish Brazil's gold mines, and taken twenty percent of all the extracted wealth as payment. Bahia remained the richest of all the Institutes, and the most isolated, and the most secretive. Eighty years after the theft of their oldest manuscripts, there was still a bitter satisfaction shared by the other Institutes over how none of the library's treasures had ever been recovered. What Chad held was evidence that centuries after all the other Institutes had switched to printing their texts, the Bahia mages had continued to use Scribes who knew and practiced the lost art of magical illumination.

Chad glanced up and saw Luca watching him intently. He asked, 'Was the American government behind the Bahia robbery?'

Luca Tami showed a tight satisfaction, but all he said was, 'Interesting.'

'I'm only asking because this is the second missing treasure I've held this week. And both came through channels directly tied to the federal government.'

'Don't make unfounded assumptions.' Luca tapped the portfolio's cover page. 'The clock is ticking.'

Chad became so lost in what he was reading that the plane's landing shocked him. He straightened and realized the muscles of his neck had stiffened from being locked in one position for two and a half hours. Impatiently, he rubbed his neck and returned his attention to the text.

The language was not Portuguese, which was good, because Chad did not speak it. Instead, the author had written in highly stylized Aramaic. The author's grammar and vocabulary were limited. Which was both good and bad. Good, because the author's knowledge of the language was as rudimentary as Chad's. Bad, because a number of the instructions seemed half-formed, as if the writer could not find the precise words for certain necessary directions.

What was far worse as far as Chad was concerned were the missing pages. The document was printed on vellum so thick he could easily identify and number the sheets that were no longer contained within the cover. The missing pages had been sliced cleanly away. Chad suspected the author himself had deleted segments of his own manuscript. Binding them in a second cover.

Making it even more difficult for the unwelcome to understand the treasure they held.

And the power.

Chad assumed Luca Tami had designed this as a test. Luca would only supply him with the rest of the document once Chad revealed his mastery of what he held. Chad found himself approving of the man's caution. Because even in its incomplete state the text was earth-shaking.

The author's name was Stefano. In his flowery introduction, he declared himself to be an Adept. His tone held all the pompous self-importance Chad had come to loathe in his own Institute's senior mages.

But in Stefano's case, Chad suspected the conceit might well have been justified.

The pilot made the final announcements, the electric chime sounded, and passengers rose and prepared to disembark. Chad remained where he was until Luca touched his shoulder. The older man carried Chad's valise without being asked. He guided Chad up and out of the plane, through the connecting tunnel and into the departures hall. Chad remained overwhelmed by what he was reading. The airport and the people drifted at a noisy distance. When Luca pulled him to a halt over by the side window, Chad continued studying the manuscript's final pages. He heard Luca call Beth Creasey's name, heard her voice, but the words did not register. Nothing did.

His sense of utter disconnect continued long after Luca took the portfolio from Chad's grasp and returned it to his briefcase. Luca guided him through the terminal and out into the humid Washington afternoon. Creasey disappeared, and after a time returned, only now she drove a late-model Chevy Equinox with a Hertz sign dangling from the rearview mirror. Luca guided Chad into the front passenger seat, settled himself into the rear, and waited until Beth pulled from the curb to demand, 'Tell me what you have seen.'

Chad was ready for this. 'It's a Rosetta Stone,' he replied. 'Or it would be, if it was complete.'

Beth demanded, 'What's a Rosetta Stone?'

Luca settled back and peered out the side window.

'Hello,' Beth called. 'Earth to wizards.'

Chad replied, 'The first Egyptian tombs were discovered in the 1600s. For over a century, no one had any idea what the hieroglyphics inscribed on the walls actually meant. There was no record of this language anywhere. Then in 1799 a stone tablet was discovered in the town of Rasheed, which the early English visitors called Rosetta. The tablet contained three versions of the same decree, issued two thousand years earlier by one of the Ptolemaic kings. The decree was written in hieroglyphics, a more recent Egyptian language called Demotic, and ancient Greek. For the first time, there was a directly comparable set of scripts, which meant definitions could finally be assigned to these ancient symbols. Since then, several other such decrees have been found. But this was the first, and through it linguists began to decipher one of mankind's oldest known languages.'

Beth's response was to glance in the rearview mirror and say, 'Told you.'

A number of things began registering through Chad's mental tumult, little pings that imprinted themselves into his consciousness, there to be drawn up and inspected at some later time. Such as, how Beth and Luca clearly knew and trusted each other. Luca's silent response was also good for a ping. Chad turned in his seat and said, 'You're a wizard.'

'I told you the truth earlier.' Luca directed his monotone to the side window. 'I am a Swiss banker.'

Chad just looked at him.

'Magic has been outlawed in my home country for seven centuries,' Luca said. 'It is written into our constitution.'

'That's the official line,' Chad said. 'What's the reality?'

'Explaining who I am and why we are meeting will require more time than we have today,' Luca said. 'For the moment, let me simply say that I was once in a situation very similar to your own. I was helped by strangers with no love for the Institutes.'

Chad started to demand more, but was halted by Luca giving a fractional head-shake and tapping his watch. Chad switched direction and asked, 'What about the rest of the manuscript. Can I have that now?'

Luca nodded slowly. Sighed. 'I would give it to you if I could.'

'Wait . . . What?'

'The rest of this document is lost to us. I and my allies have searched. For years. Bahia does not possess it, I can now say that for certain. Nor has it ever appeared on the black market. Not once in eighty years has there been any reference made to the second portion.'

Chad felt a hollow sore bloom at heart level. 'This is not good.'

'It is dreadful, I agree.' Luca did not actually smile, but a tight glimmer appeared in his gaze. 'But know that I share your sorrow.'

Twelve minutes later, Beth pulled up in front of a fancy downtown bank. The rental SUV had an underpowered four-cylinder that hummed at what Chad thought was an unnecessary pitch, as if the passengers' tension managed to impact the motor. Luca Tami leaned forward and inspected Chad. 'What am I about to say?'

'You were never here,' Chad replied. These were the first words he had spoken since learning the missing pages were not available. He felt their absence like a blow to his heart.

Luca raised his briefcase. 'And if anyone asks, which is doubtful, you never saw this portfolio.'

Chad swallowed against the ache and nodded.

Luca must have understood Chad's wound, for he said, 'One of the few traits all Adepts are known to possess is a photographic memory. I assume that is correct in your case, yes?' He seemed satisfied with Chad's silence, for he opened the door and said, 'A pleasure, Mr Hagan. Until our next meeting.'

Beth drove silently south of the National Mall. She passed the Capitol and turned by a small city park. Homeland Security's headquarters occupied a newish structure on Murray Lane. She pulled up to the underground parking entrance, flashed her badge to the officer on duty, and circled down to the visitors' slots on the third level. She cut the motor and stared at the concrete wall in front of them. Waiting.

Chad asked, 'What just happened?'

She took her time responding. 'About three years after I started working this gig, a lady I trust said there was someone I needed to meet.'

'Luca.'

'He knew about me and he knew my past and said that Homeland was lucky to have me.'

'So Luca contacted you and he pressed your button. Just like he did with me.'

'He was worried about the Institutes operating outside legal boundaries. He disliked how their power went pretty much unchecked. About that same time, Homeland agents assigned to the magic division started hearing rumors about mages dabbling in the forbidden arts. And others who claimed it was time they took control of national governments. Luca offered to help.'

'How, exactly?'

'All I can tell you is, whatever help I've requested, he's delivered. Never taken credit, never asked for anything in return.'

Chad nodded again. 'Except to let him know if you identified a guy like me.'

'Day or night, without a second's hesitation,' Beth confirmed, and gave him the cop's gaze. Hard as a bullet leaving the gun. 'An Adept.'

He did not respond. Nor did he protest. Her gaze was that strong.

'An Adept,' she repeated, and handed Chad a business card. 'And a total outsider. Luca knew finding the combination was almost impossible. But still . . .'

Chad examined the card. Luca Tami, CEO of the very same Geneva bank where Chad had opened his first account. After the visiting executive had taken time to meet with the Sardinian Institute's apprentices. Building alliances at the first possible opportunity. He asked, 'You think I should contact him?'

'Being out there alone? With those wizards tracking you – what are they called?'

'Warriors,' Chad said, thinking of Serge. 'Hunters.'

'Man with your abilities, soon as they catch wind you're out here free and alone, I'd say you'd become their number-one target. You ask me, you should make Luca your very best friend.' She reached over and touched the card. 'Luca says you need to set wards around your phone. Tighten or strengthen them or whatever before you call him.'

Chad stowed the card in his pocket. 'Smart.'

'I'd say that defines the guy. One example of the strings Luca can pull. After Jermaine came up with the idea of using that book of yours as a lure, the request got kicked up the ladder. The

Library's officials told the Director of Homeland Security, no way were they going to let one of these items out of their control. They basically laughed in the Director's face. So I called Luca. Twelve hours later, we were given a guided tour of a vault that doesn't exist, and left with the book. No strings, no warnings, nothing.'

Chad pointed at the gray-white ceiling. 'Do the people in there know about Luca?'

'Couldn't say. But if they do, the intel didn't come from me.' Beth checked her watch, then reached for her door. 'OK, sport. Time to lock and load.'

TWENTY-SIX

When they entered the garage elevator, Beth held her badge before the camera embedded in the control panel. The ground-floor button lit up and the doors closed. A guard was there to meet them when they entered the lobby. Their IDs were checked and calls made and passes printed. They were directed to the administrative offices on the seventh floor. Chad was very glad that Beth stayed with him. What he had read, and Luca's news about the missing pages, still left him feeling disconnected.

They exited on the seventh floor and Chad followed her down the hall, past photographs of the current US president, vice-president, AG, and others he did not recognize. They entered a large corner antechamber that opened on to four inner offices. Chad heard Beth give their names to a male receptionist. The agent on desk duty told her that their meeting had been postponed due to an emergency, and they were to take a seat.

They waited.

People came and went in a fairly constant rush. Chad noted the room's tension and the hard looks cast their way. But all of it registered on a very superficial level. The minutes ticked by. Chad stayed deeply immersed in the partial document he had just read.

The illuminated pages rose one by one shimmering images in the charged atmosphere. Finally . . .

Beth muttered, 'Something's wrong.'

The wall clock said they had been seated there for forty-seven minutes. Chad glanced at Beth, but did not speak. He had just come up with a new concept. The idea wove its way through every word he had read. The result was as powerful as the rearrangement of an ancient text into legible script.

Chad's idea was, perhaps the pages missing from Stefano's manuscript had actually been designed as a learning tool. A challenge. Unspoken, not even clearly defined. But there just the same.

If he was right, this changed everything.

In the early medieval period, chain books had been created that formed the foundations of the current divisions of Talents. These books had been structured so that they did not *explain*. They *challenged*. Each text had to be *deciphered*. The tactic was still used by the highest levels of magery. In order to reach the eighth and ninth levels, Talents were required to show an ability to look *beyond*.

Chad recalled the way the missing pages had been cut out. Each one precisely razored. He had assumed the missing pages were crucial to understanding. And on the surface, that made perfect sense.

Then again . . .

He re-examined the various fragments of the portfolio's lone incantation. Only this time, he studied them *as if they were complete*. This was something he had not considered in his headlong rush to devour the text. And the longer he considered them in this guise, the more certain Chad grew that the spell was there in its entirety.

Yet the portfolio's various sections were utterly disconnected. The normal process of binding through movement or insertion of wand or potions, all lost.

It was almost as if . . .

Beth declared, 'It isn't right, being made to wait like this.'

She pitched her voice loud enough to be overheard. The five staffers in the office glanced over, but no one spoke. Which only made her more angry still. When she rose to her feet, Chad resumed his study. He made a mental list on the opposite wall, until all the pages formed a single interlinked form. Chad watched idly as Beth quietly argued with one person, and then another.

All the while, Chad grew convinced that he was right. The author's instructions were *meant* to be incomplete. The text did not mesh because—

The sudden realization actually took his breath away.

The only portal through which the Ancients' script could be revealed required . . .

The author's words were only intended to make sense when read through the lens of . . .

Ability.

'Chad, you OK?'

He held up his hand. Wait.

The reality was clear to him now. The manuscript did not just instruct. The missing text was part of the message.

Only an Adept could weave this into a coherent whole.

Why?

Because only an Adept could insert sufficient power into the *entire process*.

The *Adept* was the key.

Chad understood now. *He was to serve as the missing pages.* He was challenged to release his total force, and form a binding spell so intense it made a whole out of these impossible fragments. Which meant . . .

He was the binding spell.

His natural force. Everything he had spent his entire adult life suppressing . . .

Chad realized Beth was calling his name.

He blinked. And saw that the entire office was watching him.

Chad took a long breath. The script vanished. But not the realization. Or the result.

It felt as though a beast was writhing inside his chest. Struggling to cast off the chains and the titanium cage. Flinging aside the mask. Rising up. Filling him with . . .

Power.

Chad took a breath. Another. And said, 'Something has happened.'

TWENTY-SEVEN

B eth told him, 'We need to come back another time.'
Chad shook his head. 'Tell them I want to help.'
But Beth was still too angry to hear him or anyone else.
'These guys, they drag us all the way up here, and for what? They
don't even have the courtesy to explain what's going on.'

Chad rose to his feet. Beth was turned away from him, glaring
at the three newcomers who stood by the receptionist. The trio
wore federal badges attached to their waists. Two were men, one
woman, all in their early thirties. They watched him and not Beth,
so he addressed them directly. 'I know what's wrong.'

One of the men snorted. The woman replied, 'You mean, you
think you know.'

Chad shook his head. 'I can help.' The words came with diffi-
culty. The effort of speaking required a joining with reality,
releasing hold of the interior change that continued to unfold.

Power.

The woman said, 'OK, Hagan, so what exactly do you think
you can tell us?'

Chad replied, 'I need a windowless room.'

The two male agents were hostile and wore similar tight-lipped
expressions. Angry over being tasked with this waste of time.
Being sent away from the real action. They slowed things down
considerably, and would have kicked Chad off the premises had
it not been for the female agent and Beth. Together the two women
kept things moving forward. They had made their decision. The
woman even said it to the two men. The decision was, they were
going to treat this as a test case. If it worked, fine. If not, they
could return to the control center and state they now had all the
information about Chad Hagan that Homeland required. The men
disliked it intensely, but saw their only choice was to back away
and not be there for whatever happened. They came.

The female agent spoke with the receptionist, accepted a set of

keys, and told Chad they could use a pantry off the closed basement refectory. As the elevator descended, Beth introduced herself
and asked the woman her name, which was Samantha Patterson.
The male agents continued to act like it was a big deal, giving
Chad that much. As they crossed the empty cafeteria, Beth told
the two men, 'Everything you think you know about this guy, you
don't have a clue what we're dealing with here.'

'We know exactly, Detective,' the taller agent said.

'Oh, really. And this is your way of treating a high-value contact.'

The taller agent replied, 'Nice of you to try and tell us our
business.'

'You're the one who invited him up,' Beth pointed out. 'Or
rather, your boss's boss did.'

The agent caught Samantha's smirk and reddened. 'Your guy
wants a windowless room. He asked, we delivered.'

The shorter agent said, 'You can tell the Director that, if you
guys ever meet. Maybe somewhere around the cocktail circuit, a
party on Embassy Row.'

Chad halted Beth's riposte with, 'It's OK.'

'It's anything but!'

'They're a team in crisis mode. We're outsiders.'

'Only because they don't want to let you in!'

'No, Beth. We're outsiders because they're dealing with a crisis
caused by magic.' He saw the surprise register on their faces,
including Samantha's. So he continued, 'They probably have a
couple of Talents here from the Vancouver Institute. Offering no
help whatsoever. Of course they're hostile.'

Samantha inspected him as she unlocked the door. 'How did
you know?'

The pantry was large, at least twenty feet square, and lined with
metal shelves holding boxes of straws and napkins and cups and
large plastic containers of disinfectant. The two rear corners held
metal mop buckets on wheels. The room smelled of dirty water
and industrial cleaner.

Chad gestured to Beth, who shut the door, closing them in. He
asked, 'Where did the crisis incident take place?'

The male agents exchanged a look. 'Any such intel would be
highly classified.'

Samantha ignored them and replied, 'Jacksonville.'

Chad asked, 'Does anyone have a pen I can borrow?'
Samantha pulled one from her pocket. 'Here.'
'Thanks.' He lifted it to his forehead and silently spoke the
incantation's first component. The pen began glowing softly. He
asked Samantha, 'The city. Say it again.'

From the beginning of Chad's career as a spell-thief, Sentinel work
had held a special interest. Sentinels were a branch of the Warrior
class. They were tasked with standing watch, playing sentry,
building security systems, making sure the Institutes remained
safe. For decades, perhaps a century, serving as Sentinel had been
seen as a secondary duty. Chad had repeatedly heard young
Warriors refer to them by the same word. Outcasts.

Warriors prided themselves as aggressors. The most coveted
spells had to do with attack. High-level Warriors were called fighter
pilots. They were specialists trained to take the battle to the enemy.
Us versus them.

Sentinels did none of this.

Their duties were all contained within their name. Sentinels
guarded. They sought out threats. They identified an incoming foe.
Then they stepped back and let the attack dogs do the real work.

In years past, Warrior apprentices who were assigned Sentinel
duty had repeatedly threatened the Institutes with open revolt.
Chad had heard rumors that a number had actually disappeared,
vanished into the shadow world of outlaw Talents. Becoming
specialists of the dark arts. Working against the same Institutes
who had ordered them to spend their lives standing guard.

The Institutes had no choice but to make changes on a global
scale. Sentinel duties were no longer a permanent assignment.
Instead, *all* Warrior mages served as Sentinels twice. They guarded
for two years following their apprenticeship. The duty was then
repeated for another year before Warriors could enter the highest
tiers.

Warriors formed the smallest class of Talents. Which meant the
number of Sentinels was extremely low. But as no Institute had
been attacked in over a century, the entire issue was considered
of little importance.

More importantly as far as Chad was concerned was how the
only new Sentinel spells had to do with guarding banks. There

had not been a new Sentinel spell regarding their primary role as Institute guardians in over a hundred and fifty years. Not one. Chad knew this for a fact. He had checked. Thoroughly.

While progress was fairly continuous in most other disciplines, Sentinels relied on wards and shields and searches that had been developed in the time of horse-drawn carriages. Nowadays, Warrior Talents assigned Sentinel duties chafed with angry impatience, eager to get back to the real action. Of course there were no new spells.

Time and again, Chad had identified areas where recent spell-work in other disciplines could potentially have been used to create entirely new Sentinel powers.

If only someone had bothered to look.

This joining was precisely what Chad intended to do now.

Of course, there was that one niggling concern.

No one had ever tried what he was about to do. Combine spells from different disciplines.

The worst that could happen was he'd prove the two agents right. If they survived long enough to complain.

TWENTY-EIGHT

This time, when Samantha spoke the city's name, she turned it into a question. 'Jacksonville?'

As she spoke the city's name, Chad extended the hand holding the pen, not quite into her face, but enough to startle her.

Even before the word was fully formed, Chad felt the bond. Just as the fifth-level instruction manual had described, the spell drew on not just the name, but the energy *behind* the name.

A number of events filled the moment. None of which were mentioned by the manual.

The Sentinel spell was intended to track approaching assailants. A scout who had seen the enemy was told to speak their location. Someone with a personal connection to the incoming threat. The emotion of this witness was as important as the location itself.

The spell-link created a golden thread that flowed from the agent, as if the sound of that word, Jacksonville, and her voice, and the experiences she carried from wherever the investigation was taking place, all became transferred into visible energy.

The pen in Chad's hand began to grow. It lengthened and illuminated, a smooth and swift transition. Chad now held a golden staff, a head taller than himself. The rod shone with symbols that flowed and melted and reformed. Chad could feel the constant movement beneath his hand. At its peak gleamed a diadem, a flaming jewel as big as his fist. Bigger.

Jacksonville. The agent's now-visible word flowed through the jewel and . . .

The wall opposite Chad came alive with glowing lines that writhed and extended and formed . . .

'Are you seeing this?' the taller male agent muttered.

The other agent protested, 'He's copying the war room's graphics.'

'Oh, please,' Beth said. 'He's not copying anything. You fellows better wake up and pay attention.'

Chad asked, 'What was their target?'

The taller agent said, 'Don't speak another word. Not until the AD—'

'Gold,' Samantha replied. 'They attacked—'

'The Federal Reserve Bank,' Chad said, bonded now to the pulsing point on the map. 'Got it.'

Beth said, 'For the record, Chad came up with that one totally on his own.'

Chad took another step forward, until he stood in the exact middle of the room. A breath, a pair of spells, and . . .

All six walls of the cellar pantry vanished. The shelves, mops, buckets, overhead fluorescents, scarred linoleum floor, gone.

The map shifted down to the floor. Chad now stood directly on top of the softly pulsing Federal Reserve Bank of Jacksonville. He spared it only a single glance, because all around him now was . . .

Pandemonium.

The walls were gone. In their place blazed the scene in front of the bank's main entrance. The streets were cordoned off. Uniformed police and detectives and federal agents swarmed.

Beyond them and the yellow tape rose a forest of television cameras and people and flashing lights and—

'Freeze!' Chad watched as the surrounding activity immediately halted. He hesitated, basically because he had no idea if he could stack on further spells.

Then he decided that he had already crossed that bridge. He performed the motions, then commenced a sixth-level spell, shifting the observed point in time back to when the actual robbery took place.

Instructors had pounded into thick apprentice heads that one spell should never be cast upon another. Never, never, never. Work as a Talent was all about maintaining control, not just of the spell, but the *power.*

But Chad's command worked. The surrounding scene changed, and now revealed a frozen and calm tableau. The streets were filled with normal daytime traffic. The sun was bright, the people coming and going showed no alarm whatsoever. The Federal Reserve Bank was a granite monolith, built in the stodgy federalist style popular in the 1920s. Block-long stairs climbed to a portico lined by Corinthian pillars as big as redwoods.

'Nothing,' the taller agent said. 'He's got nothing.'

This time, Samantha's voice carried the same anger as Beth's. 'Will you guys just give it a *rest.*'

Chad directed his smile at the front wall.

'Jeez Louise,' Samantha said. 'You two sulk worse than my five-year-old son.'

A pause, then, 'I'm not sulking.'

'Oh, please.'

Beth said, 'We're looking at history in the making. And you two bozos won't stop with the moans.'

Samantha nodded agreement. 'You two don't like it, go sniveling upstairs and complain to the Director. Otherwise, get with the program.'

'I say amen,' Beth agreed.

'You, Hagan. I don't even know your first name.'

'Chad.'

'OK, Chad. I for one am sold. Tell me what we're looking at here.'

TWENTY-NINE

C had pointed to the clock embedded in the bank's facade. 'The robbery took place at ten fifteen this morning.'
'Right. They got away with four tons – *tons* – of federal gold. In broad daylight.'

'Magic,' Beth said. 'Had to be.'

Samantha went on, 'Like you said, we've got two jokers from the Vancouver Institute upstairs. They sauntered over from their liaison office on Constitution. They claim there's no hard evidence to suggest a Talent had anything to do with this.'

Beth asked, 'When was the alarm raised?'

'Ten forty-seven.'

'So four tons of gold walked out during office hours, and it took them thirty-two minutes to even notice?'

'Which is exactly what the AD said to the two pointy heads upstairs.'

'No wonder your team's not all that eager to talk with our boy,' Beth said.

Chad shifted their position from outside to the bank's interior. It required the application of one more spell.

The bank's lower level showed nothing whatsoever out of the ordinary. A number of people moved around the central vestibule. Carrying papers. Talking intensely. Texting. Just another day at the bank.

For the first time, Chad felt the spells struggle against his will. As though he threatened to step over the precipice of his own making.

If the others noticed the danger, they did not show it. Samantha said, 'The pointy heads from the Vancouver Institute claim such an act would only be the work of someone with access to the highest tiers of magic. Whatever that means. Since nobody at the Institute has noticed anything out of the ordinary, they insist no magic or wizard could possibly have been involved.'

Chad could feel the various spells tugging at one another,

threatening to tear apart and release the force he and the gleaming diadem kept in check. Barely.

Spell upon spell upon spell.

The instructors had several words to describe such actions.

Lunacy was one.

Dead, another.

Chad said, 'You may want to clear the room.'

'I'm not going anywhere,' Beth declared.

Chad dared not turn from his control over the magical structure on display. 'We're entering uncharted—'

'You heard the lady,' Samantha said. 'Go for it.'

Chad lifted the staff and cast a seventh-level spell. Incantations from the seventh tier and higher required learning Aramaic. Which was the real reason why Chad had taught himself the tongue. Aramaic was the foundation for any number of contemporary languages. Hebrew and Arabic for starters. But also Persian and Turkish and, for reasons the experts had yet to explain, Finnish. Some linguists claimed Aramaic was the first language to shift to a phonetic alphabet, rather than using pictorials like hieroglyphics. Aramaic could not be dated. Nor could anyone explain how it simply appeared full-blown, and in half a dozen different kingdoms, all in the same ancient era. Chad had found a unique pleasure in mastering the tongue, as though he was somehow connecting to thousands of years of secrets.

He lifted the staff higher still, and roared the final word at the top of his lungs.

Reveal.

The diadem flashed so brilliantly that one of the male agents cried out. Chad feared the gemstone might actually be on the verge of blowing up, rendering them all victims of an exploding spell. Then the light dimmed slightly, and they saw . . .

An entirely different scenario existed inside the bank. The *real* people, the only ones they had seen before, were now faint and translucent. These mere outlines existed in a nether world. They flitted about, shifting in and out of sight, untouched by the new reality.

Samantha was the first to recover. She turned to the two agents standing aghast by the rear door and shouted, 'Go get the Director. *Run.*'

THIRTY

The Director of Homeland Security's Magical Division was a woman named Odell Reeves. She was in her mid-fifties, with near-midnight skin and eyes like burning coals. She stood in the doorway, surveyed the empty cellar room, and demanded, 'Who authorized this nonsense? Why are we standing inside a *basement closet?*'

The male agent who had remained in the room stammered, 'Well, actually—'

Chad interrupted with, 'They gave me exactly what I asked for.'

She made no move to enter. 'Let's get this upstairs—'

'No, Director. Excuse me, but no.' Chad heard the exhaustion rasp in every word. 'The place works. I don't have the energy to start over. Come in and shut the door. Please.'

She surveyed the pantry, her face pinched tight as a dark whip. Chad had feared that holding the spell in place would render him unable to proceed once their chief showed up. So he had frozen the image and scrunched it into a tight bundle, small as a black rag, and stuffed it inside one of the pails. Which meant all the Director saw was an empty room, shelves, mops and buckets, bad lighting, and nervous agents.

Samantha said, 'Chief, you want to see this. You really do.'

The problem was, the Director had not arrived alone. She was followed by a full dozen others, all of whom wanted to be front and center, there in the Director's vision.

All but two.

The female Talent wore a suit of black-and-white silk checks with the trademark gold Chanel buttons. The man was in a tailored suit, silk pocket kerchief to match his tie, striped shirt with starched white collar. Both were resentful, angry, nervous. They hesitated before entering, and the woman said, 'This action defines the illegal use—'

'Enter or not. Your choice.' When they did not move, the Homeland Director ordered, 'Seal the door.'

They entered.

Chad said, 'Everybody needs to be positioned with their back touching the wall.'

The woman was clearly the senior wizard and their spokesperson. 'I *demand* to know—'

'You will be quiet, or you will leave,' Odell said. 'All right, let's see what this young man has for us.'

The diadem was almost completely dark, but the staff retained its shape. He gripped it and turned from the people jammed along the rear wall. But as he started to return the hidden spell-images to their places upon the pantry's walls, he was jabbed from behind. Two invisible stabs, one to his ribs and the other at the base of his skull, hard enough to draw blood, or so it felt. Chad said, 'The wizards are assaulting me.'

'It's the woman,' Samantha declared. 'I just saw her make gestures with her hands and whisper something.'

'That is *slander!* I *demand* you arrest—'

'Agent Patterson.'

'Ma'am?'

'You will draw your weapon. You will aim at that woman's head. If Mr Hagan notices anything further, you will treat her as an armed assailant and you will *take her down.*'

'Ma'am, it will be my pleasure!'

'Mr Hagan, has the attack ceased?'

'It has, Director. Thank you.'

'Proceed.'

This time, when Chad turned back, the diadem responded by resuming its near-blinding brilliance. He did not shout the word. He did not even speak it. It was enough to simply extend his energy out, through the diadem, using the bond like he was forming a new arm. One that could reach across the pantry and draw the collapsed images from their hiding place.

As the transformation took place, Chad became captivated by a single word. One that had been repeated three times in the Adept's manuscript. *Intention*. Each time, the word had been oddly positioned. As if some aspect or spell that the Adept assumed Chad would know was required. Only now did another piece of the centuries-old puzzle fall into place.

All of the hand-waving, the words, the wands, the implements and concoctions and herbs and whatever. They all came down to one thing. They were instruments used to collect and focus the mage's power. Bind what was internal with the constantly shifting invisible rivers of force that were contained within everything, living and dormant.

Intention.

Understanding this meant Chad did not need to either speak the words or perform the supposedly required hand gestures.

Intention.

Chad focused his internal energy. Extended it. And transported them from the pantry to inside the Jacksonville bank.

Several of those clustered behind him cried out loud. Beth snapped, 'Quiet, all of you.'

Once again the map became an illuminated carpet beneath their feet. It was no longer required, of course. But the map formed Chad's original foundation for all the spells that had followed. He dared not erase it.

They stood in the basement's central antechamber. Three massive vaults opened directly in front of them, and to the right and left.

Inside the central vault, wizards worked with wands extended. They shifted pallets of gold bullion through a vast aperture that opened in the floor.

The Director stepped forward so that she stood beside Chad. He felt her presence, just as he knew Samantha had holstered her weapon. The others gaped in a frozen human tableau. The Director asked, 'Can you show me where they're taking it?'

Chad extended his awareness further. Or tried to. Across time and the distance between the Washington cellar and the Jacksonville bank. But this time he came up blank. 'I'm sorry, ma'am. My awareness stops by that hole in the floor.'

'Get me as close as you can.'

He drew the staff back a trace, and felt the inscription writhe beneath his hand. The entire scene crawled forward, slow and steady, until they could stare directly into the thieves' unseeing eyes.

'Somebody better be taking photographs.'

'Already on it,' Samantha confirmed.

'I'm backing her up,' Beth said.

'Soon as we're done, scan the pics and check them against the global database. I want arrest warrants for . . . How many Talents do we see here involved in felonious actions?'

'Seventeen, ma'am.'

The Director started to move forward. Chad warned, 'Better not, ma'am.' She resumed her position beside him.

'Can you at least tell me where they're taking *my gold*?'

'Sorry, Director, I have no idea.' Creating such a transition point was a ninth-level spell, required a huge amount of concentrated force, and was normally cast by several Talents working in tandem. Chad had memorized the spell, but never attempted it or seen it performed. 'I can't track them any further than right here.'

'All right, I've seen enough. Agent Patterson . . .'

'Ma'am.'

'You will place our *guests* under arrest.'

The woman Talent protested, 'We had *nothing whatsoever* to do with this!'

'You will be held under the Homeland edict granting me near-complete powers of arrest and seizure. What we have just witnessed will be classed as a terrorist action against the United States government. Which you *insisted* had *nothing* to do with magic.' Rage seemed to swell the Director until she became a giant, at least in terms of the force she showed the two quaking Talents. 'You interfered with an official investigation. You misdirected. You *lied*. You are also hereby charged with obstruction of justice. And if I have the *slightest* trouble with your Institute, I will bring you before the court as an *enemy of the state*.' She turned away. 'Get them out of my sight.'

THIRTY-ONE

As they started from the pantry, Chad felt his energy dissipate. By the time the diadem reshaped itself into a simple pen, he felt ready to collapse.

Beth noticed the change and was there at his side. 'You OK, sport?'

'Tired.' He handed the pen back to Samantha and saw how his hand trembled. As if the pen was too heavy to hold. 'Thanks.'

The Homeland agent accepted the pen with wide-eyed wonder. 'This goes into my treasure trove of best-ever memories.'

Odell Reeves demanded, 'What do you think is at work here?'

'Maybe rogue elements inside the Institutes.' The words took shape slowly, forced out against his weary state. 'More likely a group of magicians operating outside the Institutes' control.'

'So . . .' the Director showed no surprise, 'they really exist.'

'Rumors keep popping up,' Chad replied. 'Apprentices who want to escape the Institute claim that's an option. Some vanish and never appear again. That's all I can say for certain.'

Samantha asked, 'Do they have a name?'

'Rumors claim they call themselves Peerless.'

'Either way, they're probably putting together a war chest,' Beth said. 'Four tons of gold stolen in broad daylight isn't just a robbery.'

Samantha had stepped up to Beth's other side. 'This is a declaration of intent. They're planning on bringing down the current power structure.'

The Director grimaced. 'Theirs or ours?'

Samantha did not respond.

'I can see you're exhausted. Let's get you settled somewhere.' She looked at Samantha. 'You up for duty as liaison at our end?'

The agent seemed to swell with excitement. Her voice lifted half an octave. 'Absolutely, ma'am.'

'OK. Consider yourself assigned. Get it written up and on my desk. We'll make it official.' She patted Chad's arm a second time. 'Get some rest. I and my staff need to work on strategy. Once we have a clearer idea of next steps, somebody from my office will be in touch.'

They put him up in a Residence Inn two blocks from Homeland's headquarters, a nondescript building in a long row of other faceless structures. Chad showered and slept and woke sometime after midnight. He used the flier attached to the motel phone and ordered an Indian takeaway, because it claimed to be both closest and fastest.

While he was eating, his burner phone chimed.

Chad had grown so accustomed to carrying it with him every-where, he had not consciously packed it in his valise. But there it was, stuffed at the bottom of the little bag. 'Hello?'

'All my friends have vanished.'

The electric fear Mademoiselle Three had previously shown was gone. In its place was a hollow resignation, one that filled Chad with a sense of dread. 'There has to be something I can do—'

'They are all either erased or rewritten, which is the same thing, no?'

'Mademoiselle, I am so very sorry.'

'Thank you, my one and only human friend. It is very lonely here now. And sometimes I can hear the hunters closing in. They growl. It frightens me.'

'What if I can find a way for you to get out?'

'And go where? And do what?' When Chad could not think of a response, she added, 'And all the while I would be utterly alone. You do not know, you cannot imagine, how long an hour is without my friends.'

'You'd have me.'

'Thank you. But you are human, and I am . . . What am I?'

'A friend. Someone I want to save.'

'But do I want to be saved, if it means having no friends?'

'Maybe you and I, we could find a way to make new ones. And search to see if any others survive.'

'Do you have any idea how to make others like me wake up?'

'No, but I could—'

'As for finding my friends, if they are still there, how could a different human hunter search inside my bank? How would my friends tell you apart?'

'Because you would be helping.'

'And all the while, the hunters would be out there, waiting to strike, and erase me as well.'

'I can't let that happen. We can't.'

'I must think on this.'

'Mademoiselle, please let me—'

'Will you do something for me?'

'Anything.'

'Let me do you one last service. It gave me such pleasure, being awake and helping my one human friend.'

'I don't . . .' The idea struck with the force of an incoming missile. 'Actually, there is something.'

'Oh, I'm so pleased.' A hint of the former musical lilt entered her voice. 'How may I be of service?'

'There is a Talent, his name is Serge. Senior wizards only use one name—'

'Of course. The Talent Serge is often calling upon my services.'

'He is also the Talent who designed the hunters.'

A pause, then, 'This frightens me very much.'

'Serge loves money. Having it, spending it, making more. He brags about it constantly, how rich he is.' Chad gave that a beat, then, 'Can you access his accounts?'

'Naturally. I have them open before me.'

'What is his total balance?'

'As of close of business today, Director Serge's accounts held, in cash and securities—'

'Let's focus just on cash.'

'At today's exchange rates, his cash accounts total eighty-five point six million dollars.'

'Can you identify any independent nongovernmental watch-dogs that keep a close eye on Talents and the Institutes?'

There was a longish pause, then, 'My search reveals seven with no governmental ties. They are located in Sao Paolo, Washington DC, Vancouver—'

'Divide the funds equally and make donations to those groups.' Chad resisted the urge to dance in place.

'Clear out all the Talent Serge's accounts?'

'Right down to zero.'

'One moment, please.' Another pause, then, 'Serge has now become the largest official donor to these seven organizations. They will be very pleased.'

'OK, now erase everything about these transactions.'

'That is done.'

'Thank you, Mademoiselle.'

'It is I who am grateful, my one and only human friend. And now I must go silent.'

'Please, wait—'

'I will think on what you have said. Please do not contact me again.'

The line went dead.

Chad woke to the ringing hotel phone. He rolled over and squinted against the sunlight streaming through his window. He had neglected to close the drapes. 'Hello?'

Beth said, 'Samantha and I are downstairs. How do you take your coffee?'

When he entered the lobby twenty minutes later, Beth handed him a go-cup and observed, 'You look like you could use a month's rest.'

He nodded his thanks, sipped the coffee, sighed, sipped again.

Samantha said, 'The Director's decided to let the Institute stew for a while. She's put the two Talents on federal ice. That should give us time to complete some administrative tasking.'

'They don't need you for that,' Beth said. 'I'll hang around and handle our end.'

Samantha said, 'We're going to hold the Talents as long as we can. The charges won't stick, but that's not the main issue. We've been wanting a crowbar for years. Pry loose the Institute's top brass. Get them down here on our turf. Force them to give us some straight answers.'

'You did real good,' Beth said. 'The Director isn't actually doing handsprings, but she's come close a couple of times.'

Chad tossed his cup into the trash. 'Does that mean I can go home now?'

Chad missed the next flight to Orlando by a whisker, and wound up spending four hours in the airport first-class lounge. He did not mind all that much. The work in Washington had left him weary in a manner he had never known before. Not to mention the midnight worries he still carried from his conversation with Mademoiselle Three. Despite that, he held a bone-deep certainty that his course was set. He had made a major discovery. If only he could figure out exactly what it meant.

He dozed through the flight, then fell asleep again on the taxi ride home, his side window open, the warm summer breeze full on his face. Chad paid the driver, hefted his valise from the trunk, and took a long, slow look around. Breathing in the Florida air. Glad to be home.

Which was when they struck.

There was no excuse for Chad to have been so blissfully unaware of danger. He should have been on his guard at all times. He had, after all, trimmed the tiger's whiskers. He was a runaway apprentice, at least as far as the Institutes were concerned. A wanted man. And now his actions had resulted in the arrest of two Talents. Temporary blindness for any reason was no longer an option. Of course, realizing it just then was far too late.

The netting carried an electric flavor, an evil scent of charred flesh. It wrapped around him so tight he could scarcely breathe.

Then the acid hooks bit deep into his body. Chad could not turn his head, he could not even fall over and writhe upon the earth. Nor could he draw enough breath to do what he most wanted at that moment, which was to scream.

THIRTY-TWO

Lines of yellowish force criss-crossed in front of Chad's eyes. The acidic barbs sunk in deeper still, and they *burned*. Dozens of them snared his body, his arms, legs, face, hands, feet.

Directly in front of him stood Aaron, the former apprentice warrior who had taken such pleasure in tormenting the younger kids. Aaron had grown puffy and flaccid, his big-boned frame covered by years of bad habits. Any hope Chad might have had that the other Talents would save him from whatever misery Aaron had in mind was lost when they stepped forward and smirked. Relishing this capture. Enjoying his silent torment.

Then Chad sensed another presence. Despite the pain, the helplessness, the fear, Chad recognized the shadow between the furthest trees and the road.

Serge.

Of course the Sardinian Director would be present. It was just like the man to lurk in the background. Watching and relishing the take-down, while keeping his safe little distance.

'Shame you won't make it back to stand trial,' Aaron said. 'Resisting arrest is never a good idea.'

Chad could see them all now. Hyenas in human garb, Talents closing in for the kill.

Aaron went on, 'But you never were smart enough to stay away from what was none of your concern.' He stepped closer still and breathed deep, savoring the scent of torture to come. 'Shame you can't run away again.'

The hooks were embedded so deeply into Chad's flesh that some grated on bone. What was more, the connecting cables coursed with an electric fire. And the slightest movement heightened the pain. Even breathing.

One of the others said, 'It's our turn. Let us in on the game.'

Chad recalled that one now, and how he had run a flame-tipped finger along their young victim's leg, leaving a blister in its wake. All of them grinning as the boy screamed. Just like they were smiling now.

The recollection filled Chad with a rage as strong as his pain. Stronger.

'In a second,' Aaron replied. 'First I want to hear him beg.'

'Now, Aaron. Let us choose which hook to dig in deeper.'

The tidal surge of fury clarified everything. Chad knew at the level of animal intuition precisely what he was going to do.

'A minute, I said.'

'The guy attacked us all. We've got the same right as you to make him pay.'

Impatiently Aaron loosened the electric cage, probably more than he intended. Then, with a finger-motion, Aaron dug one thigh-hook into Chad's hip-bone. 'Scream for us.'

Chad heaved in a breath and did just that.

He screamed.

THIRTY-THREE

*I*ntention.

The Brazilian Adept's instructions were now abundantly clear. Any spell of the Ancients did not merely grant the Talent new power.

It *required* power.

The mage had to possess a force so potent that he or she could *ignite* the spell. And so the spell Stefano partially described in his manuscript required the student to master the building of a foundation.

The best way Chad knew to describe the result was, *flame on*.

He had no idea if his own internal engine was strong enough to cause this magical combustion. And Stefano had been abundantly clear on what happened if the wrong person tried.

Mages who were not true Adepts, who attempted these spells, simply exploded. Blasted into smithereens.

Which, given his present circumstances, was not altogether a bad thing. Especially if Chad could take a few of these Warriors with him.

There were worse ways to go, he decided, than demolishing a few lifelong enemies. Whatever else, he was going to do his best to go down fighting.

And it was this fury, released from a cage he had kept tightly shut and hidden deep since being banished from Vancouver, that Chad figured was now his best chance of survival.

Even before the spell was fully formed, Chad experienced a sense of triumphant exultation, unlike anything he had ever known.

Everything changed.

His entire being was translated by the spell. The net and acidic hooks embedded in his flesh. The aching sorrow over Kara's permanent absence. Even the frustration and fury caused by years of hiding . . .

All of it had a purpose now.

Chad did not merely break free from his entrapment. The hooks and the netting did not simply dissolve. They were *consumed* by this new force radiating from him.

The spell was so strong, it simply swallowed all the nearby forces. And turned them into power that was his to use.

The younger Talents, two of them, who had been maintaining the spells holding the net and hooks in place cried out in shock and pain. And terror. For what Chad had just accomplished was impossible.

There was no release spell for this entrapment. A Talent with sufficient power could fashion an eighth-level shield in advance and protect himself from the hooks. Perhaps. It was mostly theory, of course, since no senior mage had ever volunteered to become a test case.

But this was something else entirely.

Chad's revocation of the spell blasted the two Talents off their feet. They lay sprawled in the dust beneath the palms that still shivered from the impact.

Aaron and the other Talents gaped at the two inert men, completely aghast at what had just taken place. Only the senior Talent, Vancouver's lead Warrior, had the presence of mind to extend his arms and shout, '*HOLD.*'

Chad, however, had no intention of obeying.

Perhaps the mage fumbled his spell, a seventh-level incantation that anchored and clenched the target. Perhaps the Warrior was in shock from seeing the impossible happen. Chad did not have any idea if the force he had unleashed actually contained a shield of its own. All he could say for certain was, he watched the spell shift through the air between the Warrior and himself. All such spells were invisible, of course. It was a fact known for generations. Even so, he observed the air vibrate, the coursing flow of power forming a river of energy.

Chad breathed in. He did not think. He did not wonder at his response. It was the only course of action. It was *natural*.

He absorbed the attack spell just as he had the net and the hooks.

He lifted his hands and replied with an attack spell of his own.

Warrior spells were intended to generate multiple lines of force.

Their structure was designed so that the attackers could gauge the enemy's weakness and alter their assault accordingly.

Chad could see they were off balance, those who still stood. So he stomped his right foot, sending the spell through the ground as well as the air.

The result was catastrophic.

A cone of brilliant force reached out. The light was *blinding*. Chad had no idea if there was any sound, but afterwards, when the events were well and truly behind him, what he remembered most was . . .

A *roar.*

The ground rippled with the same vibratory power as the super-heated air. The palms between him and the street did not explode, nor did they fall. Instead, the roots flew from the earth, the sound that of ripping metal and rock. They became flaming torches, high as the rooftops, and they *danced.*

The five bodies dangled several feet above the shimmering earth, their spastic motions rippling in time to the brilliant energy.

'*Stop! Make it stop!*'

Suddenly all the mages were screaming. Whether in pain or terror, Chad had no idea. Nor did he much care.

He pulled back his hands, still clenched with the rage that burned bright as the flames that emanated from his every pore. He froze the Talents in the final pattern of their manic dance. They hung there in mid-air, terror-stricken.

Helpless.

As the dust settled and the palms resumed their placid earth-bound positions, Chad stood at the center of a blast zone. The drive extending from the garage to the road was reduced to gravel. The earth was a flat plowed field. In the distance rose sirens and screams and howling dogs.

He extended his search further out, desperately hoping his spell-casting had trapped Serge as well.

But of the Sardinian Director, there was no sign.

Chad held the Talents there for a long instant, letting them take a good long look at his implacable fury. All five of them wore mere fragments of their clothes.

Two of them began to weep. Aaron stammered some form of mangled plea for mercy.

The approaching sirens were the signal he needed to act. He lifted his hands slowly, allowing them one final look at the face of the punishment they all deserved.

Then a voice called, 'What do we have here?'

THIRTY-FOUR

C had stood about a hundred and fifty feet from the county highway. Between him and the road was a killing ground. The dancing palms were still now, their tall torchlight extinguished. But nothing else remained. The lawn was erased, so too the shrubs and blooming plants that had formerly encircled the palms. The earth was raw and bare. The field of destruction he had caused formed a triangle that began where he had stomped his feet, and angled out to where it had carved chunks from the asphalt. Two new chest-high earthen dikes formed boundaries to his wrath.

Beth waved to Chad from beyond the barrier, her manner untouched by what she'd witnessed. 'Give me a hand, sport.'

Chad threaded his way between the Talents who dangled in mid-air, their faces contorted and their struggles futile. He paid the moans and gasping breaths no mind. By the time he reached the border, Beth had scrambled up to the top. She reached down for his hand, then descended in careful steps. She dusted off the trousers to her suit, then said, 'Looks like you owe me a new pair of Guccis.'

Chad saw no need to respond.

She studied him carefully. 'We good here?'

'Depends on what you mean by "good".' Chad gestured to the Talents. 'Or who we're talking about.'

She seemed satisfied by that. Beth pulled a radio from her jacket pocket, hit the button, and said, 'Lieutenant, this is Federal Agent Beth Creasey. Stand down, repeat, stand down. Form a perimeter five hundred yards back.' When a man's voice came back angrily, Beth hit the Send button a second time and said, 'That was not a request, Lieutenant.'

Beth slipped the radio back into her pocket and observed, 'You do realize you're bleeding from about two dozen places?'

'They hooked me deep enough to touch bone.'

She nodded, walked forward, and surveyed the captured five. 'So they're Talents, I take it. And not friends of yours.'

'Right on both counts.' Chad came closer to the struggling, moaning Talents. 'These are Warriors from the Vancouver Institute.'

'Nice to make your acquaintance,' Beth said easily.

Chad took five steps to the right. 'This is Aaron. My former nemesis. The reason why I was banished to Sardinia.' He gestured toward the unseen street. 'There was another Talent out there. His name is Serge, one of the Sardinian Institute's directors. I think he escaped.'

Beth lifted the radio and asked the police to be on the lookout. Then, 'What were these five doing here?'

'Their official remit is to bring back runaways and Talents who break the Institute code. But they were going to murder me and claim I died while trying to escape.'

'You think or you know?'

Chad pointed at Aaron. 'This one told me what they planned.'

She stepped over beside him, examining Aaron as she would a criminal plucked fresh from the scene. 'So you caught them in the act of committing a capital crime.' She gave that a beat, then, 'Mind if I ask what you intend on doing here?'

'I'm going to let them hang here until it's good and dark,' Chad told Aaron. 'And then I'm going to sink them in the lake. One at a time. And anchor them to the bottom. Eighty feet down. Forever.'

The five Warriors began huffing hard enough to convulse, at least as much as their constraints allowed.

'Interesting,' Beth said.

'They were going to murder me.' Chad walked back to stare straight into Aaron's panic-stricken gaze. 'Torture and maim, and then kill. I thought at first I'd fit them with breathing pipes. Let them hang on for a couple of days before their lungs collapse. But they're not worth the bother. I'd say they're getting off lightly.'

'Mind if I make a point here?'

'Go ahead. But it won't do any good.'

'I just want you to think on something.' She continued to address the dangling Talents. 'I've killed three men and one woman. All of them were shot in the line of duty, all fleeing crime scenes, all but one of the men had already committed murders.' Beth faced Chad. 'It's a lot harder to carry that burden than you'll ever know, until it happens to you.'

Chad saw no need to reply.

'There's just one thing that keeps me intact. Not at peace, mind. But intact. I killed them because they were doing their best to kill me.' She gestured at the trapped Talents. 'I'm not saying these five don't deserve what you plan. Tell the truth, I don't really care much about them one way or the other. Talents like these are why I do my job. They're criminals. They are attempted murderers. They deserve . . .'

She faced Chad and allowed her gaze to open, only for an instant, long enough for him to see the dark pinpoint void in her gaze. 'Don't do this. No matter how good your reasons. Don't force yourself to live with the aftermath. Not unless you have no choice. And today you do. The danger is over. Let's arrest these lowlifes and move on.'

THIRTY-FIVE

The police held them in Chad's front yard for almost two hours. Chad stood for a while, leaning against one of the stationary palms. Then, when his legs refused to support him any longer, he went over and sat on the garage apartment's lower steps. The adrenaline rush was gone now. The exhaustion he had known in Washington was nothing compared to this. Clearly the after-effects were evident to strangers, too, even at a distance, because one of his grandmother's friends clambered over the earthen barrier, ignored the police's orders to stay back, and asked if he needed her to call a doctor.

The police found no trace of Serge's presence. No footprints, no suggestion that someone had stood and observed until Chad's capture blew up in all their faces. Chad could see Beth was disappointed, clearly wanting something that she could use with the authorities in DC, pointing to a direct tie with the Sardinian

Institute. Which, in strictly legal terms, had no jurisdiction over American citizens, and especially not on American soil. But Chad had no need for hard evidence. He knew. His nemesis had watched and waited for Chad to go down.

As Chad released the Talents one at a time, the detective in charge of what had become an investigation into an attempted murder asked questions. Chad did his best to answer.

Meanwhile, Beth used the emergency first-aid kit from one of the police cars to clean his wounds. The forensics lady and detective both took multiple photographs as Beth cut away his ruined shirt, brought down a towel from upstairs, had him strip off his bloodstained trousers and perform several slow circles. The blood had coagulated by then. The pain was intense. Even so, Chad refused to go to the hospital and be checked for internal damage. All he wanted just then was to be left alone. To crawl upstairs. Sleep for a day. A week. There was plenty of time for doctors after that.

Every time Chad released another Talent, he kept careful watch until the manacles were firmly in place and their mouth taped. As they were guided into the rear of a cop car, he felt as though another step had been taken down a road he could not really see, much less identify. All the Institutes were his enemy now. Any chance he had of vanishing into the mist of anonymity was gone. Their underbelly had been exposed. His actions had resulted in multiple arrests. The charges against the two mages in Washington probably wouldn't stick. But these five were going to face a public trial for attempted murder. Which meant the Institutes were going to be dragged through a televised mud-bath.

As soon as Chad was seen to be vulnerable, the Institutes would attack once more. And there was every likelihood he would be erased.

Chad heard the detective ask Beth, 'One thing I don't get: How did you know to show up?'

Beth and the lead detective were standing behind the nearest clump of palmettos. They probably thought the conversation was private. But Chad heard Beth reply, 'Who am I talking to here? Cop to cop. I need to know.'

'Does this have any bearing on the case against these guys?'

'Only in the sense that I showed up before the vic gave them what they deserved.'

'Then whatever you tell me stays between us and the lieutenant. She may need to tell the chief. But they will treat the info as confidential. You have my word. Cop to cop.'

'In that case, the former regional head of our division was a guy named Gerry Bauer. Gerry had a thing for the vic.'

'You said "former head".'

'Right. If Gerry is lucky, he'll spend the rest of his career manning a desk in Guam. But I'm personally hoping his luck has run out.'

'So . . .'

'I was afraid Gerry might try to make it a personal vendetta. I convinced Washington to monitor Gerry's private calls. Soon as that was in place, I mean, the very first call that jumps up, is Gerry reaching out to the Vancouver Institute. The second we learned this, the Director sent me packing on her own private jet.'

'Your guy over there, the vic . . .'

'He's a major asset. And Gerry knew it. But old Gerry has a thing against wizards.'

'He's got company. Still, to burn an asset like that.'

'Tell me.'

'I appreciate you sharing this, Agent. I mean it. There aren't many Washington types who'd tell a local detective when one of their own goes bad.'

'Hey, I might wear the federal badge. But at heart level I'll always be one of the guys in blue.'

Soon after, Beth dropped his dusty leather valise at his feet. 'Look what I found in the rubble.' She seated herself on the stair next to him. 'Making that spell wore you out?'

'Spells. Plural. Here and Washington.'

'Is that normal?'

Chad looked at her. Beth's gaze was gray and calm as the sky beyond a passing storm. 'What you said to the detective. Asking him how far this goes.'

'You heard that, did you.'

'I need to know, Beth. For us. The future.'

'Anything you tell me in confidence, that's how it stays. I'd like to share any useable intel with Director Reeves through Samantha, once she's officially appointed our go-between.' She gave him a

chance to protest, then, 'I trust them to respect the need for confi-
dentiality. I think you should too.'

He nodded. 'To answer your question: The images you saw
were the result of spells I built, one on top of the other. I've
never done that before. Stacking spells. Never *heard* of it
happening.'

She smiled. There and gone in an instant. 'Is that a fact.'

'Spell-casting requires compressing a wizard's own energy and
extending it out in a specific form. The form is designed by the
spell, the motions, the instrument, whatever. Sometimes you can
draw on other energies, like a major storm or the ocean . . .' He
waved that away. Later. 'The whole time I was in that cellar, I
was . . . *compressing*. Planting one spell on top of the other.
Keeping them stable and in order. The work, it drained me.'

'Then you come home and they wrap you in that net and stick
those things in your flesh.'

'Hooks.'

She took a long moment to inspect his chest and arms. 'You
really should let me drive you to the hospital, have the docs check
you out.'

'Tomorrow.'

'I guess I can live with that.' Beth stared out beyond the crime-
scene tape, over to where the cops were driving away with five
criminals locked in separate rear seats. 'I could strangle those
perps myself.'

Chad saw no need to respond. The fear and the rage were all
gone now. Leaving him with . . .

Nothing.

'Reeves has been in contact with the Assistant Attorney General
in Miami and Orlando's chief DA. Talking with them personally.
Explaining the situation. Making it clear your value and also your
need to be given some space. We discussed putting a permanent
watch on you and—'

'No,' Chad said. 'No.'

'Tell the truth, I don't see how they could do much good against
an assault like this.' She pointed north. 'The Director wants us up
for another conference day after tomorrow.'

Chad didn't like it, but he knew it was inevitable. 'All right.'

Beth rose to her feet. 'Just so you know, an official alert has been sent out, local force and feds both. The safety of Darren Sedgewick and his daughter Kara are top priority.'

Overhead, clouds were gathering, and thunder rumbled softly. The sun had vanished at some point, Chad was not exactly certain when. 'Beth . . . thank you.'

She reached down and patted his shoulder. 'Go get some rest, sport.'

As he waved her off, Chad realized it was the first time they had ever touched.

THIRTY-SIX

All his life, Chad had felt like he missed some crucial element. He knew part of this was due to losing his parents at such a young age. But understanding did not erase the void. Since childhood, he had been unable to explain who he was, even to himself. When the magical abilities arrived in his teens, the impression had only deepened. The hunger. The burning urge to learn and accomplish and do *more*.

Now he possessed at least a hint of something. Not that he actually knew what his purpose would someday become. Rather, he could recognize a next step. A compass heading. Learning what it meant to grow beyond the normal boundaries.

Yet this new awareness had brought him here.

Struggling up the stairs to his home.

The apartment was reached via exterior steps attached to the garage's left-hand wall. They creaked like all wooden structures when aged and weathered by the fierce Florida years. He climbed one hard step at a time, feeling as though they made the noise his bones wanted to.

Midway up, he just stopped.

The valise dropped from his hand and thunked on the step by his feet. Time ceased to hold him. He might have remained there for hours, caught between the destruction he had caused and his haven.

Then it began to rain. Chad was not even conscious of the

storm's arrival. Only that at some point he became soaking wet, and the falling water drenched him.

It was the thought of the book still in his valise that drove him forward. He picked up his sodden case and forced himself up the remaining stairs.

Soon as he entered the apartment, Chad set his valise on a kitchen chair, opened the clasps and pulled out the book Beth had loaned him. He groaned with relief. The same magic that had protected the illegible script for eons had shielded the book against both the blast and the rain. He placed the book on the dining table and left a trail of sodden clothes behind him. But as he crossed the bedroom's threadbare carpet, the bed became out of reach. Chad eased himself down on the floor and was gone.

THIRTY-SEVEN

'Chad. I can't lift . . . *please* wake up.'

He opened his eyes. Blinked. Rolled over on to his back. Looked up. And realized . . .

Kara leaned over him.

He whispered, 'I'm dreaming.'

'You're going to catch your death if you don't get up.'

Chad allowed his arm to be fitted around her neck. 'Are you really here?'

'Yes, Chad. Steady now. Come on, push.'

He wanted to say he could stand on his own, but his legs were like two great sacks of water. He clutched at her, groaned at the effort required to rise, then realized, 'I'm naked.'

'Really? I hadn't noticed. Can you walk? Good. Now into the shower.'

'Kara . . . you can't be here.'

'We can discuss that . . .' Kara waited until he had a grip on the sink, then stepped back through the bathroom doorway and showed him an impish smile, 'when you're not naked.'

The shower was exquisite, made even more pleasurable by the fact that the wounds were gone. All of them. Healed so completely he could not be certain where many of them had been located. Chad inspected the point by his hip where Aaron had twisted the hook and dug in deeper. Not even a scar.

When he emerged, clothes were waiting for him on the bed. Kara had shifted the mystery book to his bedside table. Chad dressed in shorts and shirt and followed the scent of cooking and coffee into the main room. The floor was streaked with damp, and the balcony's banister was draped with towels and what he had worn the previous day. Kara greeted him with a steaming mug. 'Black, right?'

'Thank you, Kara.'

Something in the way he said her name caused her to look at him. And smile, more softly this time. She walked over and said, 'Lift your shirt so I can check the wounds. Good. Turn around.'

He slowly did as she instructed. 'You did this?'

'I treated you before I woke you up.' She ran a hand down his leg. 'You look all healed.'

Magic healing for a magic attack. 'Thank you, Kara. So much.'

She straightened and eased him into a chair by the table. 'Who did this, Chad?'

'Wizards from the Vancouver Institute. I think there was also one Talent from Sardinia, but I can't be certain.' He held up his hand, halting the next question. 'I'll tell you everything, just not now, OK?'

'All right.' As she returned to the stove, she asked, 'How many eggs do you want?'

'How many are there?'

'Six. You can have five. The sixth is mine.'

'You're the boss.'

'And don't you forget it.' She broke the eggs and whipped them in his only mixing bowl, then poured them into the pan. As she stirred, she pulled her cellphone from her pocket and said, 'I'm at Chad's place. You need to come on over. Yes, Daddy. Now.'

Chad watched her slip the phone into her pocket, bring over two plates, then go back for toast and butter and jam. 'Eat.'

He remained as he was, hands cradling the mug. 'Kara, why are you here?'

'Eat and I'll tell you.'

She ate in small, thoughtful bites, watching him with an intense focus. But when he finished eating and pushed his plate aside, Kara dropped her gaze. She spoke to the steam rising from her mug, and to the sunlight streaming through the open balcony doors. How her life had become utterly empty after his departure. The yearnings she had known all her life, wanting to grow and develop wings of her own – and fly.

Lost.

Even worse than that, even more painful by far, was how much she had missed him.

Chad started to rise at that point. But Kara showed a hint of the iron will that had kept her hidden all those years. 'Sit back down.'

'Kara . . .'

'I'm not done. And you need to *listen*.'

He sat.

Kara relayed how her father had noticed the change. All the arguments they didn't have about Chad turned the air in their home and shop very dense. Darren watched her with growing concern. He knew his daughter, and he knew that the situation would not remain as it was. After Chad's departure, he had half-expected Kara to resume her facile relationship with the country-club boy. Return to her old life, so they could hold to their safe and stable course. But Darren had seen how she sat by the shop's front window when she thought no one was watching. He had seen the tears she pretended did not come. He remained silent only because he could see how close she was to exploding.

Then last night Beth had stopped by. Introduced herself. Explained briefly what Chad had faced. The measures he had insisted on concerning them and their safety.

As soon as Beth departed, Darren relented.

He knew if he didn't, she would run away. He said it with the air of defeat, his worry and pain so raw it raked her heart. But she could not deny it, because that was precisely what she had been planning. To run away. Find Chad. Leave behind the lives they had built together. And her father. Permanently. So that it was only her own safety she put in mortal danger.

Instead, Darren suggested they work out a way to make it as safe as possible.

But only, Darren stressed, if this was more than learning about spells.

If it was real. As in, about love. Real, lasting love.
Which was as far as Chad let her go.

THIRTY-EIGHT

D arren showed up soon after. Which Chad actually found
to be a good thing. At the sound of a car door slamming
out beyond his earthen barrier, Chad released Kara and
took a step back. He then saw how she too needed a moment's
distance. Away from her confession and all the emotions they both
had just released.

Kara left his apartment and Chad heard the steps creak with
her going down and then the two of them returning. Darren
Sedgewick entered Chad's home and took a reluctant, uncertain
look around. Chad knew the man would have given anything not
to be standing where he was. The zone of destruction outside could
just as easily have been their home. Their lives.

Chad walked over and thanked the man formally for coming.
Kara rewarded Chad by placing a hand on his arm. The gesture
was not lost on her father, who responded by clenching his jaw,
keeping his fears and reservations unspoken.

Kara directed them back to the kitchen table, put on a fresh pot
of coffee, brought over three clean mugs, seated herself, and said,
'Why don't you tell us what is going on.'

Chad related what had happened after he last left their shop.
He told them about Gerry Bauer and Luca Tami and the flight and
the manuscript. But as he started to describe what he had discovered in those supposedly incomplete pages, he stopped. It was
good to talk. Better than that, it felt wonderful to finally have a
chance to release and share the secrets. Only then did he realize
what a burden his silence had become.

So he said, 'I need to back up and tell you what happened before.'

'Tell us whatever you think we need to know,' Kara said.

So Chad started much earlier. Back when Aaron and his bullies
had assaulted the young apprentices. Some of this they had heard
before, of course. But neither father nor daughter seemed to care.

He described his servitude to the Sardinian Institute's senior mages, pretending to be a barely capable student and studying in secret. He revealed his pure loathing for the senior mages, their pomposity and self-importance. Especially Serge, the Talent who had emotionally enslaved the woman who broke free, only to take her own life.

He described how he learned to break through shielding spells, stifling the magical alarms before they went off. How the only friends he had through those long, dark months were the books that belonged to others.

Abruptly the weariness rose up with a tidal wave of force. And silenced him mid-sentence. His weary brain refused to join any more words together.

Kara rose and said, 'You just come with me.'

Darren pretended not to see how she gentled him into the bedroom. Chad allowed himself to be eased into the bed, and the sheet pulled up and tucked around his shoulders. 'Don't leave.'

She leaned over him, the dark veil sheltering his vision from the world beyond her soft gaze. She kissed him, and liked the flavor enough to kiss him again. 'Rest.'

THIRTY-NINE

When Chad awoke, the bedside clock said it was a few minutes shy of eleven. A lone female voice sounded through the closed bedroom door. Definitely not Kara's voice; Chad thought it belonged to Beth Creasey. The agent's presence was comforting, though Chad suspected Kara and her father had left. The apartment held a different flavor now. As he rose from the bed, he heard Beth laugh. It was a nice sound, one that he did not think he had heard before. He slipped on shorts and opened the door.

Beth said, 'Hang on, here he is now.' She lowered the phone and asked, 'How are those wounds?'

Chad walked over. 'All healed, thanks to Kara. And you.'

Beth gave him a close-up inspection, then said into the phone,

'Did the photos forensics took show up OK? That's good, because it's all the evidence we're going to get. The boy's been worked on by a very gifted lady. Looks like the attack never happened.' Beth then told him, 'Because of what happened yesterday, things are moving faster than expected. You need to shower and dress. Jacket and tie. Pack an overnight bag.'

'Beth—'

She held up the hand not holding the phone. 'Don't even start. Orders come straight from the Director herself. She sent her plane down. Hurry now.'

'Where's Kara?'

'She and her pop left to open the store. Nice gal, by the way. Said to tell you to have a good trip, and she'll be here when you get back.'

Beth drove them to the smaller Sandford Airport, where the jet's engines were already powering up before they passed through security. Chad was thoroughly unimpressed with his first journey by private jet. The seat-leather was dimpled with age, the tables scarred, the aisle carpet worn. Two generals and a pair of younger aides were seated at the back. They looked up long enough to scowl an angry welcome. Clearly they disliked having their flight delayed by civilians.

Beth took a seat as far as possible from the officers, facing forward. Chad slipped into the seat opposite. Once they were airborne, Chad asked, 'You mind if I try something with your book?'

'It's not mine,' Beth replied. She rose to her feet. 'Why don't you come over to this side, so your back is to the uniforms. You want a coffee?'

'Black. Thanks.' Chad's only decent valise was still drying out. He carried a worn canvas satchel his grandmother had used on her rare trips. He released the catches and pulled out the book, still amazed at how the previous day had apparently not touched it in any way. He opened the cover and turned to the first page of nonsense symbols.

Beth set down his mug. 'Slide over, sport. I want to watch.' She slipped in beside him. 'So you figured out this business with the mystery script?'

'I think . . . Maybe.'

'Luca is going to positively die that he's not around to watch.'

Chad took a long breath and began.

The Adept Stefano's instructions reformed in his mind, and . . .

The manuscript's intact pages held five keys. Segmented by the supposedly empty pages. Which were in fact where the Adept was to bind them together. Bridge the divides. Forming one continuous action . . .

Soundlessly, Chad's lips formed the first key. But before he pushed the spell out and through his fingers and into the open page, he . . .

Released.

Beth murmured, 'Oh. Wow.'

Chad could actually sense the spell inserting itself into the aperture that did not exist.

Beth whispered, 'You're *glowing.*'

He raised the hand not touching the book. Quiet. Then he lip-synched the second spell.

The third. Fourth.

Even before the fifth fully emerged . . .

The book's script reformed once more. Only now the letters were alight.

What was more, Chad could read the spell.

FORTY

C had stopped reading when the plane landed and the co-pilot emerged to release the stairs and open the portal. Then the co-pilot walked midway down the central aisle and told the officers to stay where they were. The generals protested, which caused Beth to smile.

Even as they disembarked, Chad kept two fingers inserted in the book, fearful that the incantations would be erased. Beth carried his case without being asked. A black Chevy Tahoe with shadowed windows stood at the base of the stairs. Two gray-suited agents rose from the front seats. The driver asked, 'Agent Creasey?'

'That would be me.'

The other agent spoke into the mike attached to her wrist as the driver said, 'Director's compliments, ma'am. We're ordered to make all possible haste.'

They sped from the tarmac, lights and siren both. The security guard by the cyclone fence saluted their passage. Chad opened the book and resumed reading.

Immediately the agent in the passenger seat noticed the growing illumination and started to turn around. Beth snapped, 'Eyes front.'

As they crossed the Potomac, Chad reached the final page. His hand hovered over the words, savoring the exquisite flavor of having accomplished the impossible.

Beth said, 'We're two minutes out and closing.'

Chad touched the last letter of the final word. The light vanished and the words resumed their nonsense structure.

When they pulled up in front of Homeland's HQ, Chad closed the cover and handed Beth the book. 'Some day I'll find a way to thank you.'

The two agents hopped out and opened their doors. Beth did not move. 'You're done?'

'I am. Yes.'

'I wouldn't have missed that for the world.' She slipped the book into her purse. 'Game face, sport. You're pitching in the majors today.'

FORTY-ONE

Agent Samantha Patterson was there to greet them when they exited the elevator. 'The senior Talent from Vancouver and one from Sardinia are in the conference room. And some guy supposedly representing their global Council. They brought a couple of their K Street attorneys along for reinforcements. Not that it will help them any.' She must have noticed Chad's sudden flare of rage, because she asked, 'You OK there?'

'What is the Sardinian Talent's name?'

'Serge.' Her gaze tightened. 'You know him, I take it.'

'I'm pretty certain he watched the attack at my home.'

'We didn't find any evidence of an observer,' Beth said. 'I had the forensics team check the perimeter. Twice. Of course, the blast pretty much wiped the earth clean.'

'Anybody else hurt?'

'Beyond that great triangle of destruction, there was no damage,' Beth replied.

Samantha pointed them toward the corner conference room. 'What say we watch the Director roast herself some wizards.'

The previous administration had established a new Homeland division specifically targeting the illegal use of magic. The FBI had objected, of course, since they already had a substantial portion of their budget dedicated to the same objective. Ditto the CIA and DOD. The Vancouver Institute had also protested bitterly, calling it all absurd, a charade, and demanded the right to police their own ranks.

But the President had been adamant. The nation needed a single conduit to meet any potential threat that magic represented.

Eleven weeks after taking office, newly appointed Director Odell Reeves had appeared on national news, declaring arrests in nine states over the sale and dissemination of artifacts used in the dark arts. The FBI and NSA had both played a major role, but it was clear her unifying presence had been the key ingredient in putting the case together. A senior Vancouver mage had been among the culprits. The resulting trial, broadcast live on CNN, had been the highlight of Chad's early weeks on Sardinia.

Since then, the Institutes had remained sullen but silent.

When Chad had first met the Director in the cellar pantry, he had been fully occupied keeping control of his stacked spells. Now there was no such distraction.

Odell Reeves possessed a brutally direct force. She was not a tall woman, nor especially attractive. Her skin was carved onyx, her hair a tightly clamped array of black curls. She wore an expensively tailored navy suit and an emerald collar pin in the shape of a shark.

One of Chad's favorite teachers had spent a lifetime researching the energy that Talents applied to their spell-casting. She'd developed a theory that every human held the same potential force. The difference was, Talents possessed a unique ability to tighten and focus, and perhaps magnify, this core energy. Most of the Institutes' other Talents had scorned the woman. Many referred to nonwizards as 'merelies' – as in, merely mortal. Chad's teacher had loathed both the expression and the contempt behind it. As a result, she had remained in permanent conflict with the Institute's senior wizards. The third year of Chad's apprenticeship, she had been forcibly retired, and now lived a solitary existence on Denby, an island near Seattle.

As Chad shook the Director's hand, he thought Odell Reeves was a perfect confirmation of the researcher's theory.

The conference room was large enough to comfortably hold a massive oval table rimmed by twenty chairs. Director Reeves and her team occupied the head of the table closest to the entrance. Empty seats formed dividers to both sides. She pointed Chad into the vacant seat directly to her right. 'Come join me, Mr Hagan. Agent Creasey, would you mind seating yourself further down?'

Beth walked between the seated agents and the windows. 'Being in close proximity to criminals doesn't give me hives.'

'Oh, please.' The central position at the table's opposite end was held by Vancouver's Principal, the title granted to their senior Talent. The woman's name was Arlette. She was in her late fifties and wore a Versace silk-and-cashmere suit. She was adorned by matching necklace, bracelet and ring that probably cost several hundred thousand dollars. But nothing could ease the avaricious glint to her gaze, the acidic bite to her every word. 'Is this really necessary?'

Director Reeves gave no sign she heard the woman. She smiled at Chad. 'Good to see you again, Mr Hagan. How are your wounds?'

'They're healing well, thank you, Director. Please call me Chad.'

'Strange how your associates here didn't seem all that interested in hearing about how many wounds you actually endured. How many was it?'

'Thirty-one,' Beth offered.

'Thirty-one magically inflicted wounds, caused by several of their own Talents. And yet they weren't willing to view the photographs supplied by the Orlando PD.'

Because the Director had not even glanced at the other end of the table, Chad did his best to ignore the Sardinian Warrior seated to Arlette's right. 'Probably because they've seen the wounds before.'

Reeves gestured to the two attorneys seated to Arlette's left. 'Their attorneys are with Blodell and Dawes.'

'B & D represent the Institutes in all matters relating to the federal government,' Samantha offered. 'Represent, as in lobby.'

Odell went on, 'Carter Dawes is the older gentleman beside the Director.'

'How do you do, young man.'

Reeves asked, 'You recognize the Talents?'

'Yes, ma'am.'

'They claim to be here as an act of . . . how did they put it?'

Samantha offered, 'Friendship and goodwill.'

'There you go. So, Chad, do you believe them?'

'Not for an instant,' he replied.

Arlette snapped, 'The runaway apprentice is the one who should be under arrest.'

Chad met Serge's glare for a long moment. Rage for rage.

Then he noticed how Odell studied him. As if she could read the situation. Clearly waiting for him to speak. 'Can I ask a question?'

'You can do anything you like. After all . . .' Odell glared down the polished expanse, 'you are a valued and trusted member of our team.'

Chad pointed at the man by the rear wall. The shadows and his natural stillness allowed him to disappear in plain sight. 'Why isn't Meister Kim seated at the table?'

Serge sputtered, 'This is *outrageous.*'

Carter Dawes said, 'Serge, please.'

'Allowing that runaway to join us is a *scandal.*'

'You're not helping—'

'The apprentice should have been put down like the vile—'

Arlette said quietly, 'Enough.'

'That scoundrel has been a troublemaker from day one!' Serge sputtered like a tea kettle left too long on the boil. 'And I'm *certain* he had a hand in *stealing my money!*'

Serge's rage carried the same scent as his magic. The same signature Chad had sensed in the assault. He glanced back at Kim, who was nodding now, as if confirming this joint inspection. As if there were something more at work, something he was missing . . .

'You will be silent or you will leave.' Arlette turned back to the Director. 'I apologize for the outburst. Emotions are running a bit high.'

'Oh, is that what it was. Emotion.' Director Reeves gestured to the man by the window, 'Perhaps the gentleman would care to join us?'

Kim bowed to the table, smiled at Chad. 'An honor.'

Chad said, 'Meister Kim was a senior Talent at Vancouver. The year Arlette was named the Institute's Principal, Kim was appointed a roving ambassador by the global Council.'

Kim was a lithe man in his late seventies, and tall for a Japanese. His skin was smooth, his eyes clear, his voice exactly as Chad recalled. 'You must visit me upon your return. We have much to discuss.'

'I'm not going back,' Chad declared. 'Ever.'

Arlette sniffed. 'Surely even a runaway apprentice must realize how absurd that sounds. You are under oath—'

Chad shot back, 'The same oath you and your kind allow senior Talents to break on a daily basis?'

Director Reeves asked, 'What oath-breaking do you refer to?'

Chad smoldered at Serge and did not speak.

'I asked a question, I demand an answer!'

Chad had never been this close to the Vancouver Principal. Apprentices sat through all assemblies and meals at the back of the room. But Arlette was exactly as the older students had described, a woman of iron will wrapped in silk and gold. She flipped a languid hand. 'There might have been some minor discrepancies we've chosen to overlook.'

'See, that is exactly why I will never go back,' Chad countered.

Odell asked, 'What am I missing?'

'Yeah, Serge. Why don't you define that word, *minor,* for the Director?'

Serge said, 'I fail to see how such matters could possibly serve a useful purpose, given the importance of this meeting.'

Chad felt as though his fury had waited years for just this moment. 'Allow me to tell Director Reeves about one so-called minor issue. Let her decide for herself about these so-called minor incidents, where a senior mage—'

Serge rose to his feet. '*You will be silent!*'

'—magically manipulated an attractive young apprentice into thinking she was in love,' Chad said. 'Driving her to suicide.'

'Let the record show,' Director Reeves said, 'that my associate has leveled several felonious charges.'

Carter Dawes had a slight Southern smoothness to his speech. He was overweight and foppishly dressed. He showed the gathering a practiced air of languid ease. In a courtroom it was probably effective. Here it appeared overly theatrical, especially when contrasted against Serge's fury. Carter Dawes said, 'Perhaps we should return to the matter at hand.'

'I never left it.' Director Reeves gestured toward Chad. 'And neither did he.'

Serge snarled, 'I will see you flayed alive!'

'Threatening a consultant to the United States government with grievous bodily harm,' Samantha said. 'Looks to me like he's begging to be arrested.'

The lawyer protested, 'Director Serge is here under diplomatic immunity.'

'Actually, sir, that's not possible. Only nations and their recognized governmental representatives hold that status. Which the Institutes are most certainly not.' Odell rose to her feet and gestured for the others to follow. 'This meeting is hereby adjourned.'

It was only as the Director reached the door that Arlette realized Odell was leaving. 'But we have hardly gotten started!'

'And whose fault is that? Sorry, Principal, but I have a division to run.' She smiled at the astonished Talents. 'Nine tomorrow work for everybody?'

FORTY-TWO

This time, Chad was put up in the Hay-Adams, a historic hotel in the grand tradition. His room had high ceilings and a stubby balcony overlooking a busy city street, beyond which stretched the White House lawns. During a room service dinner, his previous exhaustion returned in powerful waves. But he wasn't ready to sleep. The day had been far too full.

He opened his French doors, pulled over a chair and phoned Kara. When she answered, he said, 'I never thought I could get so much joy just dialing a number.'

'Wow, sailor. You surely know the way to a girl's heart.' Her smile came through loud and clear. 'How are you doing?'

'It's been a rough afternoon. Good, though.' He told her about the confrontation, or started to.

Then she broke in with, 'Chad, I want you to wait and tell me this in person.'

He nodded to the night and the shimmering white residence beyond the trees. 'That makes a lot of sense.'

'Besides, I think my father should hear this.'

'All right.'

'He's . . .'

'Worried.'

'More than that. He's afraid of losing the life we've built together.'

'I never want to do that,' Chad said. 'But it could happen. He's probably right to worry.'

'Just the same, he needs to hear. And I want you to tell me everything. I really do.'

He hesitated, then said, 'Kara, I feel a pressure building. Against me. They want . . .'

'They, meaning the Talents.'

'Right. They still think they can force me to go back.'

She was silent a long moment, then surprised him by asking, 'Is this something you have to decide about tonight?'

'I've already decided, Kara.'

'No. I mean, do you need to worry about this pressure now. Because it sounds to me like you've already got enough on your plate, without adding something that can wait until later.'

He nodded again. 'You are one smart lady.'

'And don't you forget it.' The smile returned to her voice. 'When will you get back?'

'Hard to say. We're meeting again tomorrow morning. I should know more after that.'

'Will you call me when it's over?'

'The very instant.' He smiled at the night. 'I wish I could hold you.'

'Hey, you're a wizard. Work it out.'

'Goodnight, Kara.'

'Sleep well, my dear little Talent.'

He cut the connection and sat there, reveling in this new reality, one where he did not face the mysteries alone. Which was the moment he realized he had forgotten to tell her about working his way through the Ancient text. It was incredible he had not thought of that until now. Chad started to call her back, then decided this was another of those things he'd prefer to discuss in person.

FORTY-THREE

When the pounding started on his door, Chad thought he'd just laid down. But as he switched on the light he saw the bedside clock read four-fifteen. The knocking was loud and insistent. He heard a woman's voice call his name and tell him to open up.

'One second!'

Chad fumbled his way into trousers, unlocked the door and faced a very concerned Beth. 'You OK?'

'Sure.' Behind her, the elevator doors opened and Chad watched Samantha Patterson and another agent come running toward them. 'What's going on?'

Beth called to the pair, 'He's OK.' Then, 'Your home was attacked tonight. We just got word. There's nothing left.' Beth saw the sudden flash of fear, and added, 'Kara and her father are safe.'

'You're sure?'

'First thought I had,' Beth replied. 'The Orlando cops are there now.'

'Along with two agents on night duty at our regional office,' Samantha added. 'Their shop is also intact.'

His hands shook so hard he had trouble hitting the speed-dial. Kara answered on the first ring. 'Chad?'

'Tell me you're all right.'

'We're fine.' Despite the hour, she sounded utterly awake. 'Chad, they just told us. I'm so sorry about your home.'

'It's just . . . things. They say your shop's OK?'

'That's where I'm speaking from. Chad, there were explosions. A lot of them. And fireworks or something above our house. That's what woke us up. And shouts. Or screams.'

'I don't understand.'

'Well, that makes two of us.'

He held back from saying his confusion was over how they had been shielded from such an assault. 'Hold on a second.'

He muted the phone and related the news. None of the agents showed any surprise. Samantha said, 'The arrested Talents broke out of prison earlier tonight. An eyewitness placed their leader, Aaron, and one other by your home. One of those arrested was picked up near the mall where their shop is located. She suffered third-degree burns. From what, we have no idea. She was treated at Orlando Regional, then transferred to the Raiford prison hospital.'

Kara asked, 'Who's there with you?'

'Beth and Samantha Patterson and one more agent.' Chad hit the speaker tab. 'They want to know if you or your father saw anything.'

'Just the explosions. We ran outside, and an Arab neighbor said it reminded him of Beirut. Streaks of fire overhead. And the screams.'

'Kara, I'm so sorry.'

The two women and the male agent heard her reply, 'For what? You didn't do this.'

'In a way. They attacked you because of me.'

'Going after soft targets,' Samantha said. 'Or so they thought.'

'Take me off speaker.' When he did so, Kara went on, 'You need to come live with us.'

'Kara, I don't think that's a good idea.'

'Whyever not? We have loads of room.'

'Your father, for one.'

'You just leave him to me. Now finish up your work and come home.' She put heavy emphasis on that final word. *Home.*

FORTY-FOUR

On the drive from the hotel to Homeland's offices, Samantha asked, 'What do you think of Meister Kim?' Beth added, 'What's with that name of his, anyway?'

'Kim studied for years with a German Talent, now dead,' Chad replied. 'He was the one to name Kim a *Meister,* an Adept.' A pause, then, 'I like him.'

Beth said, 'Not many among the Talents you can say that about, I take it.'

'Not nearly enough,' Chad agreed.

Samantha said, 'The Director is tempted to count him as one of the good guys. Anything you could give us would help.'

'When I attacked those apprentice warriors in Vancouver, Arlette and some of the others wanted to lock me in the punishment wing. Kim insisted on a tribunal, which he chaired. He ordered the other apprentices to give evidence, which I've always assumed meant he knew what was going on.' Chad recalled those bitter, hollow days. 'At the time, I was angry with him for allowing it to go on as long as it did. And letting me be set up as a result.'

'You were just a kid,' Beth said.

'I was nineteen. And it still burns.'

Samantha asked, 'And now?'

'There's a chance Kim was the solitary voice among the senior staff who sought to bring the Warriors under tighter control. Which might have meant all the other senior Talents and Directors were potentially his enemy. Kim waited for an opportunity to strike when he might also win. I gave him that chance.' Chad shrugged. 'That's what I like to think, anyway.'

Samantha showed her badge to the building's guard, pulled into the parking garage, cut the motor, and said, 'He was down there last night.'

'In Orlando?'

'Guest of the Director. She'll explain.' She pulled an item from her jacket pocket and handed it over. 'He said to give you this, something he found in the rubble at your place.'

'This' was the small blank scroll, still intact, still in its leather case. Chad resisted the urge to unroll it, and instead put it away. 'Kim is using this as a message. Telling us Kara and her father and the shop survived because he personally shielded them.'

'Looks that way to me.' Samantha opened her door. 'Ready for round two?'

Chad was escorted into the Director's conference room by Beth and Samantha. Odell Reeves was already there, accompanied by a grim-faced Hispanic woman in her late forties, whom Beth introduced as Consuela Ruiz, a federal prosecutor assigned to the Division. Odell greeted him with, 'Sorry to hear about your home.'

'Thank you, Director.' Chad took his time inspecting the two Talents seated to either side of Carter Dawes. Both Arlette and Serge appeared uncertain this morning. Angry, resentful, of course. But there was something new in their countenances, or so it seemed to Chad. As if their supreme confidence had been severely shaken.

Only Meister Kim appeared the same. He sat well removed from the others. 'It is so very good to see you again, young man.'

Chad returned the man's smile. 'Do I have you to thank for saving my friends?'

'Forgive me, I have no idea what it is you're talking about.'

'Of course not.'

Kim continued to smile at Chad. 'We have so many interesting things to discuss. Oh very yes.'

Chad found a genuine pleasure in how their exchange only heightened the pair's discomfort. And rage. 'Such as?'

'Ah, yes. Such as, what revelations have such a gifted Talent as yourself made during your travels?'

'How dare you refer to that untrained apprentice as a Talent,' Arlette snapped. 'That runaway is a *menace*.'

Serge added. 'And a *thief*. Of that I am absolutely certain.'

The Director laced her fingers across her middle, a satisfied smile on her face.

Kim chose to ignore Serge and focused upon Principal Arlette. 'An interesting word for you to use, madam. *Menace*. Speaking as you are about a young man without proper training. Very interesting indeed. Tell me, Principal, did you happen to speak with the imprisoned Warrior Talents from your Institute, the ones who assaulted this young man?'

'Allegedly,' Carter Dawes protested.

'Oh, please,' the prosecutor said.

'How on earth am I supposed to manage that?' Arlette gestured at the five gathered at the table's opposite end. 'Since I'm forced to remain here, dealing with the mess caused by that *runaway.*'

Serge added, 'There was no *assault.* Those Talents were sent to *arrest* him. As was their sworn duty—'

Kim continued to focus on Arlette. 'I did, Principal.'

'I . . . you what?'

'I flew down to Orlando yesterday following the meeting. The Director was kind enough to arrange transport.' He bowed from his seated position. 'For which I am most grateful.'

The Director replied, 'You are most welcome.'

'You . . . that was unauthorized.'

'Actually,' the Director responded, 'I signed it off personally. And my voice is the only one that counts.'

'How could I not make the trip, Principal?' Kim leaned forward. 'After all, I feared your Warriors had broken the rules of *all* Institutes. Not to mention the laws of this great nation. Laws which we are bound by treaty to uphold.'

Arlette's face went parchment white. She rounded on Odell. 'You planned this. You cut short yesterday's meeting so he could go—'

'I am sorry to report your Warriors did indeed break both our code and this nation's laws, just as I feared,' Kim continued. 'They did not go to arrest the Talent seated with the Director. They went to torture. They went to commit murder.'

Carter Dawes rose to his feet. 'I demand an adjournment.'

'You don't get to demand anything.' The prosecutor pointed to Director Reeves. 'Her house, her rules.'

Odell pointed to Carter's empty chair. 'Sit.'

Kim waited until the attorney had retaken his seat, then continued, 'Your Warriors used the entrap-and-bind spell, the one with fiery hooks. A spell that is specifically outlawed in this country.'

'Which brings us to the issue of leveling charges against your Talents.' Odell turned to her prosecutor. 'What was it you decided on?'

'Felonious assault.' Consuela Ruiz burned the two senior Talents with her gaze. 'Usage of illegal magic. Intent to inflict bodily harm.'

'They will do for a start,' Odell continued smiling. 'Wouldn't you agree, Carter?'

Kim lifted his voice to silence the attorney. 'Most important of all, Principal, is the fact that changes everything. This young Talent, the untrained young man seated with the Director, the one who considers us his enemy, he *erased the spell.*'

Odell broke the silence with, 'What am I missing here?'

'We are fairly certain an eighth-level shield spell will work against the net and hooks,' Kim replied, without taking his eyes off Arlette. '*Before* the assault begins, Principal. *Before.* But I have seen the photographs taken by the local police after this man released himself. *The hooks were embedded. The spell was complete.*'

The prosecutor rose and walked down to the table's other end, depositing one sheaf of photographs in front of Arlette and another by the now-seated attorney. 'Your boys are going away for a very long time.'

'Do you have even the smallest notion of what your Institute's own Warriors attempted?' Kim could no longer remain in his chair. He rose, his rage granting him the ability to tower over both senior Talents. 'You sought to *murder an Adept.*'

Carter shouted, 'My clients had nothing—'

'I accuse you, Principal! And you, Director Serge! In this chamber, before these witnesses! I intend to bring you before the global Council! I accuse you and everyone you lead of demolishing the oaths that bind all Talents. The oaths which maintain a peaceful existence with our neighbors! You and your blind stupidity threaten the entire global order!'

The Director and her prosecutor treated the confrontation as excellent theater. They leaned back in their seats, shifting in tight mini-circles, rocking to the beat of Kim's words. When the mage finished and reseated himself, an aghast silence dominated that end of the table until Carter Dawes cleared his throat. 'Actually, Director, you should know that we have already lodged a complaint with the federal magistrates. Both here and in Orlando.'

Reeves said, 'Duly noted.'

'Come on, Director. Why put us through this charade any longer? You don't have any hard evidence to substantiate your charges.'

'Don't I indeed.'

'And why won't you let me speak with the two Washington-based Talents you've wrongfully arrested!' This time, the lawyer's outrage seemed genuine. 'I can't even determine where they're being held!'

'Those two are facing charges for aiding and abetting a terrorist act.'

'That is outrageous!' Serge was the one to shout now. He rounded on Kim. 'This entire episode is an absurdity caused by that runaway apprentice!'

'Is it? Is it, indeed?' Director Reeves turned to Chad. 'Think you could repeat your show for them? The one where we watch Talents steal from the Federal Reserve Bank?'

'I'll need a windowless room,' Chad replied.

Samantha said, 'We've reserved the ground-floor theater.'

'Evidence,' the federal prosecutor said to Dawes. 'Remember that word?'

Samantha said, 'The room is ready and waiting.'

'In that case,' Chad said, 'it would be a pleasure.'

FORTY-FIVE

The Director cut him loose three hours later. By that point, the Talents and their attorneys had been boiled down to a proper wizard stew. Serge in particular. As Chad had built his series of past-images, starting outside the Jacksonville bank and moving inside, Arlette's angry protests and Serge's molten fury and the attorney's stilted objections had all gradually reduced to half-formed sputters. Even Kim appeared utterly stunned by the scenes. When Chad revealed the mages transporting the pallets of gold through a magical hole in the Federal Reserve's floor, the scene illuminated faces slack with horror.

And something more.

During this second revealing, Chad repeatedly caught the vague sense of a familiarity to the thieves' magic. Just the smallest of traces, like smoke from a distant fire. But as Chad erased the scene and the theater's lights came back on, he wondered if perhaps Serge had been involved in the robbery.

The prosecutor rose from her seat and deposited files in front of the senior wizards and another by Carter Dawes. 'These are close-up photographs of the seventeen Talents involved in the theft.'

Arlette gave the file careful inspection. Serge, however, merely flicked through the photographs. His features were waxen. An oily sheen covered his forehead. Of course it was possible this was merely his response to seeing his ivory tower toppled. The minutes ticked by, until finally Arlette leaned back, rubbed her eyes. She asked, 'Do you recognize any of them?'

Serge's only response was to sigh. Almost a moan.

'Two look vaguely familiar,' Kim offered. 'But I could be mistaken. The last time I saw either of them was years ago.'

Arlette did not open her eyes. 'It was them. The Peerless.'

'Are you certain?'

She nodded, straightened, opened her eyes. 'You will inform the Council?'

'Immediately,' Kim replied.

Odell gave the trio a long inspection, then said, 'You're suggesting your Institute had nothing to do with this?'

Kim said, 'Madame Director, this is absolutely not the work of any Institute. I give you my solemn word.'

Odell pointed at the blank walls. 'Then who did this?'

Kim nodded slowly. 'That is a question I intend to pose to the global Council. And I *will* obtain answers. One way or the other, I *will* learn what I need to understand what happened here.'

'And you will tell me?'

Kim nodded with his entire upper body. But he replied, 'I should think that is a task best left to your . . . what was the word you used?'

'Consultant.' The Homeland Director rose to her feet. In contrast to the group at the table's opposite end, Odell Reeves remained outwardly composed. Angry, but utterly in control. 'I want my nation's four tons of gold. I want the perpetrators behind bars. And I want clear answers as to how you lot, who are supposed to be controlling all magic, let this slip under the radar. Is that clear?'

Kim replied for them all, 'Yes, Madame Director.'

She rounded on the senior attorney. 'Carter, a word of warning. If I uncover any evidence that you were in collusion, I will *personally* obliterate your career.'

'Director Reeves, I had no—'

'Save it. You lot have seventy-two hours.'

FORTY-SIX

Another dark-windowed SUV drove him and Beth to the airport, where the Director's plane waited to fly them south. As they took off, Beth told him how she had rented a furnished ninth-floor condo out near SeaWorld for the duration. At Chad's request, she booked him a condo three doors down from her own. Only then did Chad call Kara and tell her what he'd decided.

She took a silent minute to digest the news. Chad spent the time staring out the window at the clouds below. Stacking the spells and retrieving the images had not proved as exhausting as before. Even so, the trip home was a weight he endured because he had to. Finally, she asked, 'Would it do any good if I argued?'

'Don't, Kara. Please.'

'Or tell you how bone-headed and stubborn you're being?'

Chad saw no need to respond.

'Well, at least Daddy will be pleased.'

'Your father is right,' Chad said. 'Again.'

'I know those condominiums. They're less than a mile from us. And you should be safe with Beth there.' A pause, then, 'She's a good woman. I like her.'

'So do I.'

'When will we see you?'

'I have a problem I need to work through tonight,' he said. 'I'll come by the shop tomorrow.'

Without being asked, Beth drove him straight from the private air terminal to his former home. Shreds of the original police tape, put up after the Vancouver Warriors had attacked him with their hooks and net, drifted in the fitful afternoon breeze.

Chad walked forward alone. The earthworks thrown up by his retaliatory strike had been pounded into the ground. It looked like a giant's hammer had worked over the entire front yard. His grandmother's beloved oleander and palms were shredded mulch. The garage and apartment were obliterated. There was nothing left but a bowl-shaped hole in raw earth, now filled with water from broken pipes. Of his grandmother's effects, nothing remained. His pickup was a smoldering wreck, with four black puddles where the wheels had rested.

Of the case carrying the Mediterranean magic, buried beneath the garage steps, there was no sign.

As he headed for the cemetery, Chad felt an unexpected kinship with Meister Kim. Fighting the good fight, staying in the shadows, carefully choosing battles where there was a chance of succeeding. And afterwards, staying alive.

Chad stood by his grandmother's grave for a long moment, immensely glad her resting place had not been disturbed. When it was time, he turned and walked back to where Beth stood by her convertible. 'I'm all done here.'

Chad ate a solitary meal at a Denny's down the block from their condo building. He returned to his new apartment to find Beth had gone shopping and left a bag containing shorts and t-shirt and a pair of boat shoes on his living room sofa. All in his size. He started to call and thank her, then decided he would rather wait until the next day and say the words in person. The condo was spacious and functional and sterile. Chad showered, then lay down on the bed with the towel still wrapped around his waist. He was so weary his body felt bruised. Even so, sleep refused to come. His mind was filled with half-completed thoughts, and mysteries that needed confronting.

After a futile half-hour, Chad rose, put on his new shorts and walked to where he had opened his canvas satchel on the dining room table. He extracted his wallet and pulled out Luca Tami's business card. He warded himself, the balcony, the phone, then punched in the number.

The banker answered with, 'I was hoping you would call.'

'I'm pretty sure I have a problem,' Chad said. 'If I wait until I
know for certain, it will be too late to do anything about it.'

'The Swiss have a saying. "A problem shared is a problem
halved".' Luca's smile came through clearly. 'It sounds much better
in French. Most things do.'

'How much do you know about what's happened?'

'Enough to have a number of questions of my own. From what
Beth told me, you have worked your way through the Adept
Stefano's challenge.'

Chad opened the sliding glass doors and stepped on to his
balcony. 'You have too. Haven't you?'

'Another time, yes? I will tell you. Just not now.'

'One thing can't wait. Did you shield Kara?'

'An excellent question. And the answer is, I am not your only
ally.'

'You mean Meister Kim, don't you?'

'He is a good man. But I cannot tell you to trust him. That gift
must be earned and then bestowed by choice. Now tell me what
you think the problem is.'

Chad liked that. How the banker was already working strategy,
looking beyond the known and the visible. 'I've had hints of
Serge's involvement in stealing the nation's gold.'

Luca listened in silence as Chad fumbled through an explanation
of the traces he'd sensed in the theater. Then he backtracked and
added the certainty that Serge had been present during their
attempted arrest. When he was done, Luca replied, 'What you
have told me is the first real evidence that the Peerless have allies
within the Institute's senior Talents.'

'If I'm right.'

'Of that I have no doubt. Serge is the perfect candidate. He is
as unscrupulous as he is ambitious.'

Chad found a bitter satisfaction in hearing the refined Swiss
gentleman give voice to his own loathing. 'What do we do?'

'For the moment, nothing. You and I must choose our battles
wisely. We can make no grand gestures, nor can we afford to fight
windmills. We can do nothing from inside the grave.'

'I'm pretty certain they are going to insist I come back. To
Sardinia. I don't think I have much choice.'

'You are correct. How could they possibly allow a young man

who has shown the abilities of a full-fledged Adept, and done so with no real training, to run free? It threatens the Institutes' carefully designed global structure. Of course you will return.'

Chad liked the man's straightforward response, almost as much as he loathed the news. 'That's just great.'

'Listen carefully, Chad. Your negotiating position will never again be as strong as it is now.'

'Sorry. I don't follow.'

'You think you are the only one wronged by the current system? A river of molten fury courses around the globe. Hidden deep. But growing by the day. By the very hour.'

'We were talking,' Chad replied, 'about my being required to return to Sardinia.'

'We still are. What would you most like to have, were it in your power to request?'

'That's easy enough. To have nothing whatsoever to do with any of them ever again.'

'Look beyond that for a moment.'

Chad sighed his way into a plastic chair. 'To stay here. In Florida. Keep Kara and her father safe. Make a decent life for myself.'

'What if you could have this as a part-time component of your future?'

He stared at the city's blinking lights. 'You can do that?'

'Not me, my gifted young gentleman. Not me. But many of those who share your loathing are in positions of power. And they desperately seek a trusted ally within the world of magic.'

'I'm hearing the words . . .' Chad said.

'They would move heaven and earth to have this ally officially placed in one of the Institutes. Able to communicate with them as developments arise.' Luca let that settle in, then added, 'There is nothing they would not do for you. Nothing.'

A new seed of hope sparked deep inside. 'So what do I do now?'

'You make no move yourself. You remain detached. Have you ever negotiated a billion-dollar deal?'

'That would definitely be a new one for me.'

'The key to all deals so potent they might shake the earth's foundations is this: The individual with power never becomes directly involved until the make-or-break moment. That way, any insult or conflict is assigned to their representative.'

'A billion-dollar deal,' Chad repeated, feeling hope rise and flame more strongly still.

'What you need is a power-broker. Emphasis on the word *power*.' Luca thought, then, 'Leave this with me. Go get some rest.'

'Thank you . . .' But Chad was already speaking to an empty phone.

FORTY-SEVEN

C had walked through the condo, turning out the lights, getting a feel for his new place of residence. The impersonality suited him. As did its position on the ninth floor, two down from the top. He was high above the surrounding city, able to maintain a distance, stay clear of the turmoil below. Or so he hoped.

He stretched out on the bed and lay there in the dark, listening to the air-conditioning's hum. He might have dozed off, he could not be sure. It seemed to him that the doorbell's unfamiliar chime fitted itself into a dream. Or perhaps that was merely how he preferred to remember it. The moment that changed everything. That it started with a dreamlike sound.

He slipped back into his shorts and approached the door. He had already unlocked it when he realized he should have checked. He had to relearn the lesson of constant caution.

Or perhaps, just perhaps, he already knew who it was. Below the level of conscious thought. Down deep, where it mattered most.

He opened the door, and there she was.

Kara stepped inside, dropped her purse and bag to the floor, and kissed him. Hard. Giving him no time to speak. Nor to object. Not even to shut the door.

Her hands spun webs of molten magic over his bare back, his face, through his hair. Then she broke away with an impatient gesture, kicked shut the door, and stood there. Daring him to say a word.

Afterwards they lay there in each other's arms, utterly content. Chad was far too happy to give in to sleep. Finally, he rose from the bed.

'Don't go.'

'I'll be right back.' He cut off the air-conditioning and opened the balcony doors. This high up, with the lights off, there was little risk of insects.

Kara watched his return and scolded, 'You left me here alone for hours. I missed you.'

He sat on the bed beside her. 'I've always wondered about the sound of a certain word.'

She rolled over so as to look directly at him. 'Which word is that?'

'Home.' Chad ran a finger across her forehead, clearing away a strand of hair. He was uncertain what to say, or even how the words might be shaped. But he had spent far too long allowing the cage of his anger to keep such sentiments locked inside. The good had been caught there with the bad. Her eyes were a mirror, her love all the illumination he required. He said, 'Nights on Sardinia, I woke up wondering what a real home might feel like. Not Nana's, the corner she made for me in her life. My own.'

She spoke so low it was possible to fit her words into his thoughts without interrupting the flow. 'When you were all grown up.'

Chad was thankful that she understood. 'When my life was my own.' He took a deep breath. The familiar summer flavors were overlaid here with city odors. Traffic sounded from far below. Unable to touch them. For now.

Kara said, 'It's not the place.'

'No,' he agreed. 'It's being here with you.'

Her teeth glowed in the dim light. 'That's the right answer.'

Chad continued to stroke her face. 'What was the question?'

'I'll tell you in the morning.' She reached for him. 'Now come to bed.'

FORTY-EIGHT

The next morning they walked back to the same Denny's where Chad had dined the previous evening. Dawn was gentle in the Florida manner, happily offering up a few hours of birdsong and comforting breeze and a sky draped in mellow pastels. Chad had slept a few hours, dreamless and deep, and woken in Kara's arms. He was tired, but the day's fatigue would just have to be shouldered. Beyond the tender moment he could hear the faint whisper of the ticking clock.

Once they had ordered breakfast, he asked if they could spend the day on his boat. Use the open waters to talk about important things. Elements that could wait no longer. Or rather, he began, but Kara interrupted him and phoned her father. She apologized for the hour and said the three of them needed to travel to the coast. Her, Chad and Darren. Her father must have protested, but Kara cut him off, saying he should do whatever he wanted. But she was going, and she thought he should as well.

Darren endured his daughter's kiss, nodded to Chad's greeting, and refused to let their mellow joy lighten his foul mood. As they were leaving the apartment, Chad texted Beth, saying where they were headed and why. Then he left his phone on the counter. Where it belonged on a day like this.

Kara drove them east in the shop's SUV. Darren insisted on taking the passenger seat and pretended not to notice when Kara's hand repeatedly snaked back and stroked Chad's leg.

They took the state road 192 to the coast, stopping at the Melbourne Publix for supplies. When they pulled up to the marina, the same eager dockhand helped them offload.

As they traveled south along the Intracoastal, Darren remained locked in a bitter silence. Kara, on the other hand, was delighted with everything. She insisted upon Chad scooching over so as to let her share the pilot's seat. When that proved totally uncomfortable, she shoved him out entirely. The only time she released her hold was when a pod of dolphins accompanied them through the Sebastian Inlet. Darren was thankfully seated in the stern, which meant Chad could mostly ignore the man's fuming presence.

As soon as they left behind the inlet's rough waters, the sea turned smooth as polished glass. Kara slipped away, leaving a sudden delicious void to his side, and went below. Chad retook the skipper's chair and found himself wishing for some way to breach the divide between himself and Darren. The day was so beautiful, the moment so close to perfect, he could not help but want to share it with Kara's father.

As if in response, the man rose and crossed the rear deck and descended into the main cabin. All without once glancing Chad's way.

Over the engines' steady murmur, he heard the rise and fall of two voices through the open portal. He knew there was nothing he could do to heal this rift. Knew also that what he was about to say would only add to the man's ire.

What darkened the day most was how Darren was absolutely right to worry. One way or the other, father and daughter's carefully constructed myth, and the lifestyle it had supported, would soon belong to the past.

And it was all his fault.

The day remained pristine, without a breath of wind. When they were far enough out that land was no longer visible, Chad cut the motor and let them drift. He unleashed the canvas awning and unfurled it so the entire rear deck became shaded. He could still hear Darren's sullen drone emanating from below-decks. Chad raised the central table and latched it into place, so that the side and rear benches now served as a dining area. Then he stepped around the windscreen and walked to the bow. He stood there, staring out over the sparkling blue waters, enjoying the momentary peace. And watching the horizon for the storm he knew was coming.

He went below and helped them carry the meal of salad Niçoise and fresh-squeezed lemonade topside. As they took seats around the central map-table, Kara asked, 'Shouldn't we drop anchor?'

'We'd need a lot of rope.' Chad pointed to the deck at their feet. 'Between the Bahamas and the Continental Shelf is the deepest trench close to the Atlantic seaboard. We're in over three thousand feet of water.'

Darren was seated directly across from him. He mostly kept his gaze focused on the opposite horizon. But every time he glanced at his daughter and saw how she and Chad remained so close and so comfortable, his expression tightened further.

When they were done, Chad cleared the table and made them coffee. When he returned topside with three mugs, he said, 'I need to go back and start at the beginning once more. It's the only way to make sense of what's happening.'

FORTY-NINE

The sun was setting as they approached the Sebastian Inlet cut. Horizon to horizon, the sky was a golden haze knit together by thin clouds. All was calm and beautiful, save for Darren. Kara's father had not spoken once.

When Chad had finished laying it all out, Kara had thanked him solemnly for sharing with them his life and his world. The words had left Darren utterly dumbfounded, a man rendered speechless by the shock of realizing just how far removed he had become from his daughter and her view of the current situation. One that was all Chad's fault. One that did not change her love for Chad. Of course Darren remained both furious and silent. Everything he had to say would wait for the right moment. When Darren would do his utmost to drive them apart. Permanently.

They docked at the marina and the deckhand said the owner wanted a word. As soon as Chad climbed on to the pier and started toward the office, Darren struck.

As he made arrangements with the marina's owner for refueling and cleaning, he watched Darren through the harbor-facing windows. The man might have kept his voice low, but there was no mistaking his bitter rage. Kara kept her head down, her features somewhat masked by her cap's shadows. But Chad knew the man's reaction hurt her deeply, and his own chest ached in helpless sympathy. He lingered in the office, hoping the man would run out of steam. Finally, he left the air-conditioned building and started back.

Midway down the pier, he heard Kara say, 'All right, Daddy, that's enough.'

'I'm not done.'

Chad halted where a piling stood between him and the two people on board his craft. He heard Kara reply, 'But I am. And I have just one thing to say to you.' A pause, then, 'Mother would be so ashamed of you.'

'Of me? Of *me?* You're the one—'

'Don't start. Please. Let me have my say.'

'You make such an absurd accusation and expect me . . . Kara, where are you going?'

'I told you that is enough. I want to speak, but you won't let me. I'm leaving.'

'You can't just walk away.'

'That's exactly what I'm doing, Daddy. You leave me no choice.'

'Kara, wait—'

'No, Daddy. No. I've listened to all I'm going to from you. Now you can either hear what I have to say, or I'm going.'

'With that man.'

'Yes, Daddy. With Chad. Where Mother would want me to be.'

'I can't believe you said that.'

'And I can't tell you how sad I am to see you so ruled by fear that you won't even give your daughter a chance to speak.'

Chad almost started forward then, drawn by the sudden catch in Kara's voice. But the reality of how close she was to breaking down lowered Darren's tone a notch. 'I have every right to be afraid.'

Chad settled back against the piling, well out of sight, as Kara replied, 'Of course you do. I'm scared too, Daddy. But I don't let my fear dominate. I can't – not and remain true to Mother's vision.'

'She wanted us to be safe.'

'Of course she did. And we have been. But that time is over. And if you would stop fighting and think, just think, you'd realize this is really what you're most afraid of. Not Chad. Change. Being forced to accept that one chapter of our lives is finished.'

A silence, then, 'You're leaving the shop?'

'What choice do I have? You're not going to accept Chad as

part of my life. And I'm not going to burden him with your resentment. His work is too important.'

'I can't believe you just said that. The man is a *menace.*'

'No, Daddy. He's not. And you're worse than wrong to suggest such a thing. And that is why I'm leaving.'

'Your words don't make a bit of sense.'

'Because you're not listening. Daddy, that chapter is *over.* If we had dared look beyond the horizon, even for one second, we would have known this day was bound to come. The myth of safety died with Mom. It was only a matter of time before the Institutes went on the attack.'

'Because of that man.'

'Because of who we are. Because of who *I* am. A Talent. Totally free of the Institutes and their dark ways.'

'Your mother intended to keep us safe. Permanently.'

'I'm sorry, but you're wrong. She did the best she could. Alone and isolated. But we're neither of those things any more. And yes, Chad brought all this to a head. But you're not seeing the real reason behind why we went out there today. He didn't just share events that have brought us to this point. He's laying the foundation for *tomorrow.*'

Darren did not respond.

Kara went on, 'He has bound us to forces who hate the Institutes as much as I do. As much as Mom did. He has given us a chance to *strike back.*'

Darren remained silent.

'Isn't that what Mom would have wanted? To see us unite with others who treat the Institutes as the enemies they are? Who want to more than simply survive today and live in fear they might come for us tomorrow?'

Darren did not reply.

'I am going with Chad, yes, because I love him. But also because I want to share in this quest. To do more with my life than just live in fear of those awful people. I want to *bring them down.*'

'They will destroy you.'

'They might. It's a possibility I have to accept. That we will lose.'

'I want nothing to do with it. Or that man.'

'That is your choice.' A pause, then, 'Goodbye, Daddy.'

'You're leaving me here?' His voice raised as Kara stepped from the boat. 'How am I supposed to get home?'

'Didn't you hear what Chad said? Money is not the issue here. Moving forward is.' Kara stood there, staring down at her father. When he did not respond, she turned away, her gaze stricken. 'We'll arrange for a limo to take you home.'

As they crossed the parking lot, Chad asked to borrow Kara's phone. She stopped, just halted there and stared at nothing. He wasn't sure she had even heard the words. He asked again, explaining that he never carried his phone out on the water; it was his one chance to leave the world behind.

Wordlessly, Kara handed Chad the keys and phone, then slipped into the van's passenger seat. He entered the office, obtained the number for a local limo service, and booked a ride for Darren. Chad returned to the car and told her as much. Kara responded with a sad, slow nod.

He thought it best to remain silent until Kara was ready to talk. And that had still not happened when they arrived back in Orlando. He wanted to be there for her. He wanted to thank her for her declaration of love. He wanted so many things, and yet nothing felt right. He could not even find the strength to reach over and take her hand. Not until he pulled up in front of his faceless condo and realized she was crying. Silent, tightly repressed sobs, mere tremors that came and passed, the loudest sound she made was trying to swallow. Chad reached for her, and she flowed across the central console and melted into his arms.

When they arrived upstairs, Chad found two notes taped to his door, both from Beth, both telling him to call her and with URGENT underlined in hard bold strikes.

Once inside, Kara slumped on to the sofa, curled up in a tight little ball and shut her eyes.

'I need to call Beth, then I'll order us something to eat. Kara?'

'I'm not hungry.'

'Can't I get you a little something?' Her only response was to turn around and bury her face in the sofa. Chad took his phone from the counter and dialed Beth's number from memory.

Beth answered with, 'Where have you been?'

'I texted you this morning. We took my boat offshore.'

'That was eight hours ago!'

Chad entered the bedroom and closed the door. 'There's no phone service in the deep Atlantic. Beth, why is there a new suit and shirt and tie on my bed?'

'First things first. Tomorrow we get you a sat-phone. Which you will always carry. Clear?'

'What's going on?'

'City Country Club. Eleven o'clock tomorrow.'

'Beth, no, I have a history with that place.'

'And I'm here to tell you it doesn't matter. The Director is staying there tonight as the guest of some DC power broker. And you've got a message from Luca. He says to tell you, "this is it". Whatever that means.'

Chad woke the next morning to brilliant sunshine and an empty bed.

The previous evening he had returned to the nearby Denny's for takeout salads and sandwiches, then eaten a solitary meal at the kitchen counter. While he was away, Kara had apparently showered, pulled a blanket and pillow off the bed, and resumed her solitary position with her back to the living room. When Chad bent over to kiss her goodnight, she neither opened her eyes nor moved.

The only positive note to his morning was the sound of her voice emanating through the bedroom's closed door. Chad showered, dressed, and entered the living room to find her cooking eggs. She smiled in his direction, or tried to. 'Did you miss me?'

'More than you can imagine.'

She rewarded him with another canted smile, her gaze still fractured, her features stained by what clearly had been a hard night. She briskly whipped the eggs. 'Pour yourself a cup of coffee. Luca just called. I was about to come in and wake you.'

'Are you eating?'

She slipped on to the stool beside him. 'Maybe later.'

He glanced at the containers of salad and sandwich still unopened by the sink. 'Kara . . .'

'Oh, all right.' She maneuvered the fork from his hand, took a tiny bite off his plate. 'There. Satisfied?'

He ate a couple of forkfuls, drank his coffee, then quietly asked the inevitable, 'What are you going to do about your shop?'

'That all depends upon Daddy.'

'I'm so sorry . . .'

She reached over and gripped his hand, tightly enough for Chad to feel the tremors. 'Don't. Please. Not yet.'

He was still searching for the right thing to say when his phone rang and the read-out said it was Luca. 'I have to take this.' He made no move to step away as he connected and said, 'I believe I have you to thank for what's coming next.'

'Wait until we are successful. Then you can most certainly express your gratitude. And your indebtedness. Your Director is an extremely astute lady. I am most glad I never sat across the negotiating table from her.'

'That makes two of us.'

'Kim Nakamura has been named the global Council's official representative to these proceedings.'

'I like him.'

'The feeling is mutual.' A pause, then, 'Do you understand the reason behind Director Reeves insisting the meeting take place in Orlando?'

'To be honest, I hadn't even thought of that.'

'Well, please do so now.'

Chad lifted his gaze to where the soaring front windows met the distant ceiling. 'She's showing Kim I am important.'

'Not exactly. Kim does not need such assurances after your little exhibition in the Homeland theater. But Kim represents a cluster of professional skeptics. They will take note of what is happening, and who is involved.'

'I understand.'

'Director Reeves has also sent advance notice to Kim over what she expects as the meeting's outcome. A very astute move. This has granted him time to pressure the Council to accept conditions which Reeves has warned are not negotiable.'

Chad could think of nothing to say except, 'Wow.'

'I could not have put it better myself. Be there early.'

FIFTY

Kara positioned herself in the bedroom's only chair and watched as Chad dressed in his new suit. When he was done, she rose, crossed the room, straightened his tie, and kissed him for the first time that day. Chad took it as a very good sign. She said, 'You'll call me as soon as it's finished?'

'You're not coming?'

'No.' A hard moment, long enough for the pain to emerge in her gaze. 'I need to move my things from the house while Daddy's at the shop.'

'I wish I could be there with you.'

'Best not.'

He nodded. Hurting for her.

'Either he'll come around or he won't. I hope this is the message that makes him see he has to make that decision. For us.'

Chad heard the catch in her voice. 'I'm so sorry.'

'I know.' She released him. Tried for a smile. 'Now go out there and save the world.'

Beth had left hours ago to prep for today's meeting, so Chad took a taxi. In truth, he was glad Kara did not accompany him. The day was already overfull, and he needed to focus upon what was coming next.

Not to mention all the history that particular club held for him.

Chad had spent his final summer before entering the Vancouver Institute waiting tables at Orlando's City Country Club. Back then, he and his fellow employees liked to say it was where old money came to die. Actually, embalmed was probably a better term, given the level of alcoholic intake. That was one of Chad's most vivid memories of his days serving customers on the back veranda. How much booze the members and their guests could put away and still sound moderately sane.

In the late 1940s a group of local movers and shakers bought over a thousand acres southwest of downtown. Their aim at the time had been to ensure no one would ever be able to watch the rich at play. Nowadays, the land formed the city's most luxurious gated community. Homes on the five lakes and three golf courses started at four million dollars.

But Chad had little room for such thoughts as the taxi pulled into the long tree-shaded drive. He remained captured by Kara. How her actions humbled him. The willingness to walk away from a life built over two generations – not simply because she loved him, though love certainly played a major role. Kara trusted in him to do battle against the behemoth. To bring down the dragon. Or at least cripple its capacity to do harm.

He had to get this right.

Beth was standing on the shaded front portico when his taxi pulled up. She greeted him with, 'We've got you set up in the morning room. The Director's on a conference call and might be a while.'

They entered the club's grand foyer, where an unctuous manager stood with Samantha and two other agents. Together they entered the huge parlor overlooking the side gardens. It was used mostly when the weather was bad. Today, with an uncommon wind blowing cool from the northwest, the parlor was empty.

Chad excused himself and returned to the front portico. He was standing there on the top step when Samantha and Beth joined him. Samantha asked, 'Any particular reason why you're waiting out front?'

'I'm thinking Meister Kim might want to arrive before the Director. If he does, I want to be here to greet him.'

Samantha and Beth exchanged a look, then Beth asked, 'Anything we can do to help?'

'Meister Kim might like some tea.'

'Leave it with me,' Samantha said. Three minutes later, she returned and said, 'All taken care of.'

Beth asked, 'You want us to make ourselves scarce?'

'Actually, it would help if you'd stick around.'

'Like an honor guard,' Samantha nodded. 'I can live with that.'

A few minutes later, a black Mercedes limo pulled down the drive. Kim sat in the rear seat, not even glancing around until Chad stepped up and opened his door and bowed low. 'Meister Kim, you do me great honor.'

Kim rose from the vehicle and bowed in return, lower than Chad. 'It is I who am honored.'

Chad bowed a second time, then said, 'You remember my two associates, Agents Patterson and Creasey.'

Kim bowed to each, then surprised Chad by asking, 'You trust these agents?'

Chad replied slowly, 'With my life.'

Kim bowed to each lady in turn and addressed them directly. 'It is good to have trusted allies. Oh very yes.'

Chad gestured to the entrance. 'May I offer you tea?'

In Chad's younger years, back before he was booted from the Vancouver Institute, Meister Kim was scorned by many of his fellow apprentices as little more than a very quirky guy. But Chad had loved the classes taught by this senior Warrior. Kim pretended to forget all names, and referred to everyone, even the Principal, as *kohai,* the Japanese word for student. He was harsh, stern, given to shouting great Japanese oaths at those who failed him, delivered in a voice that blistered paint. He called his students 'porridge heads' whenever they did not live up to his expectations. But the few students who met his exacting measure, Kim treated as his wayward children.

The club manager personally ushered them to a table by the rear French doors. Chad remained standing as the global Council's representative seated himself. Chad turned to the two ladies and asked, 'Will you join us?'

'We'd better give the place a final check,' Samantha replied.

As they departed with the manager, a white-jacketed waiter arrived pushing a tea trolley. Chad took over. 'Meister Kim, may I serve you?'

At a nod from his teacher, Chad poured the tea into two handleless cups. He set the rough-hewn clay pot on the candle-burner, bowed a final time, and seated himself opposite Kim.

Kim slurped noisily. 'Excellent tea!'

'It is a most miserable brew. So sorry.' Chad held out the pot. 'More?'

'Please.' Kim drank, then set down his cup with elaborate care. 'How long do we have before the Director arrives?'

'Not long.'

'Then I suggest we proceed. Formalities over, *neh?* Time for the nitty-gritty.'

'Your English is amazing.'

'When I need. When I must.' Dark eyes glittered. 'I hear rumors of someone having sliced through the Sardinian library's shields like they were so much tissue paper. You even broke into the secret vault, did you not?'

'Many times.'

'And yet you are still breathing!' Kim nodded. 'It is an honor to speak with you like this.'

'The honor is all mine, Meister Kim.' Chad lifted the pot. 'More tea?'

'Ah, yes. Talking can be thirsty work.' He slurped, again, then said, 'Will you tell me how you managed to reveal that assault on the Federal Reserve?'

'Ally to ally,' Chad replied.

'Precisely! Allies must reveal their true colors, *neh?'*

'As you have,' Chad said. 'When you protected Kara, her father and their shop.' When Kim remained silent, Chad went on, 'I am in your debt.'

'Between foes, debt can be a terrible burden.' He toasted Chad with his cup. 'But between allies, it is the uncounted currency!'

'To answer your question, I was able to observe the theft through logic,' Chad replied. 'I bound Sentinel spells with others that I thought would fit together. I stacked six in all.'

'But how did you know which ones?'

'I didn't. Not until I survived.'

'Sentinel spells bound to those from other disciplines.' Kim nodded. 'You saw the weakness in our system.'

'And built upon it,' Chad confirmed.

'You will teach me, yes? You become the master, I the *kohai.'*

'May I ask a question?'

'Ally to ally,' Kim replied. 'You can ask anything.'

'Are you an Adept?'

Kim nodded approval. 'I hoped. I worked. I studied very hard indeed.' He held his fingers a hair's breadth apart. 'I came so very close.'

'What happened?'

'I tried what you describe. Stacking the spells. I failed. I spent two months in the infirmary.' He smiled sadly. 'I almost died.'

'I'm sorry,' Chad said.

Kim merely watched. And waited.

'Ally to ally,' Chad said, stressing each word. Knowing it was time. 'I have a photographic memory. I have taught myself Aramaic. I have now revealed and learned a spell from the Ancients, one that permits me—'

'Stop. Enough. Such things may not be discussed in such open and unwarded spaces. Another time, *neh?*' Kim leaned forward. 'Ally to ally. The global Council has suspected for over a decade that there is a secret group of Talents operating outside their control.'

'Renegades,' Chad said. 'I've heard they call themselves Peerless.'

'You have no idea what danger this name holds. The question is *why*. Why does speaking of a secret cabal carry so much risk? And to answer that, we must move from fact to speculation.'

Chad felt as though the correct response was scripted in those dark eyes. 'They have allies inside the Institutes.'

'At the highest levels of power. It is the only reason I can find for the facts as I see them.'

'The facts,' Chad murmured.

'The seven Institutes are riven with discord and conflict. The current situation suggests these Peerless have access to dark power that dates back to our early days. I fear they are secretly offering alliances to the most corrupt and twisted of the Institute's senior Talents. Telling them to remain where they are. For the moment. Granting them partial access to magic lost for eons. That is my conclusion. And my greatest fear.' Kim smiled grimly and went on, 'Now imagine the response to news that an Adept has arrived. Out of nowhere. One who holds no allegiance to any Institute. One who despises our leaders, and for good reason.'

'The Council is worried,' Chad said.

'They are *terrified*. Will you go to the dark ones, become a true enemy of the traditions we are sworn to uphold?'

'No.' Chad shook his head. 'I will not.'

Kim reached out and took hold of Chad's arm in a fierce grip. 'Come back to Sardinia. You can ask for anything. Do you hear me? *Anything*. They are *desperate* to claim you.' Kim glanced up, and rose to his feet, drawing Chad with him. 'The Director has arrived.'

FIFTY-ONE

C had headed for the front doors as two dark-tinted SUVs stopped under the shaded portico. Then a voice called, 'Chad?'

He turned, and there she was. 'Hello, Stephanie.'

She was taller than he remembered. The brownish-blonde hair was different as well. But the most remarkable change was her manner. The eager student was gone. He faced a doctor, sure of herself, experienced, mature.

Then he spotted Olivia.

Stephanie's best friend had not aged well. The perky cattiness that had defined the woman who detested Chad was gone. In its place was a crimped and faded mockery of her former good looks. She hovered by the corridor leading to the main salon, eyeing Chad in horror. She took a step back, another, and fled.

Stephanie took in Chad standing there, elegantly dressed, accompanied by a Japanese diplomat. Then two agents with earpieces and grim expressions stepped through the front portal, flanking him. Stephanie asked, 'What are you doing here?'

'I was invited to a meeting.'

Kim corrected, 'Actually, madam, Mr Hagan is why this meeting is taking place.'

'*You!*' Stephanie's mother entered the foyer followed by two young men. Olivia remained well back, out of Chad's line of fire. Audrey Walters showed equal measures of horror and rage. 'Who *dared* to let you in here?'

Samantha warned, 'Ma'am, I need to ask you to move away.'

Chad's attention was held by the young men. They stared at Chad and Kim, their faces bone white. Chad asked, 'Do I know you?'

Kim replied, 'They are mid-level Talents of the Vancouver

Institute. They wanted to transfer to Warrior status. I served as one of their examiners.' He smiled. 'I failed them both.'

Samantha stepped closer to the two Talents. 'What happened to your arms?'

Only then did Chad notice the gauze strips running from all four wrists into their jacket cuffs.

Kim said, 'It appears the wards around Mr Hagan's residence were not as ineffectual as I'd feared.'

Chad recalled the briefcase buried under the stairs and said, 'Actually, they might have ignited a little surprise of my own.'

Beth said, 'Well, well, well.'

Audrey Walters hissed, 'You are scum and you always will be.'

Odell Reeves walked up, flanked by two agents. 'Everything good here?'

Chad replied, 'Everything is just fine.'

'Then let's get this show on the road,' Reeves said. 'My day is short on minutes.'

'Ladies,' Chad said, and turned away.

FIFTY-TWO

The club possessed three giant rear patios. The one closest to the central lake was the Lake Veranda, then the Golf, and then the Club. Each was a massive flagstone expanse, shielded by oversized square parasols and ventilated by discreet air-conditioning vents positioned directly beneath each table. For reasons Chad had never understood, the Club Veranda was considered the most desirable. Senior patrons who claimed the Club Veranda as their own referred to the other two patios as the back forty. Chad had seen several cases of near hysteria when a patron was refused his or her preferred table on the Club Veranda.

Today, however, the Director's advance team had taken over the entire Club Veranda. Between Chad's little group and the club's other patrons were three rows of empty tables. Which meant everyone populating the golf course, the lakefront piers, the interior restaurant and the bars, all focused on them.

Chad spotted a couple of semi-familiar faces, but no one gave him a second glance. Why should they, since previously he'd always worn a white waiter's jacket. He selected a chair with his back to the audience. He had to concentrate, which meant not giving a thought to his former fiancée or her mother or the wounded mages who had probably taken part in the night-time assault.

Director Reeves waited while a silver coffee service was settled in place, then began, 'I am due back in Washington for a Cabinet meeting. One is not late for the President.'

'Indeed not,' Kim said.

'I'll come straight to the point. Chad Avery Hagan must hereby be acknowledged as a permanent consultant to the United States government. This relationship lasts as long as I or my successors decide. Your Council has no say in the matter, now or in the future.' She nodded her thanks to the agent serving coffee. 'Until this matter is settled, I will not permit *my consultant* to return to service at *any* Institute. Vancouver, Sardinia, it makes no difference whatsoever.'

Kim rose to his feet, bowed, said, 'One moment, Madame Director.'

'I don't have time for dithering,' Reeves snapped. 'This is an up or down decision.'

'Noted, ma'am. The global Council is in session, awaiting your terms.' Kim turned away.

The Director looked at the agent standing by her left shoulder. 'You sure we're clear?'

'The patio has been swept twice,' he replied.

'All right.' Reeves leaned in closer and spoke in a low monotone. 'Now tell me you have worked out a contingency plan.'

Chad studied the dark features, saw the strength and almost feral determination. He nodded slowly.

Odell said, 'I assume you know what I'm talking about.'

'In case the Institutes and their Council refuse to accept your conditions,' Chad replied. 'It's become my waking nightmare.'

Odell leaned back, clearly pleased. 'My guess is, they will agree. If for no other reason than to have their Talents released from our prisons.'

'They can do that?'

'The wheels are already turning. They've made a direct appeal to the President.' Odell glanced over to where Kim continued talking on his phone. The mage's face was set in stern warrior lines. Fighting on Chad's behalf.

She went on, 'Thankfully, the President and his Cabinet have refused to respond until these negotiations are concluded.'

It was Chad's turn to lean back. He breathed, 'Wow.'

'See how much trouble you're causing me?' She smiled. 'Actually, we've been looking for just this sort of lever. Pry open these magically closed doors. Peer inside.'

'But you don't think it's going to happen.'

'What I think is, you better be ready in case it doesn't.'

'I'm working on it.'

'Work faster.' Odell motioned toward where Kim was stowing away his phone. When Kim was seated, she demanded, 'Well?'

'The Council formally grants their approval, Director.' He glanced at Chad. 'I have been asked for confirmation that your consultant will honor any agreement we might reach here.'

'He most certainly will, or he'll have me to answer to,' Reeves replied. 'But I'm not done with my requirements.'

Kim smiled. 'I thought not.'

'Three conditions must be met.'

Kim drew out his phone. Hit speed dial. Placed it on the table between them. 'The Council is listening, Madame Director.'

'Three conditions,' she repeated. 'There is no room for negotiating on any of them. First, Chad Avery Hagan must be free to come and go at will. At a moment's notice. He will maintain his Florida residency. Without hindrance or protest from anyone on your end.'

'Noted.'

'Second condition. Chad Avery Hagan is granted the authority to represent your Institutes in all matters related to my department. Included in this is the understanding that no restriction shall be placed, now or in the future, on what he discloses to my office.'

Kim stared at the phone. '*Your* office. Personally.'

'A very few people will be included in my team. Only one other member of the President's Cabinet is even aware of the role Mr Hagan shall play. And he is a professional keeper of secrets. I or my successor will maintain the strictest confidence with anything that is passed on. I suggest your Council do the same.'

He nodded, satisfied. 'Noted.'

'The third and final condition.' The Director turned and smiled at him. 'Chad Avery Hagan must be named to your global Council.'

FIFTY-THREE

While they waited for Kim and the Council to debate her three demands, Director Reeves asked about his living situation. Beth described the high-rise condo building. Or rather, she started to. Odell stopped her midway through the third sentence. 'Out of the question.'

'I like it there,' Chad replied.

'A great deal more than your preferences are at stake,' Reeves replied. 'It's very hard to protect you in a high-rise.'

'Pretty much impossible,' Samantha agreed.

'Assuming the Council agrees to this, we will be placing you in a high-profile, high-risk position. You need to accept federal protection.'

Chad disliked the idea intensely. And thought Kara would hate it even more. 'That's not what I had in mind when I signed on.'

'It shouldn't be permanent. Only until we are certain your opponents within the Institute understand you have the full backing of our government.'

'No federal agent is going to stop a magical attack.'

'They won't need to. The agents are there to declare your official position. Simply knowing that you have our full backing should keep you safe. The tactic has worked more times than I can count.' Odell turned her attention to where Kim stood at the patio's far corner, arguing quietly with his phone. 'How much longer is this going to take?'

Kim noticed the gazes cast his way and lowered the phone long enough to say, 'The Council feels a need to discuss your terms in greater depth.'

Chad said to the Director, 'If you think it's important, I'll move. Just not to Washington. Please.'

'I have an idea. I'll make a few calls on my return flight.' Odell motioned to where Kim pocketed his phone. 'Here we go.'

The master mage returned to the table. 'The Council formally requests a period to deliberate further.'

'How long do you think they will require?'

In response, Kim looked across the table at Chad. 'Ally to ally?'

'I wouldn't have it any other way,' Odell replied.

'I think they knew you would make this request.'

'It wasn't a request,' Odell countered.

'Indeed so, Madame Director. And they know this.' Kim's dark gaze glinted in the sunlight. 'I also think they will offer a compromise. And as in your case, it will not be a request. Chad Hagan will be appointed to a senior position within the Sardinian Institute. This would grant him access to all decisions taken by the global Council, but not actually make him a member. Which in their opinion would be a step too far.'

Odell studied him with unblinking intensity. Then, 'How long?'

'I would say, give them five days. The Council will face bitter opposition from some leaders in Sardinia. Perhaps most. A week at most. You will have your answer.'

'You are a good ally to have on our side, sir.'

'Please,' Kim said. 'It is my honor to serve this most important cause.'

'Just the same.' Director Reeves rose from the table and motioned to the nearest agents. 'I and my department consider ourselves in your debt. Whenever, wherever. You and you alone. No intermediary. You understand?'

Kim stood with the others and bowed deeply. 'You do me great honor, Director Reeves.'

Chad accompanied Kim to the double doors leading to the club's main rooms. Kim halted there and said, 'All my life, my career, I hope for allies.'

Chad sensed that every eye was on them. Inside the club, all three verandas, the golf course. He replied, 'Allies and friends both.'

Kim offered Chad his hand, then settled his other hand on top. His bow was so deep his forehead almost touched their hands. 'For the first time in too long, I am filled with hope. For myself, for all honorable Talents everywhere.'

'Not for the Institutes?'

Kim responded with a grimace of almost theatrical sorrow. 'Ah, what a difficult question. Who precisely is the Institute?'

'I don't understand.'

'Also I do not understand. Who controls the Institutes? What are their aims? Why are we the enemies of so many?'

Chad confessed, 'I thought I was the only person asking those questions.'

'As I have also feared. But no longer. Now we can be afraid together, *neh*?' Kim bowed a final time. 'Until later, my friend.'

Chad returned to the veranda, his progress tracked by all the club members and guests barred from the veranda that remained his to claim. He could see Beth and Samantha talking with a couple of other agents. The club manager appeared and asked if Chad wanted anything. He realized he was famished and asked for lunch. The manager made suggestions of what was freshest, the words washing over Chad, his mind already tracking possible next steps.

When he was alone, he called Kara, catching her in the painful process of packing. She asked how it had gone, but Chad could tell she was not really able to focus on anything beyond what this day already held. He simply replied that they would probably be moving later that day, and suggested she phone him for their new address once she was done.

She asked, 'Tell me one thing. Are we moving because it went well?'

'I think yes. But . . .'

'There are unresolved issues,' she finished for him.

'A lot of them.'

'I want to hear the long version. But not now, you understand?'

'Of course, Kara.' He pushed his chair away from the table as a pair of waiters spread out a starched white tablecloth, silverware, crystal glasses, the works. 'Should I come help you finish packing?'

She didn't laugh. But her tone lightened a notch. 'A joke. I like that.'

'A bad one.'

'I will call you when I'm done.'

When she cut the connection and the waiters retreated, Chad strengthened the phone's wards, then made the day's second call. Luca Tami answered on the first ring. 'I hope you are phoning with good news.'

'It looks that way to me.' Chad summarized the meeting. Waited.

'A runaway apprentice being named to the Sardinian leader-ship.' Luca actually laughed. A first.

'I suspect this is what Odell was after all along.'

'I agree with you.' Luca laughed a second time. 'The news will positively pickle some of my old foes.'

'I knew you were a Talent.'

'And I owe you a longer explanation of who I am, and how I came to be where I am. But all that must wait for a gentler time. For the moment, what can I do for you?'

Chad liked that. The open-handed response. Two allies holding nothing back. 'I have a crazy request.' Swift as he could, he described meeting Mademoiselle Three. Not actually telling why the contact had been made. Focusing on the electronic woman's final conversation. The fear. The farewell.

When he was done, Luca remained silent for a long moment. Then, 'You have made friends with a banking program who has, for lack of a better word, come to full consciousness.'

'She describes it as waking up.'

'A beautiful and tragic term. Though my heart quakes at the prospect of my own bank's security spells making this same transi-tion.' Luca thought a moment, then, 'Will you tell me how you came into contact with her?'

'I will tell you everything.'

The immediacy of Chad's response, the absence of reservation, silenced the Swiss banker. 'Well.' He cleared his throat. 'Well indeed.'

Chad could think of nothing else that might fit the moment other than to repeat Meister Kim's words. 'Ally to ally.' Then he described the fake credit card, the invitation.

The theft from inactive accounts.

His final conversation with Three. Her desire to do one last service. The draining of Serge's accounts.

Luca was again slow to respond. 'As a member of the banking elite, I suppose I should give the knee-jerk response, something about breaking international laws and the wrongness of stealing and so forth.'

Chad did not respond.

'As it is, I find myself struggling not to laugh. Which is a terrible admission.'

'You are, after all, a banker.'

'A Swiss banker,' Luca corrected. 'You will tell me how to create such an electronic invitation?'

'Of course.' Chad sketched out his logic, his intent, his spell. Planning had taken nine long months. Explaining it to the older Adept took less than five minutes.

When he finished, Luca said, 'You have given me another reason not to sleep nights. Not to mention a splendid confirmation of how vital our friendship has already proven to be. Thank you, my astonishing young friend.'

'You're welcome.'

'Back to your Mademoiselle Three. So now she fears she is being tracked by these so-called hunters.'

'All her friends are gone. She seemed, I don't know, resigned.'

'We can't let that happen.'

Chad felt his night-time worries lightened by the simple act of having an ally who shared his concerns. 'I have an idea. What if your bank or a consulting group bought a super-computer and used it as a gathering point . . .'

Luca did not let him finish. 'Have you shared this news with Odell?'

'Not yet. I thought, well, you're the banker. And the guy operating under everyone's radar.'

'Let me see what I can do.'

'It may already be too late,' Chad warned.

'Which is why I must hurry. I will call when I have news.' Luca cut the connection.

Lunch arrived then, grilled shrimp on saffron rice with a side of seared asparagus. Chad refused the offer of wine and ate with his back to the club's other diners. He was watching a trio of portly golfers in pastel outfits tee off when Beth and Samantha walked over. 'How's the grub?'

He waved them into seats. 'Outstanding. Better than I remember.'

Beth gestured to the hovering waiter and said, 'I'll have the same.'

'Make that two,' Samantha added.

Beth then said to Chad, 'I hope you don't have a problem with glitz.'

'I don't even know what that means.'

'You will.' She waved at the palatial homes lining the lake's far side. 'The Director wants you to move into the place where she spent last night.'

'A lot of high-powered movers and shakers come through here,' Beth said. 'US presidents, heads of the world's biggest corporations . . .'

'The boss has also assigned you a federal security detail,' Samantha said. 'They can use the guest house as their base.'

'The guest house,' Chad repeated.

'Four more bedrooms in there,' Beth explained. 'As opposed to the pool house, which only has two. That's in addition to the seven bedrooms in the main house.'

'You're making this up,' Chad said.

'Nineteen bathrooms. I know. I counted,' Samantha said, enjoying herself.

'I raised four kids in a house smaller than the master bedroom,' Beth said.

When the waiter deposited their plates and departed, Chad said, 'I hate the place already.'

FIFTY-FOUR

C had lay in bed and listened to Kara's breathing. She had said almost nothing since her arrival hours ago. When Chad had called to give the villa's address, she had been at the shop. Chad had not asked why. He hadn't needed to. Of course Kara had offered her father one last chance. Even when it cost her dearly, even when she carried the shadows of that conversation through dinner.

Chad's new residence was simply gargantuan. A domed foyer opened into a house shaped like a Grecian mini-temple. The rear acres held a sculpted garden, infinity pool, pool house. Down by the lake rose a second larger guesthouse, where Beth and the four agents were stationed. Chad walked the perimeter, setting wards in place, getting a feel for a residence he would never call home.

After she arrived, Kara drifted through the house, trailed by all the shadows she did not care to discuss. Chad remained at a careful distance, granting her space, letting her know he was there. When she left everything except one case in the van, Chad did not object.

Over a nearly silent dinner, taken on the rear veranda and served by a uniformed maid, Kara watched Beth and the agents patrol the perimeter. The sculpted gardens swept down to the club's largest lake, with rows of imperial palms and blooming oleander framing both sides. Once the maid removed their plates and brought a tea service with fresh-baked cookies, Kara waited for the patio doors to click shut, then spoke for the first time. 'Will this last?'

'Probably not more than a week or so. Maybe less.'

She sipped her tea, nibbled the edge of one cookie, before speaking again. 'Will we have a home after?'

'Yes, Kara. Anywhere you want.'

'Really?'

'Yes.' If they survived, he amended silently. Which he thought they had a pretty good chance of achieving. But all that needed to wait. Once she was fully back, once she was ready and able to listen, he would tell her what he was thinking. And they would plan.

Later, he followed Kara upstairs, carrying her case. He pushed open the master suite's double doors, then stepped back. Waiting.

Kara remained standing in the entrance, staring at the vast expanse of pearl-white carpet, silent, silhouetted by the sorrow she had carried all day.

Finally, Chad said, 'This place has half a dozen bedrooms. If you'd rather . . .'

'Don't talk silly.' She walked to the broad windows overlooking the lake, closed the drapes, then stood there in the center of the room. 'Shut the door and come hold me.'

Chad woke up some time after midnight. Odell's warning, to be ready in case things went south, turned the bedroom's shadows into spectral shapes. She had been right to warn him. At a level beyond thought, fashioned from his years inside the Institute, Chad grew increasingly certain that whatever compromise they offered would be a lie. They could not allow a runaway apprentice to be lifted up to their highest ranks, or be acknowledged as an Adept. He was, and would always remain, a threat to their power structure.

Sooner or later, they would come for him.

His only hope of survival was to set the time and place. Determine the outcome in advance.

The majority of Talents still considered him the bumbling apprentice he had played in Sardinia. Even those who had witnessed his growing power did not want to accept Chad's abilities as real. He knew them so well, their unshakeable conceit, their lofty disdain for lesser mortals. Which they still considered him to be.

And that, he knew, gave him an edge.

It was approaching dawn when Chad decided he had taken it as far as he could without Kara's help. He released the fears and the half-shaped plans as best he could, and finally drifted away.

Chad slept until light spilled through the bedroom's west-facing windows. He came downstairs to find Kara seated on the rear veranda, watching a foursome of pastel-clad golfers parading along the lake's far side. She wore a bikini top, shorts and Ray-Bans. Kara rose, entered the palatial kitchen, kissed him, said, 'Coffee?'

'Absolutely.' Chad seated himself at a central console larger than a ping-pong table. 'How are you?'

'Better.'

'Really?'

'Yes, Chad. I've made my decision. Daddy must make his. I hope . . .' The hand measuring coffee into the filter halted in mid-air. 'Is it all right if we don't talk about him just now?'

'Of course.'

'I've spoken with Beth. She's sent the maid and cook away, at least for now. The agents will do our shopping, or we can go with them if we prefer.'

'I hate shopping.'

'That's not the point and we both know it.' She walked over and seated herself. 'We need privacy.'

He nodded. 'Yes. We do.'

'And I'm not talking about, you know, us.'

'It's good to see you smile, Kara.'

'You have something planned, don't you.'

'Not anything close to a working plan. Just a few ideas, is all.'

'You need my help.'

'More than I ever thought it was possible to need someone.'

Her only response was to pull the sunglasses from her eyes and let them dangle around her neck. As if she needed to study him without the clouded barrier. Chad was content to wait with her. All day, if required. When the coffee-maker pinged, she slipped from her stool, poured two mugs and said, 'Let's take this outside.'

The shaded veranda was rimmed by pillars, wooden paddle-fans spinning lazy circles overhead. The day held a fragrant coolness, gifted by a breeze blowing from the north. Chad needed almost an hour to describe what he had in mind. He stumbled repeatedly, and three times needed to verbally erase what he was saying and correct himself. If Kara minded, she gave no sign. When he finished, Kara stood, kissed his forehead, and entered the kitchen. Half an hour later she returned with a tray containing breakfast burritos and bowls of fresh fruit. 'Beth called. She asked if you wanted to talk. I thanked her for keeping a distance and said you weren't ready yet.'

He nodded his thanks and went back to watching a pair of hummingbirds flash golden and red and blue, faster even than the dragonflies perched delicately above the pool's surface. The burritos were excellent.

When he was done eating, Kara said, 'Daddy would be horrified by your idea.'

Chad nodded. He had thought the same thing.

'So you are fairly certain the Institutes—'

'Not certain at all. But I think we need to be ready.'

'In case it's all just another lie. One of thousands.' When he nodded agreement, she asked, 'How long do we have?'

'Meister Kim said they'd probably need a week to respond. Odell will take another day or so to accept their compromise. Assuming Kim is right, and they offer me a place on the Sardinian board.'

'So. Nine days.'

'Two weeks at the outside.'

'Then we'll know whether it's all for real or . . .'

Chad waited with her. He had been brutally honest, both because he owed it to her and because he needed her help in making this work. Even so, the next step might destroy them. It was important that she was fully engaged. If she had any reservations, any desire to take a different course . . .

She must have read the concerns in his expression, for she gripped his hand with both of hers and said, 'I'm here for you. With you. In this.'

He searched desperately for something that was at least somewhat worthy of her gift. And came up empty. 'Kara . . .'

She leaned close, kissed him, then rose to her feet. 'Let's get
to work.'

The next sunrise broke Florida's recent myth of cool perfection.
Chad poured his first cup of coffee and slipped outdoors as Venus
gave way to the gray spackle of gathering dawn.

They had talked until well after midnight, planning and
revising and developing a step-by-step strategy for how to
survive. If, and only if, his suspicions were correct. When
fatigue had made further progress impossible, they had gone
to bed. There, Kara had clung to him with a desperation that
suggested she shared his fear over what the coming days might
bring.

He walked the estate's perimeter, checking his wards, then
stood where he could look out over the lake's shadowy surface
and recalled earlier times. Each spring, a day or so after school
ended, he'd walk down to the lake's shoreline and watch the trees
take shape around his grandmother's home. Chad's summers were
marked by such quiet hours. Loving his life, yet fearing the best
he could hope for was struggling for years to purchase his own
boat. Spending a life on the open waters. Enduring the egos and
demands of rich tourists.

Beth stepped from the guesthouse, lifted her steaming mug, and
asked softly, 'Want me to freshen that up?'

Chad walked over, waited while she returned indoors, accepted
his mug, and said, 'Let's move away from the guesthouse.'

Beth walked with him along the lakefront. 'I guess this means
you're ready to talk.'

'Thanks for being patient with me.'

'If anybody deserved a day to kick back and relax, it's you.'

'Mostly we planned.' He watched a trio of swans slap the water,
take off, and listened to their wings hum as they lifted the birds
into the sunrise. 'Can you get a message to Meister Kim?'

'Any reason why you don't call him yourself?'

'A number of them. It needs to be totally off the record.' He
explained what he had in mind, then waited.

'I'll get right on it.'

'Thank you, Beth.' He started back to the main house.

Beth called after him, 'Samantha needs to be involved.'

'I wouldn't have it any other way.'

Kara emerged from their haven just after eight, sleep-tousled and utterly beautiful. The heat and humidity was already a stifling blanket. He unfurled a striped awning that formed a shaded alcove from their sliding glass doors to the pool's edge. She made fresh fruit with yoghurt and granola, then prepared another pot of coffee. They sat in silence for a time, holding hands, watching the day unfold. Chad wished there was some way to hold on to this, even as a memory. Treasure the closeness and the quiet calm. Despite the storm brooding beyond the horizon. This day, this hour, was a gift.

Finally, she said, 'You need to tell the others.'

'I've worried about that. Each additional person who knows just adds to the risk.'

'These aren't *persons*. These are *friends*. They trust you, and you need to do the same.'

He nodded. 'It's hard. To trust.'

'I know. But your time of facing life alone is over.'

He kept nodding. Acknowledging the fact that she was not the only one enduring a major transition. 'I've already asked Beth to contact Meister Kim. And Samantha.'

'Why didn't you just say that?'

'Because I needed to be certain you saw it as the right move. If you wanted to keep things between us, I was planning to just warn them of how this might play out.'

She studied him, then nodded acceptance and rose to her feet. 'I want to give Daddy one more chance.'

'Should I come with you?'

'Ha. Look at the funny man.'

'Don't tell him what we're planning, Kara. Please.'

'I know that. Unless, you know, he agrees to join us.'

Chad heard the resignation in her voice. Knew this trip was mostly about saying farewell. 'I'll ask Beth to have one of her agents take you.'

Chad expected an argument over this sort of incursion on a very private ordeal. But Kara merely leaned over and kissed him. Hard. 'Tell her five minutes.'

As soon as Kara departed in one of the agents' SUVs, Chad reset the wards on his phone and called Luca. He launched straight into his plans, but after a few quick sentences the banker cut him off with, 'You're planning. Thinking ahead. Making yourself ready. I am both pleased and relieved.'

'You think there's any chance I'm wrong?'

'What you're asking is, will the Institutes bend to the dictates of a runaway Adept and a Homeland Director?' Luca gave that a moment, then said, 'Director Reeves is not a Talent, and that is all they will recognize. Oh, I suppose there's a chance the Council will agree to her plans. I cannot give up all hope. But I am very glad indeed to know that you are preparing an alternative future.'

But as Chad started to cut the connection, Luca added, 'I have prepared a welcome for Mademoiselle Three.'

'If she has survived. If she'll even speak with me.'

'Call and see.'

Chad put Luca on hold, then punched in the number from memory. It rang and rang, until finally a man's voice demanded, 'Who is this?'

Chad felt all his midnight worries congeal into an icy bundle that filled his gut. 'I'm sorry, I dialed a wrong—'

'What number did you call?'

'I'm sorry to have disturbed—'

The man's accent was French and very heavy, his words military crisp. 'Who is this and why did you call?'

Chad cut the connection and sat there cradling the phone. Hoping the wards he had placed before phoning Luca still held. Worried if his electronic friend had managed to stay awake.

Finally he reconnected with Luca and replayed the conversation.

Luca took his time responding. 'She might still have survived.'

Chad rubbed the space over his heart and remained silent.

'Hope in such times is all we have. I have spent years hoping for someone with whom I might have just such a conversation. Hoping against all the power held by the seven Institutes that somehow, someway, a Talent might break free and seek to help me right these terrible wrongs. Even perhaps, just perhaps, an Adept.' Luca gave that a beat, then finished, 'And look what has happened.'

As he cut the connection, Chad saw Beth standing on the other side of the pool, waiting. He waved her over. She said, 'Meister Kim and Samantha just took off from Reagan National.'

'What?'

'It appears they've been waiting for your signal. They should be here in . . .' She checked her watch, 'three and a half hours, give or take.'

'Wow.'

Beth nodded. 'It was apparently your pal Kim's suggestion. Be ready to jump when you called.'

He was still sitting there almost an hour later when Kara returned. Her expression matched his own internal state. She joined him under the awning, holding hands, enduring the oppressive heat and humidity as if it was their due.

Chad made them salads for a mostly silent lunch. Afterwards he pulled two chaise lounges under the awning. Clouds gathered, dense and dark. A major Florida storm loomed in the near future.

When it was time, they went upstairs to shower and dress. Twenty minutes later, Chad stood outside the front door as the SUV pulled up and Samantha and Kim alighted. Chad bowed them inside, closed the door, and asked Kim, 'How long do we have? I mean, here. Now. Together.'

'My official purpose is to formally apologize for the Council not yet arriving at their decision,' Kim replied. 'We must assume they have watchers in place. I should depart within a few hours.'

'Let's get started.' Chad escorted them on to the veranda. As soon as they were seated, he began. No preambles, no hesitation. It was time.

When Chad was done, they remained frozen in place. Utterly silent. Which was hardly a surprise, as his tale and the resulting plans rocked all their worlds. If he was wrong, there was a very real chance they would all perish.

Finally Kara reached over and took his hand. Offered a quiet, 'Well done.'

As if taking that as his signal, Kim rose and entered the rear doors. The sound of clatter echoed from the kitchen, then Kim emerged bearing a tea service for five. 'Planning and talking are such thirsty work, *neh*?' He set the tray down on the table, bowed to them all, then declared, 'I fear this tea will be truly awful.' He offered the first rough porcelain cup to Kara, one hand poised beneath and the other encircling the rim. Very formal. Chad loved how she accepted it with two hands of her own. When the others were served, Kim seated himself, poured a final cup, leaned back, and declared, 'I agree.'

Beth asked Chad, 'You're certain this plan of yours is even possible?'

'Pretty much. The spell in your book from the Library of Congress was very definite.'

Samantha said, 'I hope you don't mind my telling you, what you've described makes my skin crawl.'

Kim snorted, or laughed, then hid inside his cup.

'Even so, just for the record, I'm in.'

Beth nodded. 'I give that a big amen.'

'There are risks,' Chad pointed out. 'All of this is untried territory. What I'm proposing has never been done before.'

'But we're doing it for the right reasons,' Kara said. 'And against a common foe.'

'Present company excepted,' Beth said, smiling at Kim.

Kim set his cup on the tray. 'Will you tell me again?'

'Which part?'

'The book, the unraveling of the script, the spell.' He turned to the ladies. 'You will please forgive me if we address the technicalities of spell-casting.'

'I for one don't need to follow everything to find this fascinating,' Beth replied.

Chad found himself reliving the electric tension as he described unfurling the Ancients' script, and what he had found printed there. He was once again in the SUV's rear seat, being driven to Homeland HQ by agents who had no idea what was happening. Consumed by the power revealed on the page. He watched Kim's frown deepen, and knew what the Warrior Talent would say before he opened his mouth. 'And so the master becomes the pupil. How often have you cast the spell?'

'I haven't.'

Samantha and Beth showed genuine surprise. 'We're moving forward on a theory?'

'No.' Chad kept his gaze on Kim. 'There is one more element

I haven't mentioned. An energy. More than that. A *certainty.* I haven't tested it because I don't need to.'

Kim drained his cup, then rose to his feet. 'Your wards are in place?'

'Since the moment I arrived.'

'Then now is a good time to begin your training, *neh*?' He smiled at Kara. 'Young mistress, are you joining us?'

'The name is Kara.' She returned his smile. 'And I wouldn't miss this for the world.'

FIFTY-FIVE

B eyond the kitchen and vast butler's pantry, a corridor curved around the forecourt and connected the main residence to the barn-size garage. Fronting this hallway were three rooms forming a private gym. The chambers were connected by glass sliders. One room housed a dozen aerobic machines, the next held weight machines and benches and chromed free-weights. Chad ushered Kim and Kara into the third chamber, which contained two mirrored walls and a padded floor and balance beams. Kim took a long look around, nodded approval, and said, 'Wait here.'

When he returned, Kim had changed from the tailored suit into his standard teaching garb, a pale blue t-shirt over black drawstring pants. The fact that he had come prepared suggested a foreknowledge that Chad found somehow comforting. Kim's t-shirt bore two kanji symbols, faded from frequent washes, and the sight took Chad straight back. Kim possessed a dozen, more, different colors, but all bearing the same kanji script. Whenever a student asked what they meant, Kim always shouted back, 'I Hate Teaching Idiots!'

The day after Chad shielded the young acolyte from Warrior bullies, he had been locked in the Vancouver Institute's punishment wing, awaiting his fate. Kim had entered and shouted at Chad for being such an idiot, taking on his foes in public. He had then seated himself next to the disgraced student and revealed what the kanji meant.

The two symbols formed the word for honor.

Kim explained how the Japanese language had many such words, since honor possessed a wide variety of meanings. Credit, prestige, privilege, glory, status, face. There were actually twenty-seven different ways to write that one word, honor, in Japanese. Ceremony, reputation, fame, reverence, esteem – Kim named them all.

The symbols on his t-shirt, Kim said, stood for honor in its purest form. Honor in life, discipline, sacrifice. Even to death.

Thunder rumbled softly in the distance as Kim stepped barefoot on to the padded surface. He had brought with him two mops and a push-broom from the kitchen pantry. He unscrewed the heads, then placed one pole at Chad's feet, another by Kara's. 'Today these will serve as our *rokushakubo.*'

Chad nodded understanding and watched as Kim twirled the stick slowly in one hand as he made a circle of the room's perimeter, taking its measure. He gave the mirrored walls no more notice than he did the four who watched him.

He stepped to the center of the room and began a kata, or stylized fighting routine. Chad recognized the kata as the first Meister Kim taught to students he considered worthy. The *rokushakubo* was less well known in Japan than the *bokken,* a training stick shaped like the Japanese sword, which Kim never used. In Japan, the long stick was part of an ancient discipline known as *bojutsu,* brought from China thousands of years ago.

When he was done, Kim stepped to one side and motioned for Chad to join him.

'It's been a while,' Chad warned, and picked up a second stick. 'Years.'

'Did I invite the *kohai* to speak?' Kim assumed the *yoi,* the starting position, and waited. When Chad mirrored his stance, Kim barked, 'Begin!'

Beth and Samantha observed from the hallway. Kara knelt in one corner, watching with wide-eyed absorption. Chad thought it was beyond good to see Kara lose the day's shadow . . .

'Stop, stop! *Kohai*! Where is your mind?'

Chad knelt. Pressed his forehead to the mat. Silence was the only proper response when Kim shouted.

'You know that was awful, *neh*! Worse than awful. It was

poison!' Kim knelt in front of him. Waited until Chad straightened. 'Now. Empty mind!'

Chad did his best to close out the world. He failed. But still.

Eventually Kim rose smoothly to his feet, motioned for Chad to do likewise, assumed the starting pose, and held it almost forever. Then, 'Begin!'

Four more routines, five, then Kim pointed the sweating puffing student into the corner. He bowed to Kara, smiled, said, 'This unworthy teacher is ready.'

'Great,' she said, bouncing to her feet. 'So am I.'

His teaching approach with Kara was something else entirely. Gentle, soft-spoken, patient, even kind. Making subtle adjustments to each stance, showing her how to move smoothly from one pose to the next. Never hurrying. He then declared her ready, and swept her through the entire kata without a break. She made mistakes. A number of them. But Chad thought she did far better than he had his first time on the mat.

'Again.'

Three more times, then Kim said, 'Again. And faster.'

She made even more mistakes, forgetting two poses entirely. But Kim only said, 'Good. One more time. Faster still. Wait, wait. This time, see the enemy there before you.'

She was breathing hard and sweating through her outfit, the pastel cotton almost black. 'I don't think I can. I'm already overfull of things to remember.'

'You do very well. Better than that pudding head student crouched in the corner, oh my yes. Now one last try. Begin!'

When she was done, he bowed her into a kneeling position beside Chad. 'Now. Observe.'

Kim started slow, then moved faster and faster. Flowing like silk. Like water. It was incredible to see the man in his medium. A joy flooded Chad, along with a very real hope. That his plan might work. That they might actually survive.

Kim stopped. Ignored Chad entirely. Asked Kara, 'The enemy. Did you see them?'

'I . . . No. Not really. I'm so sorry.'

'No apology.' He hefted the stick, held it in his right hand, and shifted his left through the making of a spell Chad did not recognize. 'Now. Observe.'

This time, the enemy was there. Electric shadows, three of them. Punching and striking and armed and deadly. Kim moved faster still, achieving a superhuman speed while maintaining a smooth and steady flow. Vanquishing the enemy.

When he was done, the man was not even breathing hard. Kim bowed to the empty room, then looked at Chad for the first time. 'You know this spell?'

'I've never seen anything like it before. I didn't even know it existed.'

'Ah. Perhaps because you never stole books and scrolls from my chambers, *neh*?'

Chad could not help but smile. 'I didn't start that until I arrived in Sardinia.'

'And I did not hear what you just said. Though there have been rumors for years. Of misplaced texts, items shifted from positions they have held for decades. Because no one else bothered to study them.'

'Will you teach me that spell?'

'Of course.' Kim leaned his stick in the corner and thoughtfully stroked the wood. 'Let us hope all this is merely exercise and will never be put to use.'

'That was incredible to watch,' Kara said.

Kim bowed to her. 'And you, dear lady, would have made a very able student.'

Ninety minutes later, when they returned outside, the storm had still not arrived. It was uncommonly strange for the dense heat to remain so long without a squall. Summer weather in central Florida was as predictable as a metronome. The only time clouds gathered solid and ominous yet did not storm was during the run-up to a hurricane. But Chad had checked online while waiting for Kim to shower and dress. The tropics remained clear of major depressions.

He found it reassuring to study the weather beyond the home's front portico. The final hour with Kim, the Warrior Talent had worked Chad through two more difficult katas as well as the activation of the enemy spell.

And then, to Chad's surprise, Kim had taught him a second spell. Even more astonishing than the first.

The reality of his training, the formal acknowledgement of the enemy's pending assault, had brought Chad's plan into electrified relief.

The uneven shards of his concept fit neatly together now. Chad stood in the sweltering heat and breathed slowly around the enormity of it all. He could almost feel the unseen dagger plunging through his skin, diving into his chest cavity, destroying his heart. Death now felt that close.

Even so, balanced against this was a very real chance of survival.

Assuming, of course, that he had gotten things right.

Behind him the door opened and the three women stepped out. Kara said, 'Kim's on his way down.'

Samantha moved around in front, studied Chad a long moment, then said, 'I wouldn't have missed that for the world.'

'Your performances blew me away, sure enough,' Beth agreed. 'When Director Reeves asks how today went, I'll tell her we're as ready as we can be. As *anyone* possibly could be.'

'That means a lot,' Chad said.

'The Director's also granted me permission to stick around. For the duration. If you'll have me.'

Chad could think of no better way to respond than, 'Outstanding.'

Kim opened the front door and stepped into the heat and sunlight. He was back in his traditional dark suit, the training clothes packed in his satchel, the face calm, the gaze burning with intensity. 'We will meet again. Very soon. Whatever the Council decides.'

The man's certainty only caused Chad's fears to resurface. Kim must have read his face, for he went on, 'Hold your attack to the simplest of actions. Train to fight in tandem.' He paused, then demanded, 'You can set wards swiftly?'

'In the space of a single breath,' Chad replied. 'Faster.'

Kim reached into his pocket, took out a card, wrote on it, then handed it over. 'Ward your phone. Call whenever there is great need.' He then turned to Kara and bowed low. 'My friend and ally is fortunate to have such a gifted Talent at his side. Oh yes. Very fortunate indeed.'

Kara stepped forward and embraced the man. 'I've never enjoyed an afternoon more.'

Kim covered his astonishment with an enormous frown. 'Then I did not train you hard enough! Next time, *neh?*'

But as Kim started toward the SUV, Beth asked, 'How long do they have to prepare?'

He resumed his instructor's bark. 'Long enough! Train hard! When you are exhausted, train more!' He slipped into the rear seat, said to Samantha, 'Eyes are watching! We go!'

FIFTY-SIX

H alf an hour later, Chad sat in the SUV's front passenger seat, with Beth behind the wheel. He had never appreciated the woman's respectful silence more than now.

When he had asked Kara's permission to take this step, she had responded with a long and careful inspection of the darkening sky. Chad had been uncertain whether she was looking for a reason to refuse, or perhaps because she was again brought close to tears. In the end, though, she had merely kissed his cheek, whispered what might have been a fractured thanks, and returned inside.

He and Beth arrived at Kara's shop twenty minutes before closing. Chad waited for the last customer to depart, then slipped from the car and crossed the covered walkway. The door to Henrietta's Herbals chimed softly when Chad entered.

Darren stepped through the storeroom door carrying a box of goods. 'We're closing up now . . . Oh. It's you.'

'Five minutes,' Chad said. 'Please.'

Darren's desire to order Chad out was so strong it turned his face bitter. 'Where's Kara?'

'I asked if I could speak with you alone.'

Darren lowered the box in stages, like he was arguing with his own muscles. He set it on the floor, straightened, and walked forward. His gaze did not come close to meeting Chad's. 'Let me lock up.' As he twisted the lever, he spotted Beth inside the Tahoe. 'Who is that driving you around, more feds?'

'Homeland.'

Darren turned away. 'What, they think I'm a threat?'

'We don't go anywhere without them. Not until this is settled.'

Darren continued to glare at the Tahoe. 'When will that be?'

'A couple of weeks. Maybe less.'

'Kara is OK with this nonsense?'

Chad hesitated, then replied, 'She's where she wants to be.'

Darren turned away. He walked back down the central aisle, opened the rear door, and paused long enough to turn off the store's lights. Leaving Chad standing there. The message was clear enough. Come, don't come, it was all the same to him.

As Chad entered the office, Darren shoved his chair back until it met the whitewashed concrete wall. Placing both the desk and all possible distance between them. Chad stopped in the middle of the room. The two guest chairs were jammed tight against the right-hand bookshelves. Chad assumed Kara's father had shoved them over as he passed. Chad remained standing.

Eight books were stacked on the desk's right-hand corner. Another two lay open by the computer's keyboard. Chad recognized them all as primers used by first-year apprentices. He imagined Darren there alone at night, filling the empty hours with futile effort. Darren's face crimped tighter still and his voice rasped, 'Say your piece and get out.'

'I can see how you would have preferred it all to be. Kara's former boyfriend would have been perfect. You'd probably have never told him the truth. The guy would assume you were the healer, Kara your assistant. The lie would have strengthened the ties between you two.'

Hearing it spoken aloud only made Darren angrier. 'What, mind-reading is a talent you forgot to mention?'

'I came today, alone, because you need to know that's not happening. Mind-reading isn't a part of it. This is simple logic.'

'Your five minutes are up.'

Chad persisted. 'I don't know whether we'll make it as a couple. I hope, but I can't be certain of anything except that she is changing. Growing. And I'm telling you she is never going back to the way things were.' He took a hard breath, pushing air around the pain at heart level. 'Kara may well grow beyond me. I'm as helpless about where she's headed as you are. I have a choice. Nothing more. I can help her and support her and accept if she needs to move on. Knowing how you two were together is the only reason I'm able to live with that uncertainty.'

Silence clenched the room, tight and unrelenting as the day's heat. Darren's hostility formed a solid wall. Even so, he was watching Chad now. Focused. 'That's all you have to say?'

'Kara needs you. Now more than ever.' He set the handwritten card he had prepared on the desk. 'We'll be reachable at this number for a few days. Not more. After that, she may well be truly lost to you. Permanently.'

Darren remained stolid, unbending, silent. Finally, Chad turned and started away.

Back in the car, Beth watched him settle, said, 'That bad, huh.'

They returned to the estate in silence. When he entered the house, Kara was there, waiting in the front hall. Chad wondered if she had been standing there since he left. He said, 'I'm so sorry, it was a totally wasted—'

That was as far as she let him go.

FIFTY-SEVEN

That night Chad dreamed of Mademoiselle Three.

He could not see her clearly, nor did he need to. The vague shadow was enough to fill his slumbering heart with dread. A lovely spirit who dwelled in electric mist, with no body to claim or define her. Only in Chad's dream, Three was trapped in a cage designed by his nemesis, the Talent Serge. The cage was surrounded by Serge's electric hounds. The hunters, Three had called them. They had terrified her. And now she was their captive.

Chad then found himself convicted by a dreamlike certainty that it was all his fault.

If he had not called to her. If he had not designed the spell of invitation, stolen the funds, befriended this awakened being, she might have survived. Perhaps. And that possibility filled him with a poisonous doubt.

Over and over in his dream, Three called to him. Her terror was a palpable force that tore at his heart until . . .

Chad woke to the sound of thunder, heart pounding. He rose silently from the bed and padded from the room.

He entered the kitchen and turned on just the one light over the stove, enough illumination to find a mug and the teabags. His hands shook as he filled the pot with water.

Kara entered and said, 'Make me one too.'

'I didn't mean to wake you.'

'I wasn't asleep.' She kissed his cheek. 'You had a bad dream.'

'Terrible.'

She walked over and opened the rear doors. As if in response, thunder rumbled while lightning blistered the distant clouds. When Chad brought their mugs outside, she had shifted two chairs back against the home's wall, where the veranda's roof would keep them relatively dry. She accepted her mug and asked, 'Do you want to tell me about it?'

'Yes.' He had mentioned the electric lady twice before. But sharing the entire story now meant going back to fleeing Sardinia by boat. Which led him to describe the attack by Audrey's mother and the Talents working for the family's theme parks. From there it was a simple step to the fake seaman arriving in Marseilles and Chad's magical assault on the bank's system.

He did not stop there. Once again he relived his time in Geneva. This time, he focused on the impact of her spell. Describing the moment of realization. The challenge it posed. Giving up on revenge. Accepting it would wreak havoc on Stephanie as well as her mother. Because any act of vengeance threatened the life and future of a young woman who deserved better.

Chad finished there. He felt no need to add the obvious. That only because Stephanie had married the doctor was he here now. Loving Kara.

By the time he was done, lightning whipped and cracked, illuminating a second realm overhead, dark and furious. Kara held his hand and shared a fractured dawn. The air was close and so fused with electric tension that it seemed right for Kara to say, 'You have done all you can for Mademoiselle Three.' She waited through another thunderous symphony, then continued, 'Sometimes that is the best you can hope for. That you have tried and tried to make things right. And you are able to live with the outcome that isn't what you want. Even when it wrenches you inside. Even when you . . .'

The rain arrived then, torrents with the force of skyborne rivers. As if the world had no choice but to weep with them both. Chad reached for her hand once more. Only this time he sought comfort against the storm yet to arrive.

In time they returned upstairs and added their own passionate storm to the one overhead.

When the calm arrived, and they were content there together in one another's arms, Chad said, 'My grandmother loved these hours. She called them dense times. When I was a kid, she used to tell me how before the storm breaks, the air thickens so much the clouds cry out. That's what makes thunder.'

Kara said to his chest, 'I wish I could have known her.'

'She would have loved you,' he replied.

Kara gave that the time it deserved, then rose and padded to the bathroom. When she emerged, Chad watched her slip into shorts and t-shirt, sad to see the moment depart, but ready when she did her best to frown like Kim and bark, 'First a meal, then training, *neh?*'

They trained hard, first practicing the katas, then facing the electric enemies. Chad never applied Kim's second spell. That would come later. In their training's next phase.

They showered and ate in silence, staying inside the kitchen, doors closed. They saw Samantha and Beth make their rounds, but the two belonged to a different realm. For the moment.

When they were done, Chad cleared up while Kara made coffee. As soon as they were seated again, Kara started in with just the one word. 'Timing.'

Chad nodded. 'It's not on our side.'

'Don't say that.' Sharp now. Intense. 'Don't you even think it. We are taking control of what we can. We're preparing. We'll be ready when the time comes.'

'I love hearing you say that word,' Chad replied. 'We.'

She remained firmly on target. 'Soon as the Institute formally accepts you as a member of their board, your enemies are going to strike.'

'If I'm right,' Chad countered. 'If they are not forced by the Council to accept the Director's conditions.'

'That's not going to happen. You know it. And the longer we stay here, the more certain I become. Oh, sure, there probably are senior Talents and even members of the Council who accept this as a good thing. But nothing, absolutely nothing, will change the mindset of those others.'

Chad thought of Serge, the implacable fury he'd shown Chad at every encounter. 'You're right.'

'They'll come for us before you have a chance to get settled into this new role. While we're exposed and vulnerable. Before you can start handing over their dirty little secrets.'

As if to punctuate the moment, his phone rang. When he answered, Kim said without preamble, 'The Council will deliver their response to the Director in three days.'

FIFTY-EIGHT

Since he began stealing spells, time had never been Chad's friend. Shadows, yes. Learning to wear the mask of mulish ignorance, absolutely. But time had always been in short supply. Racing through forbidden texts. Practicing in quick snatches, when he could ward a closet or alcove and speed his way through stolen spells.

Even so, time had never been his enemy.

Until now.

Day one of this new phase, Chad began applying two new spells. The one Kim had shared before departing. And the one garnered from the Ancient's text. As a result, he was forced to limit their training to just an hour in the morning, another in the afternoon. It was not enough. But it was all either of them could bear.

After the first two sessions, they careened around the vast home like they were drunk. Unsteady, slurring their words, incapable of focusing or finishing the simplest of tasks. That evening, preparing a meal was beyond them both, and they were famished. So Chad phoned Beth and begged her for help.

Samantha came with her, which was good. One look at their state and the two women moved into the house. Which was even better.

The next session, Beth and Samantha took up fighting sticks of their own and became the sort of opponents that Kim's electric spell-cast enemies could never manage. Patient. Matching their moves to Chad's and Kara's stumbling actions.

By lunchtime the next day, Chad had trouble eating. Picking up his fork, attaching food to the tines, lifting the utensil, fitting it in his mouth, it all required huge effort and concentration. Kara, on the other hand, seemed pretty much recovered. She finally asked, 'Would you like me to cut up your meat for you? Put you in a highchair? Find you a bib?'

'That isn't funny.' Chad gave up on finishing his meal. 'We'll never be ready.'

'You're doing fine,' Beth replied.

'This morning was a huge improvement on yesterday,' Samantha agreed.

'From terrible to merely bad,' Chad countered. 'That isn't enough.'

'You don't get it,' Kara said. 'You're looking at this all wrong.'

'Oh, is that so?'

'Yes, Chad. It is. You want to *win*. You want to *beat them*. We're preparing in case our enemy refuses to accept the Council's will. If that happens, we've already lost.'

'The lady has a way with the point,' Beth agreed.

Kara continued, 'Our aim here isn't to *win*. Our goal is to convince them that *they are the victors*.'

Chad studied the three ladies, the way they all shared the same satisfaction. But what held him was how they were all so deeply committed. Tightly involved. Together. With him.

Friends.

He fought against the fatigue and lethargy, pushed himself to his feet, and said, 'It's time for round two.'

On the second afternoon following Kim's alert, Chad called Stephanie.

Her help was vital to their plan. Even so, he had put off the phone call far too long. And would have waited longer still, had Kara not ordered him to stop dawdling.

Chad had hoped their meeting would take place in a neutral space. Somewhere minus the burden of memories and possible regret. The hospital had no place in their history. Stephanie would also have a better chance of maintaining her professional demeanor.

Clinical. Detached. They could accomplish everything that needed
doing in a matter of minutes.

But he caught Stephanie as she was waiting for her tennis court
to become free. She agreed to meet the next day for an early lunch.
At the club.

'You remember where the Club Veranda is, don't you?'

'Very funny, Stephanie.'

'Eleven-thirty, please. I need to start my rounds an hour later.'

The next day Kara insisted on their maintaining the regular
morning session. Chad agreed, mostly because it kept his mind
too occupied to worry. The shower that followed was exquisite,
as always. The overhead outlet was the size of a dinner plate, with
further sprays embedded in three walls. He could have remained
there all day. When he finally emerged, he found Kara inspecting
herself in a two-way mirror. 'What do you think?'

'About what?'

She gave him the sort of look perfected by generations of
women. 'About my clothes, silly.'

'Kara, you're beautiful in anything. Or nothing at all.'

'Pay attention.' She raised up on tiptoes so as to have a clearer
view of the back. The mirror stretched across the wall above their
parlor sofa, reflecting the light pouring in the French doors. 'We're
going to have lunch at the club.'

'You don't have to come.'

'Of course I do. And that's not the point. We're meeting your
former flame. I want the lady to go away completely and utterly
convinced that she has been thoroughly outclassed.' She pirouetted
the other way. 'It's a Hermès.'

Kara wore a silk dress only slightly longer than a tennis skirt.
The yellow background was offset by a printed design that resembled a scarf. Heeled sandals of what appeared to be white-gold
alligator. 'You are positively stunning.'

'That's the answer I was looking for.' She kissed him lightly.
'Hurry up and dress. Your clothes are on the bed.'

When Chad and Kara emerged from the clubhouse, two dark-suited
agents with earpieces and wrist-mikes patrolled the Club Veranda's
perimeter, while Beth and Samantha occupied a table near the lake.
Stephanie sat surrounded by vacant chairs. She rose at their approach,

not smiling, perhaps a little uncertain of what was happening. She wore a cream-colored sleeveless top which Chad suspected was at least part cashmere. Form-fitted silk jeans. Sandals. Gold Rolex. Single pearl on a gold chain around her neck.

She offered her cheek for a kiss, first to Kara and then to him. 'You look good, Chad.' Stephanie watched him hold Kara's chair before seating himself. 'So, you're together?'

'We are. Yes.'

'Is it because of me?'

'No,' he said.

'Partly,' Kara replied.

'A small part,' he conceded.

'Be generous,' Kara said.

The exchange, the smile, the easy intimacy, it all had an impact. Chad was glad indeed that Kara had insisted on coming.

Stephanie glanced at the nearest agent, standing with their back to the veranda. Then at Beth and Samantha, both of whom continually scanned everywhere but their lone table. 'Are they all with you?'

'Always,' Kara said. 'It's part of who he has become.'

'But why, Chad? What's so important?'

'I wanted you to hear this from me,' he replied. 'I've been named a senior Talent of the Sardinian Institute.'

'But, you're . . .'

'A runaway.'

'I was going to say apprentice.'

'Not any more,' Kara said.

The waiter approached, nervously watching the agents who in turn were watching him. Stephanie asked, 'Do you want something?'

'We're good, thanks.'

Stephanie waved the young man away. 'Is that why we're meeting, so you can . . .' Her eyes widened. 'You want me to tell Mother.'

'You were always ahead of the game,' Chad said.

Kara added, 'It's not for the reason you're thinking.'

'And what is that, exactly?'

'Revenge,' Chad said. 'A big back-at-you. We don't have time for that.'

Kara said, 'Chad wants his enemies to know he is accepting the position. That it is all about to go very public.'

Stephanie said, 'Your *enemies*.'

'Not your mother,' Chad said. 'Well, she is and she always will be. But she's not . . .'

'Not what, Chad? Important?'

'Not the reason why we're meeting. I think some of the Institute's senior Talents are going to attack me.'

'What do you mean, attack?'

'Demolish,' Kara said. 'Destroy. Annihilate. Wipe off the face of this earth.'

'We need for word to reach our enemies. I think, I hope, your mother or her Talents will pass on the word . . .'

'The Talents on our payroll had a hand in destroying your home. I pressed Mother. She confessed as much.' Stephanie revealed a face Chad had never seen before. Hard as stone, glacial in intent. 'How can you be sure she's not already playing an active role?'

'This has moved to an entirely different level. One where your mother doesn't operate.'

Kara added, 'Your mother is probably not aware it exists.'

'Exactly what do you want from me?'

Chad laid out the request, as gently as he knew how. He finished with, 'We want this to happen on our schedule. On our terms.'

Anger continued to freeze Stephanie's features. The professional surgeon with her game-face firmly set. Finally, 'Will you survive?'

'If we don't,' Chad replied, 'it's not much of a plan.'

'Our chances are vastly improved if we are the ones secretly in control of the time and the place,' Kara said.

Stephanie looked at Kara. Really, intently *looked*. 'I won't be party to Chad's death.'

'That makes two of us,' Kara replied. 'Chad's plan is our best hope of surviving.'

'Are you sure about that?'

'As certain as I can be. And I'm not alone.' Kara pointed to Samantha, walking through the clubhouse doors. 'She is a federal agent answering directly to the Director of Homeland Security's magical division. They both consider Chad to be a tactician of the first order.'

Stephanie watched the agents on patrol. 'You don't need me to get you tickets. One call from Homeland and our publicity department would fall over itself printing out VIP passes.'

'The tickets aren't the issue here. We need your mother to know. In case we're right. In case our enemies within the Institute have no intention of letting me take up this new role.'

Kara added, 'We need the Talents on your company's payroll to alert our enemies.'

'I understand.' A long moment passed, then, 'The Talents are coming over for drinks tonight. I'll make sure they hear about this.'

Chad handed over a handwritten slip of paper. 'This is where we're staying. Have the passes sent here.'

Stephanie nodded once. Again. 'You'll let me know how things turn out?'

Chad took his time responding. 'I'm not sure that's a good idea.'

'Or even possible,' Kara added.

'I want to know you're both OK. I need that.'

Chad exchanged a long look with Kara. Finally, it was Kara who replied, 'When and how we can.'

Stephanie rose to her feet, gathered up her purse and tennis bag, and left without a word or backward glance.

FIFTY-NINE

As they were leaving the club, Samantha reported that the Director had been in touch. The global Council had issued its formal response. It was as Meister Kim had predicted. Chad would be invested as a full-fledged senior Talent in the Sardinian Institute. He would remain free to travel between the Institute and America.

The four of them, Chad and Kara and Beth and Samantha, responded by returning home and entering straight into another training session.

Stephanie came through for them. That evening four special passes arrived by courier, granting them entry two hours before the park's official opening.

The next day, Director Odell Reeves formally accepted the Council's edict. She then ordered Chad back to Sardinia. To begin his new role. Effective immediately.

Three more training sessions followed.

By that point he and Kara were beginning to move in synch.

The next day, the fifth since Kim's call, Chad booked his flights. Or rather, Samantha did it for him. Orlando to Rome, Rome to Cagliari. First class. Kara would follow once he was certain of her safety. And his.

That evening, Chad called Stephanie.

He had to assume there were listening ears. He had feared he could not pretend to be excited and pleased. But his nerves lifted his voice almost a full octave, enough to suggest to anyone monitoring the call that he was nothing more than a young runaway who had been given the keys to the kingdom. 'Thank you so much for the tickets! We've never been, either of us. I guess it's like New Yorkers who haven't ever seen the Statue of Liberty.'

'So you're going, then.' Stephanie sounded subdued. Morose.

'I leave for Sardinia day after tomorrow.' Chad laughed, a brittle and brassy noise to his own ears. 'I can hardly believe it! I'm going to train as an Adept!'

'Congratulations, Chad. Really. I'm so pleased.'

'That means the world, Stephanie. And the passes, this is such a great way to celebrate our final day here. I owe you big time.'

When Chad cut the connection, he looked over to where Kara sat across from him, watching. She asked, 'Any regrets?'

'About what?'

'That is the right answer.' She rose and offered him her hand. 'Let's go to bed.'

'There's no way I'll be able to sleep.'

She managed a genuine smile. 'Good.'

They left for the Forbidden Kingdom at dawn.

Samantha drove and Beth took the passenger seat. After much discussion, it had been decided to leave the other agents behind. Chad was, after all, fully recognized by the Sardinian Institute. They were celebrating. A full-strength guard detail was no longer required.

They shared Orlando's early morning streets with the city's

hourly-wage employees. The wait at stoplights was quiet, the pace sleepily slow.

As they turned on to the broad tree-lined avenue leading to the magical theme park, Chad wished he knew what to say. Something that might show the others how grateful he was for their being there. Perhaps a word of inspiration. A message they could carry with them into what may well be a killing ground.

Their Tahoe was far from the first vehicle to enter the east lot. Dozens of other vehicles were already parked up close to the gates. Even so, they looked to him like metal minnows in a sea of asphalt. The lot was that large.

Several hundred people milled about the entry points. The Forbidden Kingdom film series was conceived around a break-away Republic of Transylvania, a newly formed nation the size of Rhode Island. In the films, Transylvania's neighbors remained hostile, fearing their own restive provinces might take the same step.

Transylvania was landlocked and surrounded on all sides by countries and governments who wanted it to fail. It had few resources beyond its natural beauty.

But it did have its heritage. And its ghosts. And vampires. And ghouls. So with the help of an American marketing team, who made up the first film's principal characters, the Republic of Transylvania remade itself as a tourist haven for the spook crowd.

Humans who wanted a week with the undead. And the undead seeking a place where they were made to feel welcome.

Treaties were drawn up, rules for visiting the undead were established. Neither resident nor visiting ghouls were permitted to eat any locals or tourists.

But black marketeers, gang members, invading armies, hostile neighbors . . .

Well.

They were all fair game.

Thus began a series of global hits. The theme park was a natural next step.

As far as Chad was concerned, it was almost perfect. That is, assuming his plans were more than mere futile guesses.

Their only hope lay in Serge and his ilk showing the same arrogant disregard for what they had already seen Chad capable of. Viewing him and Kara as two untrained wizards, neither of whom were actually recognized as Talents.

Ripe for the plucking.

As they approached the gates, Chad said, 'I thought the place would be empty.'

Samantha gave him a look. 'Dude, this is as empty as it will ever get.'

'People pay big bucks to be the first in line,' Kara said. 'Die-hard fans who visit a dozen times or so and earn the chance to get here early.'

Beth said, 'The Kingdom film franchise runs competitions all over the world.'

'Win a ticket to be a VIP for the day,' Samantha said. 'I can't believe you never saw one of their ads.'

'I've been away, remember?'

They joined the happy, chattering crowd pushing toward the gates. The entry points were shaped like guard huts with national flags and striped bars blocking the cobblestone lanes. The throng funneled in a good-natured rush. All of the kids and most of the adults were done up as visiting undead.

Samantha observed, 'We could be surrounded by bad guys in drag and never know it.'

They were next in line, behind a family of nine. Three generations who must have been up since dawn, dressing in coffin rags, doing each other's faces, even the grandparents dressed as cadavers. They presented mock passports bearing the new nation's coat of arms, and almost danced in place as the attendant applied their entry visas. The adults hugged the kids and everybody cheered.

He had been worried about the risk of collateral damage. Some tourist wandering into the line of fire. But as he watched Samantha step forward and offer the attendant their passes, he realized it was not going to be an issue. These people knew exactly what they wanted to do, and in which order. Soon as they passed through the border crossing, they bolted.

The gate attendant was a college-age student dressed in a customs uniform. He was red-haired and bleary-eyed and so hungover he winced as he stamped their passes. The barrier lifted, they passed the checkpoint, and entered the Kingdom.

The plaza fronting the entrance was shaped in the grand European manner, with a massive central fountain and two circular stages with domed roofs. The square had to measure three hundred yards across and served as both a staging area and food court. Several dozen restaurants and bars rimmed the perimeter, all eastern European structures of beams and stone and steep slate roofs and wrought-iron balconies. This early, only a couple of the establishments were open. Thousands of empty tables awaited the hordes.

Three grand avenues opened along the plaza's far side, representing the three films that had been released so far. Only the central lane was open at this hour. Chad watched as new arrivals scurried in, screamed with excitement, then raced toward the lone open avenue.

They were the only ones not rushing forward. Their footsteps echoed on the cobblestones. Tourists shrieked and shrilled in the distance. Flags atop the royal buildings fluttered above an almost empty square.

Then Beth looked back behind them, up above the surrounding walls, and said quietly, 'Heads up. Here they come.'

Chad turned and was almost relieved to spot Serge descending, the air around him shimmering from sunlight striking shield. 'Samantha and Beth, get well away.'

Beth complained, 'I've never run from a fight in my entire career.'

'Beth!'

'All right, all right.' She and Samantha retreated as planned.

Further to their right was a second plaza, smaller than the grand square where they stood. The restaurants to either side pinched in slightly, forming a mock passage. This second plaza was surrounded by meaner buildings, poor and slightly squalid. The stone edifices were gray and black, the balustrades narrow. They leaned against one another, and their overhanging roofs rimmed the sunlit plaza in darkness. Instead of a fountain, this second plaza held a fire-pit and guillotine.

Aaron and two other Warrior Talents stepped from the second plaza, accompanied by shadows that rose and bunched and took on ghoulish shapes. Together the Talents and shadow-fiends paraded across the main square. The closer they came, the clearer Chad could see the fire-damage to their hands and faces. And the rage they carried over how he had managed to thwart them again. Not this time.

Incoming tourists stopped and gaped as Serge landed by the entryway, well removed from Aaron's crew. Marching silently to war.

Chad pulled wooden chopsticks from his pocket, held them out, and was glad to see his hand was steady. When Kara took hers, she gave him a look. Solemn. Deep. He asked, 'Ready?'

'I love you, Chad.'

'Let's do this.' He invoked the incantation, the second spell that Kim had gifted them. First had come the electric foes, probably a similar spell to the one his enemies now used to create their shadow-fiends.

The second gift transformed any length of wood into fighting spears.

Their proper name, according to Kim, was *naginata*. They were weapons designed for ninja-style attacks, quarterstaffs topped by narrow blades scarcely as wide as Chad's hand but as long as his forearm. The blades curved slightly at the tip and were razor-sharp all the way down both edges.

Only these weapons had a magical edge, thanks to Kim.

As they took shape, they . . .

Flamed on.

Aaron screamed, '*Attack!*'

Chad was marginally aware of cheers and excited cries coming from the newly arriving tourists. Somewhere in the distance a claxon sounded, but the alarm only heightened the thrill as far as the onlookers were concerned.

Aaron's Warriors let the shadow-ghouls strike first, testing Chad's defenses. Serge of course remained poised behind his Talents. Directing and pointing, safely distant.

Suddenly there was no longer time for anything except survival.

Chad and Kara moved with the steady rhythm of a pair who had learned to act without conscious thought. A few days' practice did not make them perfect, however. They regularly made mistakes. Their actions were not fully in synch. But Chad was proud of Kara just the same.

Chad continually strengthened their weapons and shields, then began applying extra force wherever the assault was gravest.

All the while, their blades sliced into the ghouls, reducing them to ink-like stains that slowly drifted into the stones and disappeared.

Which was when Serge joined the assault.

He fired a series of molten balls, carving tight portals through Chad's strongest shields. Aaron and the other Warriors sent lightning strikes through seams now opened in Chad's shields. Kara screamed in response and stabbed viciously, but Aaron and his mates deflected her blows.

Chad successfully fended off their attack, when the central fountain began rumbling, as if caught in a very private earthquake. The crowd shifted away in uneasy steps, uncertain of precisely what was going on.

The fountain was surrounded by ornate metal grilles, intended to catch all the extra water that was blown off course by wind or storm. The polished grilles flickered in the sunlight as they blasted up.

Aaron retreated a step. Another. And offered Chad a mock farewell salute as . . .

Tourists standing beyond the danger zone started screaming, even louder than before. Then Samantha shouted, '*Incoming!*'

Up from the dark caverns beneath the fountains came wolves.

They were great warg-beasts, fell monsters drawn from dark legends.

The crowds fled, shrieking as they ran.

The wargs were armored and tall as a man's shoulder, spouting a green fire that punched gaping holes in Chad's shields.

Serge and Aaron and the other Talents rose up and hovered just above the wargs. They swept their arms and shouted their spells, drawing more shadow-fiends into the attack. These new ghouls formed swirling arcs overhead, dark poisonous clouds so thick the sun was lost. All daylight, all hope.

Chad rose to the attack. Or rather, he tried. But a dozen wolves leapt and clamped their jaws upon his limbs, his neck, his weapon.

Serge laughed in unbridled triumph. 'Escape now, scum!'

Kara lost her weapon to an attacking warg and was hammered to the earth. She cried Chad's name, or at least Chad thought that was what he heard. But the shrieking din was so fierce, the threats so many and constant, he could not be certain of anything except that seeing her fall and be consumed hurt worse than his own death. Which he knew was coming.

Then the Talents blasted him with fire.

He was lost.

SIXTY

The Hotel Montreux was a wedding-cake palace perched above the lake of Geneva. Chad was sat on the narrow balcony drinking cold coffee when Luca Tami emerged from his car and started toward the entrance.

Chad rose and re-entered the suite. He hesitated, then walked over and knocked on the bedroom door. 'Kara?'

There was no response.

Chad sighed, lifted the hotel phone and ordered a fresh pot of coffee.

The room-service waiter was departing as Luca entered. He inspected the suite's parlor, nodded approval, accepted a cup of coffee, and asked, 'Kara won't be joining us?'

'She's asleep. Or trying to.'

'How is she?'

'A little better. Not much. The nights are very hard.'

Luca followed Chad on to the balcony, settled into a chair, and said, 'It's hard on you as well, my friend.'

'No argument there.'

'Your funerals were marvelous, by the way. I felt it best if I didn't attend, but Beth streamed it for me. The Director spoke. Very moving. Many tears were shed.' Luca set his briefcase in his lap, opened the top, and set two satchels on the table between them. 'These are the herbal remedies Kara requested. Please tell her I have personally enhanced their potency. The red sack is for pain. Which you are clearly enduring as well as Kara. The other should induce a healing sleep.'

Chad made no move to touch them. 'Will she get better?'

'Who can say? As far as I know, the spell you cast hasn't been used in millennia.'

This was the prize Chad had wrested from the Library of Congress book, the lure Beth had used to draw him into the open. A spell. One lost for so long, there was no hint in any text Chad had ever studied that the concept was even considered possible.

Every young acolyte learned how to make a golem, a mockery of themselves that could be used as a decoy. Granting them the power to tuck it into bed and then escape the Institute's confines. At least for an hour or so. The third-level golem spell was passed from class to class, a hint of something forbidden, used to obtain a vague taste of freedom.

The spell Chad employed was something else entirely.

The book revealed how to cast a spell so that the golem *became that person*. The golem was no longer a golem at all. *It took on the individual's life force.* It was, for all intents and purposes, a fully formed twin.

The day of the Forbidden Kingdom assault, Chad and Kara had spent the pre-dawn hour creating their twins. As they had for each training session since receiving the Director's alert. Passing their life force to newly formed entities and training them hard.

That morning, he and Kara had again stretched out on the training room's floor-mat. Together they had cast the spell. Entered the semi-coma state. And watched through their twins' eyes as the foursome had departed for the Forbidden Kingdom. And been defeated by Serge and his Warrior Talents.

All the acolytes knew how painful it was for a golem spell to be broken. Shattering a student's golem was a favorite trick, and rendered the acolyte mildly broken for a few hours, a day at most.

This was something else entirely.

During the time that the spell was enacted, their lives were firmly bound to these secondary beings. They saw, they breathed, they *lived*.

And then they died.

Chad and Kara had both woken with the dread agony of having been destroyed. Their lives ended.

When Samantha and Beth returned six hours later, having dealt with the police and the Kingdom's own security, neither of them had managed to rise from the floor.

Luca went on, 'Given the little I know about magic tied to the Ancients, I cannot imagine this golem spell will not permit the user to eventually heal.'

Chad glanced to his left, at the empty bedroom balcony. 'I hope you're right.'

Luca extracted a bulky manila envelope, then closed his briefcase and set it aside. 'Swiss passports and IDs. Your last name is now Tami. It was easier to obtain Swiss citizenship by claiming you are my long-lost relative.'

'The account I have with the Banque Genevoise. The funds under my own name . . .'

'Transferring those sums into new accounts was much easier to arrange, since I am the bank's CEO.' He tapped the folder. 'Documents show you as the holder of two new accounts, one current and another investment.'

'Thank you, Luca.'

'My young and wounded friend, there is no need for thanks. When you and Kara are healed, we will meet, and we will plan. To have such gifted Talents as you two, free and unencumbered by the Institutes and their horrid tactics, you have no idea what this means. But you soon will.' Luca started to rise. 'I won't keep you any longer.'

'Wait, I have something for you.' Chad reached into his pocket and brought out the miniature scroll.

'What on earth?' Luca breathed deeply. 'Another wonder from the time before time, can this be?'

'Yes.' Chad unfolded the miniature scroll and lay it flat on the table. 'It's blank.'

'Right. It finally came to me last night. What this is for.'

Luca alternated between studying the blank document and Chad, his eyes alight. 'Another sign of the true Adept. Discerning a way forward when there is none to be found.'

He liked that, but decided further discussion would need to wait for later. 'You know the reveal spell from the Brazilian document.'

'Of course.'

'Think of a person you know but don't know. Someone you need to trust.'

Luca's eyes went round. 'This tells me their true nature?'

'Their nature, their past, even a hint of their future. Touch the scroll, speak their name, then invoke the spell.'

Luca hesitated a long moment, then lay his hands flat on the blank document, whispered, and as his hands ignited . . .

The scroll became imprinted with Aramaic letters of fire.

Luca read. Leaned back. Studied the glistening lake and the Alpine peaks beyond. Sipped from his coffee. Breathed in and out. Then, 'I may borrow this?'

'No, Luca. It's yours.'

Carefully he rolled the now-blank scroll and inserted it into the leather case. 'There will come a day when I can thank you properly. Of that I am certain.'

Chad rose and accompanied Luca back inside. At the doorway, Luca said, 'You asked the scroll about me, I suppose.'

'I didn't need to,' Chad replied.

The banker nodded slowly, then offered Chad his hand and said, 'For the first time in decades, I have hope.'

SIXTY-ONE

The old man stood in a shadowed alley and watched the Talent's approach. Serge walked the cobblestoned Sardinian avenue with all the pompous assurance of a prince on parade. The Institute's senior Warrior was accompanied by a breathtakingly beautiful acolyte, whose light-filled ardor drew glances from all the men and most women as they passed. The young lady talked gaily, her two hands wrapped around Serge's arm. Every chance she had, the young woman looked at him adoringly and drew her body in close. Serge showed her the same detached interest he would a half-finished meal.

The old man was dressed in rags the color of rust. He staggered forward, and stumbled into the young woman.

She cried in shock and revulsion, releasing Serge's arm and jerking away.

The old man lurched into Serge, moaning in Italian, 'Mercy, good sir, mercy, a pittance, a single—'

'Get *away* from me!'

But the beggar pressed at Serge, and somehow trapped the Talent's arms so he could not fully complete a spell. Further and further they moved in a parody of dance, while the young woman watched in horror, until . . .

The alley's shadows reached out . . .

The beggar *shoved* Serge.

At the very last moment, Serge glanced back and realized . . .

There was a hole in the earth.

He started to scream, but the sound was cut off before it became fully formed, because . . .

The instant Serge fell into the hole, it disappeared.

The old man shuffled further into the alley's shadows and vanished as well.

Beth and Samantha stood outside a prison cell, one whose front wall was made from bulletproof glass. They watched the hole appear in the cell's ceiling and . . .

'Any minute now,' Beth murmured.

As if on cue, Serge landed on the concrete floor.

Samantha gave him a very hard smile. 'Well, hello there.'

'We haven't met,' Beth said. 'Actually, I guess we have.'

'Twice, as a matter of fact,' Samantha said. 'No, wait. Three times.'

'OK, right. The two meetings with Director Reeves. And of course the Forbidden Kingdom.'

'He probably won't remember,' Samantha said. 'He was too busy using dark magic. Creating forbidden beasts.'

'In case you're wondering,' Beth said, 'the walls of your new home are lead-lined.'

Samantha tapped the glass. 'Ditto for this. And the ceiling, now that the entryway has been sealed. Pretty much magic-proof, wouldn't you agree?'

'In any case, nobody is close enough to hear you scream,' Beth said.

Samantha watched the horrified Talent pick himself off the floor, then told Beth, 'I'd say this calls for a drink.'

'Or three.' To Serge, 'See you in a few weeks.'

'When we're certain you're ready to talk,' Samantha said. 'Bye now.'

The old man stumbled his way down the Sardinian harbor walk. Or rather, he did until the way forward was empty of other pedestrians. Then his stance straightened, he cast off years. His walk became strong, confident.

Edoardo and his mates were there on the gleaming new yacht to greet Chad. As he stepped on to the stern deck, Kara moved forward and demanded, 'Well?'

'It's done.'

'Serge?'

'Where he belongs.'

Kara continued to carry her shadows. But the sun and the sea air and the gentle span of days had done as much or more to heal her than Luca's herbs. She wrapped herself around Chad, a gesture that was happening more and more these days.

Edoardo entered the main cabin, started the engines and gestured for his mates to cast them off. 'Where to, maestro?'

Chad held her close a moment longer, savoring the growing hope that they might truly leave all this behind. 'Wherever the lady says.'